KNIGHT FOR A LADY

*Brides By Chance
Regency Adventures
Book Three*

Elizabeth Bailey

SAPERE BOOKS

Also in the Brides By Chance Series
In Honour Bound
A Chance Gone By
A Winter's Madcap Escapade

KNIGHT FOR A LADY

Published by Sapere Books.

11 Bank Chambers, Hornsey, London, N8 7NN,
United Kingdom

saperebooks.com

Copyright © Elizabeth Bailey, 2017
Elizabeth Bailey has asserted her right to be identified as the author of this work.
All rights reserved.

No part of this publication may be reproduced, stored in any retrieval system, or transmitted, in any form, or by any means, electronic, mechanical, photocopying, recording, or otherwise, without the prior written permission of the publishers.
This book is a work of fiction. Names, characters, businesses, organisations, places and events, other than those clearly in the public domain, are either the product of the author's imagination, or are used fictitiously.
Any resemblances to actual persons, living or dead, events or locales are purely coincidental.

ISBN: 978-1-913335-07-6

Chapter One

Heat shimmered on the air. His shirt was sticking to his chest under the increasingly uncomfortable frockcoat. His cravat all but choked him and his breeches chafed.

Niall cursed under his breath. He was deucedly uncomfortable, recalling with longing the days back in camp when he and his fellow officers would have stripped to their drawers on a day like this and thrown buckets of water over each other. Instead, captive now to a civilian life, he must endure the discomfort and do the pretty to Tom's bride and her friend who had chosen to walk into the village.

The youthful Lady Tazewell had hailed him with undisguised pleasure as he emerged from the smithy.

"Lord Hetherington! How delightful! We had not expected to see you until the dinner hour."

Niall executed a bow, trying to sound gratified. "Ladies. A trifle of business only."

"Oh, and we are after trifles too, are we not, Jocasta?"

Lady Tazewell glanced at her friend and back to Niall. "Delia and I are busy with white work, you must know, Lord Hetherington."

"Yes, and we have run out of thread."

Niall groaned in spirit, but some response was called for. "Ah, an important mission, no doubt."

Lady Tazewell gave a giggle and her eyes danced. "An important excuse, Lord Hetherington. We could not be expected to remain indoors on such a day."

To his chagrin, both ladies, in light muslins and armed with parasols against the sun, looked perfectly fresh and not in the least troubled by the heat. Irritation got the better of him. "I'm astonished Tom sanctioned such an expedition in this hot weather. What if one of you were to be overcome?"

Lady Tazewell's tinkling laugh rang out. "Pooh, we are not such poor creatures!"

"Nevertheless, I would advise you to return by way of the woods rather than the road. It is bound to be cooler."

"Now that is an excellent notion, don't you think so, Delia?"

"Oh, yes. Your woods are so pretty too."

Miss Burloyne was eyeing him in a distinctly predatory fashion, and Niall's sense of self-preservation kicked in. He cast about in his mind for an excuse, but he was too late.

"Why do you not accompany us, Lord Hetherington?"

"Delia! We could not possibly incommode him. I am sure he has far too much business on hand, do you not, Lord Hetherington?"

This was uttered with an arch look that clearly demanded a reply in the negative. The last thing he wanted was to dawdle through the woods, especially when he cherished a strong suspicion that he was under fire. But Tom was now his neighbour as well as an old school friend, and Niall knew him to be punctilious in all matters of courtesy.

Resigning himself to the inevitable, he gave a small bow. "Only my horse in need of shoeing. If you will allow me to escort you, ladies, I can very well come back for him."

Miss Burloyne turned pink and Lady Tazewell's smile embraced him. Niall stifled another groan and turned his steps in the opposite direction to the tavern, where he'd been headed in hopes of a cooling draught of ale.

Together they traversed the village green, making for the woods that bordered Itchington Bishops and came out into the grounds of Tazewell Manor.

How it came about, he was unable to fathom, but Niall found himself walking next to Miss Burloyne while Lady Tazewell tripped along the path a little ahead, having secured his unwilling attention to her friend with an airy comment.

"Delia is an expert needlewoman, you must know, Lord Hetherington. You must have her tell you about the exquisite embroidery she is engaged upon." With which, she skipped away, intent upon examining wildflowers apparently, leaving him prey to her gushing guest.

"Oh, it is a mere nothing, sir. I am merely fashioning a landscape scene. It is meant for my father for Christmas, if I can finish it in time and have it suitably framed. But I have set it aside in any event."

"Why is that?" Niall asked, without the slightest real interest.

Miss Burloyne gave a laugh which jarred in his ears. "To help Jocasta with her white work, of course."

Lady Tazewell's mischievous face peeped back at them over her shoulder. "I am so unhandy with a needle. Poor Marianne — my sister-in-law you must know — used to complain of my impatience."

"Yes, but now Jocasta is mistress of her own establishment," chimed in Miss Burloyne, "she cannot escape the duty. I am only too happy to do what I may to lighten the load."

Niall's sense of being in purgatory increased. Was this the style of conversation to which he was reduced? He dredged up a suitable comment. "Ah, indeed? But do tell me about your landscape."

Nothing loth, Miss Burloyne launched into a vivid description of the work, to which Niall paid little heed. By means of interpolating an occasional grunt of assent or interrogation, he was able to allow his mind to wander.

Not that Miss Burloyne was in any way objectionable. Pretty enough, though unremarkable, with the distinct disadvantage of freckles and sandy hair. She lacked the vivacity of her friend Jocasta, an attractive brunette with a pert but taking manner. Tom obviously doted on her. Unsurprising, since Niall understood they'd been married less than a year. But if young Lady Tazewell was matchmaking on her friend's behalf, she was doomed to be disappointed. Niall was not hanging out for a wife. Not yet awhile.

Let him, for the Lord's sake, learn the ropes of estate management and become better acquainted with his tenants before he succumbed to parson's mousetrap. Although marriage was inevitable now he'd inherited the earldom.

The weight of depression that plagued him threatened a return, and Niall thrust it back. Why everyone should suppose him to be over the moon, he could not fathom. It was tragic, rather. And a heavy responsibility he'd never imagined would come to be his. Who could have supposed that Roland Lowrie — as hale a man as you could wish, as Tom Tazewell had been able to testify — would be carried off by a fever, along with his wife and both his hopeful young sons? The entire family wiped out.

The news had reached Niall in November of the previous year, on the eve of battle against the forces of the Maratha Empire in India. He'd fought at Assaye in September, under the command of Lord Arthur Wellesley in support of the British East India Company — one arm in a campaign waged on several fronts across the region. He had barely taken in his new fortune by the end of a hard-won conflict, and it was after Christmas before he was able to sail for England. By the time he arrived at Lowrie Court in the early summer of 1804, the estate had been neglected for the best part of a year.

The lawyers had taken time to trace Niall, going back several generations to locate the distant relationship. But cousin he was, and none had been more astonished than Colonel Niall Lowrie to find himself an earl. Astonished, and horrified. Instead of continuing in a profession he loved for its gypsy life and freedom from social shibboleths, he must exchange adventure and excitement for the tedium of the country and the boredom inherent in the kind of social chitchat in which he was currently engaged.

"Do you not think so, Lord Hetherington?"

Startled, Niall looked round at Miss Burloyne and spoke without thought. "I beg your pardon? I was not attending."

Her face fell, and he was at once irritated and guilty. Before he could fashion an apology, Lady Tazewell cried out in a voice of clear urgency. "Heavens, what is this? What can have happened?"

Niall glanced towards her and his eye caught on a figure lying half across the path. Striding forward, he passed Lady Tazewell and dropped down on one knee beside the still form.

It was female, and a glance down her clothes informed Niall that she was genteel, if less than fashionable. He looked at her face and found it deathly pale, the eyes closed, mouth a little open. Her arm had fallen away to one side and Niall reached towards her ungloved hand, setting his fingers to her wrist.

"Is she alive?"

A faint pulse rewarded his search and he nodded, only half aware of the two ladies hovering over the prone figure. Niall touched the back of his hand to her face, and found it warm to the touch and a trifle damp. "I think she may have been overcome by the heat." He looked up at the two anxious faces. "Stand off a little, if you please. I must check for broken bones."

"What, you are going to examine her?" This in a shocked tone from Miss Burloyne.

Impatience rode Niall. "Of course. I'm no surgeon, but I'll soon tell if she has broken anything."

With a firm touch, but with care, he felt each limb in turn, running his hands over the woman's legs without a qualm. She was woefully thin, he discovered, but her bones appeared to be intact.

Niall picked up her hand and began to chafe it, glancing up at Lady Tazewell as he did so. "Do you know her, ma'am?"

"I've never seen her before. But I'm not yet acquainted with everyone round about."

"But you'd know if she was from the village, surely?"

Niall's eyes were once more on the woman's face. She looked to be more than a girl, her gown of nankeen-coloured muslin demure in style, her hair confined behind, though it had clearly come loose in the fall. It was dark, her pallid face accentuated by the contrast. Niall surveyed the hollow cheeks, noting blue smudges under the eyes and grooves from nose to mouth unnatural in one so young. Niall had seen enough of wounds and illness to recognise the signs. Had the young woman been subject to the same fever in the village that had carried off his predecessor?

As he watched, the dark lashes quivered, the lips moved as if in speech, and her eyes fluttered open.

Niall leaned over her. "Do not try to move as yet. I believe you must have swooned."

Consternation entered her eyes, of a curious light colour somewhere between grey and blue, and she started up.

"No, keep still!"

She sank back, staring up at him. "Who are you?"

"I am Hetherington. Don't be alarmed. We were walking this way and came upon you lying here."

Her eyes blinked up at him and passed to the still trees above. She put a wavering hand to her head and as she shifted, evidently caught sight of the two ladies standing a little way off.

"Oh! Who —? This is… I must get up!"

Agitation entered her voice, and Niall caught her as she struggled to raise herself.

"If you must rise, allow me to assist you. We don't want you fainting again."

"Th-thank you … very kind…"

Her voice was a thread and Niall, his arm about her shoulders, felt her sinking.

"No, you are not yet well enough. But we must get you off this dirt." With care, and some difficulty, he slid his other arm under her knees. "Put your arm around my neck."

She obeyed and Niall made to rise with her in his arms, evoking protests and exclamations from his companions.

"Gracious, Hetherington, can you manage her?"

"Should we help?"

Niall shook his head. "Easier if I manage her alone. But if you will look about for a likely tree trunk perhaps?"

The two girls twittered as they cast about in the immediate vicinity, and Niall was able to adjust his balance and get to his feet, his burden safely ensconced. He shifted the weight in his arms and found it lighter than expected.

"You are skin and bone! Have you been ill?"

Her head had fallen against his shoulder, but she raised it slightly.

"Lately, yes. I am … I am not as well recovered as I thought. I am sorry to be such a nuisance."

"Don't be foolish," Niall said in a peremptory tone, and was surprised to hear a tiny gurgle of laughter. He grinned down at her. "Well, you sound a little better at least."

"My mind is clearing."

"Excellent. Now if we can sit you down somewhere —"

"Over here, Lord Hetherington!"

Looking in the direction of Miss Burloyne's voice, Niall found her gesturing and saw the two ladies had indeed discovered a tree stump. Lady Tazewell was standing behind it, her open arms indicating its suitability for a seat.

It was a little way into the woods and his boots crunched fallen twigs and debris as he made his way towards it, skirting the trees. Reaching the spot, he set the girl down, taking care to keep hold of her shoulders until she seemed able to sit on her own. She grasped the edges of the stump and glanced at him.

"Thank you. I can manage now."

Looking at her wan face, Niall was not convinced. "Are you sure?"

"Yes, indeed. If I sit here for a space, I will be better directly."

Niall released his hold, his hands ready to grasp her again at need. But she remained upright, if a trifle wobbly.

The other ladies came in closer.

"There! Poor thing, was it the heat?"

"You look dreadfully pale still," said Lady Tazewell, eyeing the girl in a critical fashion. "I wonder, should we take her to the Manor, Lord Hetherington?"

The girl began to look a little agitated. "Oh, no, pray don't trouble. Let me not keep you. I shall be perfectly able to walk back to the vicarage presently."

Lady Tazewell's face registered surprise. "Oh, you must be the Reverend Westacott's niece. He said you were expected."

A tiny smile, then a frown. "I am Edith Westacott. And you must be Lady Tazewell."

"I am, and this is my friend, Miss Burloyne."

Miss Westacott looked from one to the other. "You are all very kind, but please don't interrupt your walk on my account."

Niall cut in swiftly. "Nonsense! You obviously can't be left to walk back to the vicarage alone. I will escort you when you are better."

"We will all escort you," came brightly from Lady Tazewell.

Miss Burloyne looked less satisfied, but Niall crushed this suggestion without hesitation. The last thing the girl needed at this juncture was two chattering magpies at her side.

"I think, Lady Tazewell, you and Miss Burloyne would do better to return to the Manor. I must go back to the village in any event, remember. You may leave Miss Westacott to me."

A flash of annoyance showed in the youthful Lady Tazewell's countenance, but she was forestalled.

"I cannot impose upon you, Lord Hetherington. Pray don't—"

"Save your breath, ma'am. I am coming with you." Niall gave a small bow. "Ladies, we shall meet at dinner."

Niall thought he detected disappointment in Miss Burloyne's face, and mentally gave thanks for Miss Westacott's unexpected appearance in their path. Lady Tazewell was putting out a hand to the sufferer.

"An unfortunate way to meet, Miss Westacott. I hope we may soon have a more comfortable encounter."

The girl took her hand briefly, and Niall noted caution in her tone.

"Perhaps we may. Thank you."

Relieved Lady Tazewell had taken her dismissal in good part, Niall watched the two ladies trot away, unsurprised to see them almost instantly with their heads together. No doubt speculating upon Miss Westacott's arrival in the district. He turned back to her. "How do you feel now?"

"Oh, I am a deal better."

Niall eyed her pallid countenance. "You don't look it."

She lifted a hand to her face and fingered her cheeks. "You do not see me at my best, I'm afraid, my lord. I have lost a deal of weight, you see."

"So I should imagine. Was it the village fever?"

She looked startled. "Village fever? No, indeed. I have not lived in the village for years."

"Ah, I see. I only wondered as my cousin and his family succumbed to it some months back."

"They lived here?"

"At Lowrie Court, yes. I have only lately arrived myself."

"Lowrie Court? Oh, you are the new lord! I had not thought… I was so sorry to hear of the tragedy."

"Thank you, but I cannot pretend to more than ordinary regret for so many lives lost. I had never met my cousin."

She did not respond. She must have been acquainted with Roland, but was clearly reticent of speaking further on the matter. Even less willing to talk of it, Niall said no more.

Presently Miss Westacott began to fidget, rubbing her thumbs against her fingers. Niall frowned. Was this embarrassment? But why?

"You seem a little troubled, Miss Westacott."

She glanced up, and he was again struck by the curious colour of her eyes.

"I am ashamed to be such a trouble to you, sir. I should not have ventured out. Only I felt so oppressed that I…"

Her voice died and she again looked conscious. Intrigued, Niall ventured a question.

"Oppressed? By the heat?"

"No! Oh … yes, it — it is excessive. Too hot really to be walking when…"

"When you are not quite well yet," Niall put in easily. The girl was clearly in some agitation of spirits. If he did not miss his guess, it had little to do with the weather.

"It was foolish of me, just as you said."

Niall gave a small bow. "Accept my apologies. I spoke rudely."

"Oh, no, I did not mean…" She drew an obvious breath. "Pardon me, my lord, I must sound like a ninny. I am not as a rule so incoherent."

"It is no wonder. You were in a deep swoon. There is no saying how long you had been unconscious."

She stared up at him, consternation in her eyes. "Surely it could not have been many minutes?"

"Well, you did not regain your senses for several minutes after we found you. I had time to check for broken bones and I chafed your hands for some time."

The pale cheeks ran a trifle pink. "I have given you a deal of trouble, my lord."

"Now don't start that again." Niall gave her a reassuring look. "Let us dispense with that nonsense once and for all, if you please. It's no trouble. I am a soldier, you must know, quite used to dealing with the unexpected."

She eyed him in a manner Niall could not regard as anything but wary.

"I might have guessed, had I been a little more in my own mind." A smile brightened her countenance. "The military bearing is unmistakable."

"Alas, I am no longer a man of the sword."

"You've sold out?"

"I had no choice."

He closed his lips, irritated to find himself drawn into talking of his affairs. It struck him Miss Westacott's conversation had little to do with fripperies. Refreshing. He could even look forward to escorting her back to the vicarage.

"Do you suppose you are ready to undertake the journey home now?"

Miss Westacott at once resumed the look of consciousness and Niall regretted having spoken.

"Yes, indeed. We need not dawdle here any longer."

She made to get up off the tree stump and Niall at once went to her aid, taking her arm in a strong grip and putting a hand to her back. She tottered a little and then steadied, straightening her limbs with a determined air.

"Thank you, my lord. I think I may manage now."

Niall ignored this. "Slip your hand through my arm. Good. You will alert me instantly if you feel yourself weakening, is that clear?"

She peeped up at him, emitting the tiny laugh he recalled from before.

"I understand you perfectly, sir."

Niall guided her through the trees, keeping a gentle pace, his tone rueful meanwhile. "I beg your pardon, Miss Westacott. I am too used to being in command."

"I can see that."

There was a tease in her voice and he had to laugh.

"Observant of you."

"Well, it is rather obvious, you know."

"I don't doubt it. I was trying to be ironic."

"Oh, I had not realised. You must blame the disorder of my mind."

Niall glanced down at her. "There is nothing disordered about your mind, ma'am. You are as sharp as a knife."

She laughed out. "I am glad my condition has not obscured that fact." And then a note of penitence entered her voice. "Oh, no, I must not tease you. You have been immeasurably kind."

"Don't spoil it, Miss Westacott. I much prefer your bite to your protestations of gratification."

Again the tiny laugh. "I see I cannot please you, sir. I shall confine my remarks to the commonplace."

"Heaven help me! I beg you won't. I've not been so much entertained since I came to this Godfor— this village."

"Oh, dear. I must request my uncle to increase his prayers for the Almighty to reappear."

Niall burst out laughing. "But you are delightful, Miss Westacott!"

The figure at his side stiffened on the instant, and Niall felt as if he escorted an effigy. She did not answer, and he was struck with the realisation he had blundered.

"What is it? May I not compliment you?"

Her eyes flashed a look, once again full of consternation. Her voice took on apology. "Oh, no! Forgive me, I … it was not…" He heard an indrawn breath and there was resolution in her tone. "Let us talk of something else, if you please, sir."

But the mood was spoiled and Niall could think of nothing whatsoever to say.

Chapter Two

Inwardly chiding herself, Edith cast about for some innocuous topic she might introduce. Foolish to be so sensitive. He'd meant nothing by the remark and her involuntary flinch was unjustified. She rarely had herself so little in hand. It must be the result of her swoon. And again, she must blame herself for venturing forth.

"Stupid, stupid."

"I beg your pardon?"

Edith had not realised she had muttered aloud. Conscious once more, she made an effort at lightness. "I was giving myself a mental shake, sir, for my foolishness."

"Which particular foolishness had you in mind?"

A choke of laughter escaped her and she glanced up at her escort. His look was innocence itself, but she was not deceived.

"I shall not fall into that trap, my lord. I am perfectly aware you are roasting me."

His lips quirked and a tiny flutter disturbed Edith's pulse. She quelled the rise of attraction. Lord Hetherington and she could have nothing to do with one another.

Nor, now she had leisure to observe with a less chaotic mind, could she count him a handsome man. He was swarthy rather, his complexion a trifle rough and weather-beaten, his left cheek and jaw marred by a disfiguring scar. But his features were strong under a mop of curling auburn locks little concealed by the beaver hat.

No, these attributes could hold little appeal. Yet his air of command and a sense of barely contained vigour gave off an energy that drew Edith, as if she might drink of it to resuscitate her depleted vitality.

"Are you growing tired?"

She gathered her scattered thoughts. "No, indeed, sir. I am managing very well. It is but a step to the village now."

She could already see the church spire through the trees and breathed a sigh of relief. Despite her words, the effort to remain steady on her feet and not succumb to the debilitating weakness that still plagued her was taking its toll.

Her strength failed abruptly and she stopped, clinging to Lord Hetherington's arm. "A moment, my lord. Let me catch my breath."

"You are tired! Why did you not tell me?"

She did not answer, grateful for the swift arm that came about her and allowing her companion to take her weight as she leant against his strength. She took slow breaths as her physician had taught her, letting her limbs relax until the breathlessness subsided.

She was glad of his lordship's silence, and thought he must have an innate understanding of her need for a brief moment of peace. Presently she felt able to take her own weight again and she straightened, feeling Lord Hetherington's hold relax.

"Better?"

"Much, thank you. I beg your pardon. I lose my breath a little too easily."

"So I apprehend." Obedient to the pressure of his arm, she began walking again. "How long is it since you left your bed?"

Edith could not forbear sighing. "A little more than a week. I was obliged to take to my bed after my arrival, I'm afraid."

"Had you journeyed far?"

"From Bath. But it was not so much the length of the trip. I was not entirely well when I made it, you see."

A grunt of dissatisfaction came from beside her. "What you mean is you got up from a bed of sickness to travel to this place. And that, my dear Miss Westacott, was definitely foolish."

Stung, she retaliated before she could stop her tongue. "It was not of my choosing, sir! Had any other course been open to me, I would not have started out at all."

She felt him stiffen beside her. "Accept my apologies, ma'am. I didn't know."

"Of course you did not. Yet you made assumptions you had no right to make." With difficulty, Edith controlled her spurt of temper. "Pardon me… I am prone to impatience since…"

"Not a terribly patient patient then?"

Her irritation vanished as she laughed. "You, sir, are an unfeeling wretch!"

"Alas! Come, you are beginning to sound more like yourself."

"I don't know how you know that since you scarce know me at all."

"Oh, I think I have your measure, Miss Westacott."

Incensed, she threw him a glare. "Do you indeed, Lord Hetherington? Upon the acquaintance of a bare half hour, if that?"

"But an eventful half hour, ma'am. There is nothing like a crisis to pare away the façade under which we all take refuge."

The cynical note was pronounced, and Edith's hackles relaxed again.

"You appear to take a jaundiced view of humanity, my lord."

"Soldiering brings out the best and the worst, ma'am, with little room for affectations. I confess to some distaste for the frivolous attitudes I have encountered in civilian circles."

"Not a very civil civilian then?"

He broke into laughter. "Touché, Miss Westacott!"

A warm glow invaded Edith's bosom, and she was obliged once again to suppress a feeling of being drawn to the man. It was fortunate perhaps that they entered the village at this moment, taking her attention in another direction.

"If we take the lane to the left of the green, it is the shorter way to the vicarage. I may enter by the back gate."

"Then by all means let us go that way."

As they neared the turn leading to the back of the vicarage, Edith bethought her of her uncle. "He will be distressed."

"Who will?"

She'd spoken aloud again. She made haste to explain. "The Reverend Westacott. My uncle, you must know. He has been immeasurably kind. He insists upon my remaining with him, though I can't but feel…"

She faded out, annoyed with herself for so nearly speaking out about her personal affairs with a virtual stranger. Not that she felt it so, recalling his words. They were scarce acquainted, yet she'd been within an ace of confiding in him.

Lord Hetherington appeared not to notice her hesitation. "I have not yet met him, so I am glad of the opportunity."

She regarded him frowningly. "You've not been to church since your arrival?"

He grimaced. "I regret to disappoint you, but no. I dare say it is a habit I must cultivate."

"But you must have had a chaplain in the army?"

"Indeed, but I have not been to church as such in an age."

To one brought up under the aegis of a pastor, such neglect seemed almost irreverent. But Uncle Lionel had stressed both tolerance and charity, and she must not judge. Instead, she indulged curiosity. "Was it a harsh life, soldiering?"

"At times. I did not regard it."

An odd tone in his eyes struck her, and she spoke without thinking. "You revelled in it."

His head turned sharply. "Yes! What made you say so?"

She could not resist. "I have your measure, my lord."

He eyed her, his expression somewhere between amusement and exasperation. "I am undecided how much I care for having my words thrown back at me."

"Then it is well we are within a stone's throw of my home, sir." She took hold of the gate and moved away from his side, holding out a hand. "I must thank you, my lord, for —"

He ignored the hand, leaning to unclick the latch. "I will see you into the house, Miss Westacott."

"There is no need, I assure you."

"Nevertheless, it will better suit my conscience to assure myself you are safely returned to your uncle's care."

Edith was left with nothing to say. She allowed him to tuck her hand back in his arm as they walked up the path that led down the back garden. Before they reached the main door at the back of the house, it opened and her uncle's round bespectacled face appeared, followed by his portly little form hurrying to meet them, a worried frown between his brows.

"Ede, my dear child! To be out in this heat! What were you thinking of? And who in heaven's name is this?"

Releasing her hand from her companion's sustaining arm, Edith moved towards the vicar.

"This is Lord Hetherington, Uncle Lionel, who has kindly lent me his arm. I'm afraid I fainted in the woods."

"Fainted!" Her uncle caught her by the shoulders, his critical gaze examining her face. "My dear, dear child! What in heaven's name possessed you? I wish you had asked me…" He faded out, catching her into a stifling embrace for an instant. Keeping his arm about her, he put out a hand to her rescuer. "I have not the pleasure of your acquaintance, sir, but you have my heartfelt gratitude. My poor girl here is not fit to be walking in such weather."

Expecting this sentiment to be echoed by his lordship, Edith was surprised when he disclaimed as he took her uncle's hand.

"I gather Miss Westacott was in need of air and solitude, sir. I cannot blame her, though perhaps it was a little incautious."

Edith had to laugh. "A little! When you have been scolding me for foolishness?"

"Did he so? Then I shall refrain, my dear Ede, but I don't mind telling you when I spotted you from the window, I was quite put about."

"Yes, I can see that, sir," Edith said on a laugh. "I'm sorry to have worried you. But allow me to make you properly known to each other."

Lord Hetherington flung up a hand. "Let us dispense with formality, if you please. You are the Reverend Westacott, sir, and I regret I have not — er — called upon you earlier. I am still grappling with estate affairs."

Her uncle's face took on the look of solemnity she knew well.

"The Lowrie family! Too, too tragic, sir. An estimable gentleman and his wife so amiable."

Edith heard her uncle without surprise. She knew his distress to be sincere, for he had known the Lowries well, and indeed had officiated at their nuptials, so he'd told her. Edith remembered Roland Lowrie as a youth, but had never met his wife. Her uncle's smile reappeared.

"And so you have taken the title, my lord? We have all been wondering who it might be — myself in particular naturally — although Lord Tazewell has been kind enough since to fill me in a little."

Lord Hetherington's frown caused Edith to cut in before he could respond.

"We must not keep his lordship. I have delayed him enough."

Her uncle took this up with all his usual buoyancy. "Indeed, yes!" Seizing Lord Hetherington's hand again, he wrung it with fervency. "I am heartily in your debt, my lord."

"Nonsense! It was my pleasure, and I was at leisure. I am only waiting for my horse to be reshod."

"At Jackson's? Then you must allow me to offer you refreshment while you wait. You must be parched, sir. I cannot think why we are standing about in this way. Ede, my dear child, do you go in and sit yourself down before you fall down."

Hustled into the cluttered hall, Edith did not know whether to be glad or sorry to see Lord Hetherington tacitly accept the invitation, entering the house in the wake of her uncle, who waved him forward with an airy hand.

"Come in, come in, my lord. We do not stand on ceremony in this house."

Within a few minutes, Edith was thrust into the comfy sofa in the haphazard family room at the back of the house, while her uncle waved Lord Hetherington to a seat opposite, near one of the leaded casement windows, which were all open to the elements on this hot day. The vicar bustled across to the bell-pull, tugged upon it and returned to hover by his guest.

"Will you take ale, my lord? I shall order the lemonade for you and me, Ede. I know Mrs Tuffin was making a fresh jug, but his lordship may prefer a stronger brew."

Lord Hetherington looked amused. "I will take a glass of your lemonade, sir. I dare say it will be more refreshing."

"I find it so certainly, but then I am not one of your keen topers, sir. At any moment I may be called out, and a clear head is essential. Now where are my spectacles?"

"You are wearing them, Uncle Lionel."

He put up his hand and fingered them, bursting into laughter. "I shall forget my head one of these days."

Edith could not resist a glance at Lord Hetherington, relieved to see he was rather amused than irritated by her uncle's insouciance.

He caught her glance. "Are you feeling a little recovered, Miss Westacott?"

"Goodness me, I was forgetting," her uncle broke in at once, coming across to lay a hand to her brow. "Should you not lie down for a space, Ede?"

She took his hand and squeezed it, more to stop him fussing about her than anything else. "I will do so presently. I am already feeling much more myself."

"But see you do rest, Miss Westacott. Or rather, I must trust your uncle to ensure you do. It's obvious to me that you are as yet too debilitated to be gadding about the countryside."

"I was hardly gadding about. And merely because you chose to assist me does not give you the right to order my movements."

"Ede, how can you talk so, when his lordship is only concerned for your welfare?"

Closing her lips with difficulty on a tart retort, Edith was further incensed when his lordship chose to throw her a teasing look.

"Just so, sir. But I fear Miss Westacott is impatient of restraint."

Fortunately for her temper, Mrs Tuffin bustled in, already armed with a large tray on which reposed the big jug filled with the pale liquid garnished with a battery of lemon slices and sweetened with honey.

"I thought as you'd be wanting this, Reverend, soon as I saw Miss Ede coming down the path."

"Well thought of, Mrs Tuffin. But you are always ahead of me. What I would do without you, I cannot imagine."

She bobbed a curtsy, simpering, "As if I didn't know what you like, Reverend, after all this time."

The ritual, repeated ad nauseam on a daily basis, revived Edith's sense of entrapment and she had all to do to prevent herself from screaming.

Mrs Tuffin was bobbing at the guest. "And would his lordship prefer ale, sir?"

"No, no, Mrs Tuffin, he is going to take lemonade with us." Surprise entered her uncle's voice. "But you know Lord Hetherington?"

"No indeed, Reverend, but a body can't be about in the village and not discover who's who."

"Of course, of course. It's my housekeeper, Mrs Tuffin, my lord."

"So I gathered."

Edith was glad of the respite afforded by this little piece of byplay and the housekeeper's subsequent distribution of the lemonade. She took her glass in a hand that was not altogether steady and was glad of the excuse of her recent faint. Her uncle would take it for the result of that instead of her inner turmoil.

His care and kindness, for which she must be eternally grateful, had nevertheless become suffocating as her strength began to return. The dread spectre of the past was hardly worse than that of her potential future. The dawdling life of the village would not suit her in the least, but she knew not how to counter her uncle's insistence that this time she must see common sense and make her home with him as he had entreated her to do years ago.

For this present, while she was too weak to think of how to acquire another position after the debacle in Bath, she was obliged to accept his enthusiastic hospitality. But kind though he was, love him as she did as the surrogate father he'd been from her childhood, Edith could not think without abhorrence of remaining under his roof for years, and turning into one of these twittering village spinsters with nothing to do but make herself useful about her uncle's parishioners. Teaching, if she could hope for another school to take her on, or a private family in need of a governess, was preferable to such a life. Unfortunately, her uncle saw it as drudgery and could not be brought to understand that it gave her a degree of pleasure to use her intelligence in the cultivation of young minds.

She came out of her reverie to find her uncle and Lord Hetherington engaged in a discussion about the resumption of hostilities in India in April, against Holgar, who had not been a party to the treaty the previous December with his fellow Maratha rulers.

"We had hoped Adgaon, which was my last engagement, would have ended the war, so I had deemed it a better time to have sold out than it might have been."

"Well, well, we must hope Wellesley and Lake may do the trick this time without your assistance, my lord."

"Indeed." Lord Hetherington set down his empty glass and rose. "I must go, sir. My horse is shod by this time, I imagine, and my agent will be champing at the bit."

"Eddows? An excellent man you have there, my lord. He has kept the place going all these months."

"So I apprehend." He stepped across to Edith, looking down at her, his expression quizzical. "I trust you will suffer no ill effects, Miss Westacott. Take care of yourself."

She took the hand he was holding out. "I must thank you, sir."

"You must not. A trifling service."

Aware as she had not been before of the warmth of his touch, Edith withdrew her hand, glad her uncle took this up.

"Trifling? No indeed, my lord. We are indebted to you. But let me see you to the door."

He bustled out and Lord Hetherington, with a valedictory smile towards Edith, followed him. She watched him go, noting the straight back and the riot of auburn hair that must have been a devil to tame in his soldiering days.

A desire to run her fingers through those curls attacked her and she banished it on the instant. What, had she run from one hideous deceit only to fall into error all over again? No, she was done with it. No man should be permitted to capture her imagination, especially one as far above her station as he could be.

Chapter Three

Insipid as the evening was, Niall felt the more irritated for the comparison he could not help making between the ladies at the Manor and the one at the vicarage. For this he must blame Lady Tazewell who, inevitably he supposed, brought up the afternoon's misadventure.

"I do hope Miss Westacott did not suffer for her swoon. Was it the heat?"

Niall nodded at the liveried servant who was waiting to spoon soup into his dish.

"It seems she has recently been ill and is not yet fully recovered."

Miss Burloyne exclaimed at once. "Poor thing! I thought she looked to be out of frame. But she was able to walk? You did not have to carry her?"

Surprised at her interest, Niall looked across the table. "She was a little unsteady, but she remained on her own two feet, yes."

"I suppose you were obliged to take her arm, though?"

"Don't be silly, Delia, of course he must have done so," chimed in Lady Tazewell. "Was she very ill? She looked distressingly skinny."

"Oh, very skinny indeed. Quite gaunt, in fact."

Surprising in himself an impulse to refute this as a slur, Niall curbed his tongue, instead turning the subject. "A fortunate encounter, as it turned out, for I was able to make the acquaintance of your vicar, Tom."

His host looked up from his bowl. "My vicar?"

"Reverend Westacott."

"Yes, my dear fellow, but the vicarage is in your gift, not mine."

Startled, Niall stared at him. "Are you telling me the village is not part of your estate?"

Lady Tazewell chimed in at this point. "Is it not, Tom? Good gracious! And I have been visiting Mrs Ash's old mother in her cottage in the belief it was my duty."

Her husband gave her the doting smile that made Niall feel positively ill.

"An excellent thing too, my love, for until Hetherington here has a chance to — er — to…"

Reddening at the ears, he faded out and Niall intervened, having no desire to encourage the ladies in the subject of his potential marriage.

"But how is this, Tom? I thought I had understood the boundary between our lands, but it seems I was mistaken."

Tom laughed. "The truth is the villagers consider themselves part of the manor of Tazewell and have always done so. It is not part of the entail, however, and my great-grandfather sold the village and its environs to Roland's great-grandfather. A bribe or a debt, my father thinks. Or it may have been the Lowries wanting to extend their lands. This is not our principal seat, as you may know, so…"

"It was not thought shocking to sell the land, I apprehend?"

"Quite so."

Niall was still grappling with the implications when Lady Tazewell, a twinkle in her eye, laughed across at him.

"Then it appears it was very proper, Lord Hetherington, for you to rescue Miss Westacott."

"Yes, indeed," agreed her shadow. "A matter of duty even."

The hopeful note in Miss Burloyne's voice was not lost on Niall. He acknowledged the sally with a faint smile, addressing himself to his meal. But the image of Miss Westacott's wan features came into his head, and he recalled the incident with a lift of pleasure.

In a matter of minutes, she had proven herself more than capable of intelligent conversation, adding a dry wit and a deal of courage. Whereas Tom's magpie of a bride, vivacious though she was, had nothing beyond the commonplace in her head. As for Miss Burloyne, whom he could not acquit of setting her cap at him, a more tediously empty-headed wench he'd yet to meet.

He could see why the somewhat staid Tom had been captivated, for the lady Jocasta Crail, as she'd been before her marriage according to her fond husband, was a pert little piece with a sunny temperament and a bubbly personality. She had evidently learned the knack of twisting her spouse around her little finger early on.

For himself, the prospect of a life in company with a woman who could talk of nothing but furbelows, fashions and gossip — unless it was a catalogue of her friend's attributes designed presumably to make him think her a suitable wife — was anathema. When he came to marry, as he now must since the succession had to be secured, he wanted more of a helpmeet than a decorative addition to his estate.

At that moment Tom, breaking off what he was saying, cast a glance at his wife as she giggled over some joke with Miss Burloyne. Lady Tazewell caught her husband's look and the smile she gave him was both intimate and full of affection.

Niall felt obliged to revise his cynical view. Perhaps there was more to the girl than he had thought. But if she imagined he would succumb to the lures she was throwing out on behalf of her friend, she was mistaken.

The evening was not completely wasted. It was more pleasant to dine in company than at his own board in solitary state, and the meal of substantial courses was excellent. Niall enjoyed two sorts of roast, but refused the pigeon pie in favour of a particularly good hare in cream sauce. He managed to avoid a syllabub but partook of the dish of snow cream pressed upon him, which he found fresh and light.

Since Tom, who had come into this minor property of his inheritance when he came of age, knew far more about managing estates than he did, Niall was able, when the ladies retired, to get some of his more urgent questions answered.

Lord Tazewell did not encourage his guest to linger over the wine, however, and all too soon Niall found himself besieged once more when his hostess insisted upon Miss Burloyne entertaining the small company with a song. Since she accompanied herself, playing an ancient harpsichord, Niall realised he was being shown yet more of her accomplishments.

Miss Burloyne's voice, like her person, was pleasant enough, her playing adequate. Yet the performance lacked spark, even to one unused to hearing much more than a fiddle and raucous male voices around a campfire. In a word, Miss Burloyne was a dull creature and Niall could almost feel pity for her attempts to catch a husband.

He was no Adonis. The reverse, if anything, for his years in the field had roughened him in both face and manner, as he was obliged to admit. Yet this earldom, irksome though it was to him, had made him prey to spinsters of the ilk of Miss Burloyne.

Unlike Miss Westacott, who clearly had no designs upon him. He recalled how she had pokered up at even a mild compliment and at once felt intrigued. It occurred to him that he now had the perfect excuse to revisit the vicarage. An apology was due to the Reverend Westacott.

Estate business kept Niall from carrying out his resolve for two days. He lost no time, however, in demanding of his agent why he had not told him of his interest in the village of Itchington Bishops.

Eddows, an energetic fellow who showed little evidence of his advancing years beyond a grizzled head of hair and an occasional moment of deafness which Niall suspected was largely selective, peered up at him in the direct way he had from his inferior height and pursed his lips.

"If you recall, my lord, you requested me to spare you the details until you'd had a chance to acquaint yourself with the general pattern."

Niall did recall it, reflecting for the first time that his attitude must have caused the man a deal of difficulty. His conscience smote him. "I did, didn't I? I beg your pardon, Eddows. I've hampered you somewhat with my megrims."

The man's mouth relaxed. "Not at all, my lord. I have merely to continue to do what I have been doing for years until you direct me otherwise."

Niall could not repress a grin. "That has put me firmly in my place."

A bark of laughter escaped the agent. "I did not intend it so, my lord. I can well appreciate how the burden has come upon you without preparation or warning. You may rely upon my hand on the reins until you feel competent to take them yourself."

Horrified, Niall threw up a hand. "My dear Eddows, you may wait a lifetime! No, no. You would do better to train a man to replace you than rely upon me."

An austere look was cast upon him. "I believe I am good for a few years yet, my lord."

"I certainly hope so. I would be lost without you, my friend."

Eddows looked gratified. "However, I had intended to ask your lordship if you would object to my son becoming my apprentice. He is down from the university and I am hopeful of his proving useful."

"Ah, yes. I understand from Lord Tazewell that your family has served the Lowries for generations. Well, I am not minded to break with tradition. By all means, employ him as you see fit."

Eddows nodded, apparently considering the subject closed. "As to your interest in the village, my lord, the boundary takes in the entire environ except the woods, which mark the start of Lord Tazewell's lands."

"Yet I gather the villagers consider themselves part of Tazewell's estate?"

A thin smile creased the agent's lips. "An ancient feud, my lord, which exists between Itchington Bishops and the neighbouring village of Long Itchington. It need not trouble you. Beyond the odd battle on either of the village greens on certain holidays when the villagers are stirred by over-indulgence, there is scant attention paid to it these days."

Niall let it go, impatience returning. "But the Reverend Westacott? He's been the incumbent of the vicarage for many years?"

"Throughout my tenure, yes. He came here as a young man."

"And never married?"

"As I understand it, my lord, he abandoned all thought of it when he took in his brother's wife and child. A naval gentleman, sir, who had the misfortune to lose his life at Toulon in '93."

"How old was Miss Westacott then?"

"She must have been ten or eleven. I doubt Mr Westacott could afford a wife as well."

Niall was tempted to enquire more particularly into Miss Westacott's more recent life. But instinct, as much as good manners, warned him she would take such impertinence in bad part. But his curiosity was aroused and he took the earliest opportunity of carrying out his intention to rectify the unintentional omission.

The unaccustomed heat had abated after a bout of rain on the previous day and Niall drove into the village in his cousin's phaeton and left his groom, who had accompanied him into his new life, in charge of the horses.

Approaching the vicarage from the front this time, he was charmed by the slate roof and old brickwork, both a patchwork of colour mellowed by time, the diamond-patterned casements and the gothic ivy-covered porch.

Mrs Tuffin opened the door to him.

"Oh, my lord, have you come to see Reverend? I'm afraid he's off about his rounds."

"Then I've timed it ill."

"Miss Ede is in the parlour, my lord, if you'd care to step in."

Niall was conscious of a strong desire to see Miss Westacott, but he hesitated. "Is she resting?"

"She's laid down upon the day-bed, just as Reverend insisted."

"Then I should not disturb her."

"Well, there's two visitors already, my lord, so I doubt you'll do that. I'll announce you."

With which, she gave him no opportunity to retract but took the hat out of his hands and set it down on the cluttered hall table, bustling to a door at the front rather than the back room he'd entered the last time.

Perforce Niall followed her. He heard his name and stepped into a bright room, surprisingly neat, where three ladies were engaged in animated conversation.

His spirits sank as his gaze took in Miss Burloyne and Lady Tazewell, seated on chairs to one side of a chaise longue, upholstered in green velvet, upon which Miss Westacott half-lay, her back against the scrolled end.

Inwardly cursing, Niall bowed and murmured a greeting to the other ladies, his gaze straying to Edith Westacott. She looked, at first glance, little improved in pallor. But as he neared, he could see a healthier glow about her eyes and cheeks.

"You look a deal better, Miss Westacott. I take it you've been sensibly resting?"

The smile he remembered came. "I've been given no choice, sir."

"And an excellent thing, too," chimed in Lady Tazewell. "Have you also come to see how she does, Lord Hetherington? I declare, we were quite put out yesterday by the rain, for Delia and I were most anxious after that dreadful faint."

"You would not have found me at all, Lady Tazewell, had you come yesterday. My uncle insisted upon my keeping my bed, though I felt perfectly recovered."

"But you've been allowed up today."

"Yes, my lord, but upon conditions, which is why you find me languishing like an invalid. It is too ridiculous and I feel a perfect fraud."

"Oh, but you should take care, Miss Westacott," came from Miss Burloyne in a voice of concern. "Your housekeeper told us how ill you've been."

"I do wish Mrs Tuffin would not keep harping upon it. Anyone would suppose I'd been at death's door."

The irritated note revived memories of the other day and Niall made no attempt to break in upon the twittering protests of the ladies. He was irritated himself, realising how he'd hoped, at the back of his mind, to resume the easy conversation he'd enjoyed with Miss Westacott. And, let him be honest, to satisfy his curiosity. But that was now impossible in the presence of the two ladies from the Manor.

Lady Tazewell caught his attention.

"When you are recovered, Miss Westacott, you must come and dine with us."

Watching Miss Westacott, Niall thought he saw a shade of annoyance cross the pale countenance, and she answered with a touch of reserve.

"You are kind, Lady Tazewell, but I don't think —"

"Now do not say you will not come, for I insist upon it. Your uncle too." A trill of laughter grated on Niall's ears. "We are so dull, Delia and I, with little to amuse us, you must know, for we have read the latest *Ladies Magazine* from cover to cover and I promise you if I am obliged to set another stitch in Tom's new nightshirt I shall fall asleep over it. Do say you will come and save us from dying of boredom."

Niall could swear his inward groan was echoed in Miss Westacott's light eyes. Nor did Miss Burloyne look to be best pleased with this effusive plea.

But he had underestimated Miss Westacott, who produced a smile of great charm. "If you put it like that, ma'am, how can I resist?"

Niall almost gave in to mirth and was betrayed into unwise speech. "You would enliven any gathering, Miss Westacott, I have no doubt."

Faint colour crept into her cheeks, and the look she threw him held an echo of that pokered reserve.

Somewhat to his relief, Lady Tazewell did not wait for what answer she might make to this. "Then that is settled. Be sure I shall expect to hear when you are sufficiently recovered to indulge us."

"You will be the first to know, Lady Tazewell, the moment my uncle allows me to stray from the house."

The touch of irony Niall detected was lost upon the youthful Lady Tazewell, who rose from her chair.

"We must leave you now, for my husband has engaged a painter and wishes me to sit for my portrait. Come, Delia. How I shall keep still for the better part of an hour, I really don't know."

"I'll read to you, Jocasta," chimed in Miss Burloyne, obediently rising.

Miss Westacott's brows rose. "But had you not exhausted your supply of reading matter?"

Lady Tazewell blushed and giggled. "Caught out! I declare, I need my old dragon of a governess to curb me." She bent down and captured Miss Westacott's hands between her own. "I said it to persuade you. Will you forgive me?"

It was done so prettily Niall no longer wondered how Tom had become smitten with the chit. Nor was the girl's charm wasted upon Miss Westacott, whose genuine laugh sounded.

"It was ill done of me to challenge you, Lady Tazewell. The habit of correction is hard to break. You will think me as much of a dragon as your old governess, I dare say."

Lady Tazewell's tinkling laughter assailed Niall's ears and he winced.

"I had forgot you have been lately a teacher. But you could never compare to my Dragon. Besides, you are much too young and beautiful."

"Beautiful? Good heavens, Lady Tazewell, you must be perfectly blind!"

There could be no mistaking Miss Westacott's astonishment. Niall, himself startled by the pronouncement, regarded her with new eyes while Lady Tazewell appealed to her friend.

"Don't you think so, Delia? Oh, I know Miss Westacott is not at her best, but only look! Are not her features quite classic?"

"Oh, desist, Lady Tazewell! I wish you will not seek to flatter me in such a way."

"But I'm not flattering you. I truly think it, I promise you." To his intense embarrassment, she appealed to Niall. "Lord Hetherington, support me in this. You are a man. You must surely see —"

"Jocasta, do stop! You are embarrassing poor Miss Westacott."

Miss Burloyne, much to Niall's surprise, spoke in a sharp tone at variance with her usual sycophantic manner. But it had the effect of arresting Lady Tazewell's raptures.

A giggle escaped her and she looked both mischievous and contrite. "Oh, dear, now I am obliged to apologise all over again."

"Just stop talking, Jocasta, and all will be well. You are incorrigible, you know."

Lady Tazewell, her eyes dancing, closed her lips firmly together. Niall was eyeing Miss Burloyne with new interest, wondering if there was more to the woman than met the eye. Miss Westacott, on the other hand, looked to be thoroughly amused.

"I must thank you, Lady Tazewell. You have succeeded in making me feel perfectly at home. I might as well be back in Bath, presiding over a clutch of schoolgirls."

Lady Tazewell burst into laughter and again caught at Miss Westacott's hands. "I wish you had been my governess. I should not have subjected you to one tithe of the mischief I gave the Dragon."

"She has my sympathies."

Which produced another gale of laughter. Miss Burloyne, evidently quite out of patience, intervened. "Jocasta, you will be late."

"Heavens, yes! Goodbye, dear Miss Westacott." She turned on Niall. "We must leave you to entertain her, Lord Hetherington."

A quick curtsy from Miss Burloyne, and the two ladies went off in a flurry of muslins, gloves and parasols while Niall held the door for them. He closed it, hearing the two voices break out into twittering chatter in the hall. Without intent, he glanced across at Miss Westacott and threw up his eyes.

"If that is a sample of what you had to put up with in Bath, ma'am, I can only say that I sincerely pity you."

Miss Westacott let out a low laugh. "She is little removed from the schoolgirl, but her heart is warm."

He came forward and took the nearest chair vacated by the youthful Lady Tazewell, speaking without thought. "The other surprised me. I believe she may be wearing a public face. I have not previously seen her let her guard down."

"Miss Burloyne? She is a year or two older, I think. But it seems a well cemented friendship."

He lifted his brows. "Evidently not enough to satisfy Lady Tazewell's thirst for amusement. I suspect you may be importuned a great deal."

"I hardly think so. I have much acquaintance with these butterfly minds. I suspect her interest springs rather from curiosity than a desire to befriend me."

"Curiosity about what?"

The old reserve re-entered her face. "I cannot imagine."

Niall frowned. "Yes, you can. Don't fob me off!"

Her eyes flashed. "Oh, are you curious too, sir?"

"Inordinately. But I shan't be so crass as to enquire into your private concerns."

The spark died and he saw her hands clench briefly.

"My story is far too mundane to be of interest to anyone."

Niall eyed her, doubting what she said. From Miss Westacott's guarded manner it was obvious there was something distinctly out of the ordinary in her immediate past. Why, for one thing, had she left her post? Not, it struck him, purely on account of her illness, though that was no doubt her excuse.

He found her eyeing him with acute suspicion and laughed. "Don't fear me, ma'am. I would not pry for the world, even though you intrigue me."

She looked away. "I can't think why."

"Then you should mend your attitude, ma'am."

Her gaze flew back to his. "In what way?"

"If you will be so prickly, you will inevitably invite question."

Miss Westacott eyed him, her expression hard to read. Her voice, when she spoke, was cold. "Did you come here on purpose to retard my recovery?"

"On the contrary, I came to see how you did."

"As you see, I am doing a deal better."

Niall did not know whether to be irritated or amused at the determined formality of her tone. He matched it. "In fact, Miss Westacott, I came in hopes of seeing your uncle."

The startled expression in her eyes gave him a moment of satisfaction he knew to be unworthy.

"Why?"

He relented, smiling. "Because I have been remiss. I should have visited him long since, but I did not know the vicarage was in the earldom's gift."

Her features relaxed. "I see. I dare say the exigencies of your role are taxing when you are unused to them."

"I had no notion how close I stood to the succession, if you want the truth of it."

The curious eyes surveyed him. "Would it have made a difference if you had?"

He was brought up short. "I've never thought of it, but of course it would not. With my cousin so young and two healthy sons, the succession should have been secure. I should never have expected to take the title."

"Indeed not. But you are under a severe disadvantage, I can see, not having been brought up to the expectation. In the ordinary way, I imagine sons are well educated in their duties by the time they take possession."

"If I am to judge by my friend Tom Tazewell, yes. Though I believe it is not always so."

Once again he came under a regard he could only describe as measuring.

"You are finding it an irksome burden."

It was a statement. Niall felt oddly elated that she understood him so readily. He shifted his shoulders in a trifle of discomfort.

"I am ungrateful. Many men would give their eye teeth for such an opportunity."

A tiny laugh escaped her. "So you are striving for a gratitude you cannot feel when all your instinct is to run away? Believe me, I can fully enter into your sentiments."

Niall warmed inside. He was tempted to probe, but the remembrance of the way Miss Westacott could poker up stayed him. He opted for simplicity.

"It's refreshing — nay, comforting — to find someone who can understand."

He was rewarded by her smile, and it struck him that Lady Tazewell was right. She was beautiful. Not striking in the way a toast of Society might be, to be admired by all. Yet the planes of her oval face, despite the gauntness of her cheeks, and perhaps her pallor, accentuated by the midnight hair, was reminiscent of the statues of alabaster from the ancient world.

Something stirred within him, and Niall's mind emptied of all thought as he stared at her.

Chapter Four

Edith met Lord Hetherington's gaze, unable to help wondering what was in his mind. For an instant she had suspected him of cherishing a slight attraction towards her. His manner, however, was so far removed from the insinuations to which she'd been subjected, to her heavy cost, she felt unable to judge. In a bid to deflect any possible move in that direction, she fell back upon formality.

"I dare say my uncle will be some time. Should you care to return on another occasion?"

"No, I shouldn't."

The harsh tone caused her to shrivel inside, reviving the memory of the dreadful day when the life she'd made had been cut short. Edith turned her gaze to the window, staring out at the village green and the bank of cottage shops beyond it. A film of moisture made the scene blur and she bit her lip, fighting against the prick and rise of tears. She had not wept since that night, and this was no moment to be succumbing to weakness.

"Miss Westacott?"

The softer note almost undid her and she could not respond.

"Miss Westacott — Edith — look at me!"

Without will, she turned her head, pulling her brows together and tightening her lips.

Lord Hetherington's rough features wore an expression of concern and she could not doubt he'd noted the moisture at her eyes.

"Was it something I said?"

She shook her head, swallowing down the persistent lump.

His frown intensified. "Good manners prompts me to leave you, but I cannot bring myself to do so when you are in such distress."

She drew in a tight breath and forced the words out. "There is nothing you can do, sir. Let it be, if you please."

He continued to eye her in silence, and the steady regard had an oddly soothing effect. Had he attempted words of comfort, she'd have been tempted to attack with anger. Presently the uncomfortable symptoms subsided and she dredged up as natural a voice as she could assume.

"I've not offered you refreshment."

He made an impatient gesture. "I need nothing."

"But I do. Would you be kind enough to ask Mrs Tuffin —" She broke off as the door opened and the housekeeper appeared with a tray. Relief allowed her to speak more naturally. "Oh, you've anticipated me, Mrs Tuffin. I was just about to ask. Is it coffee?"

Lord Hetherington jumped up and moved out of the way as the housekeeper made for the table behind the day-bed.

"Coffee it is, Miss Ede. Reverend don't like me to waste the tea."

Edith glanced at her visitor. "For my part, I find coffee revives me better. Will you take a cup, sir?"

"Thank you, I will. Black, Mrs Tuffin, if I may."

The resumption of a casual tone eased Edith the more, and she was able to answer with her usual lightness. "Is that a habit acquired in the field, my lord?"

"Probably. Cream was rarely part of our rations."

"I confess I prefer it larded with cream, though I had not been used to sugar until I came here."

Mrs Tuffin began to cluck. "You need it, Miss Ede, that's what Reverend says. You need plucking up, he says. Plenty of milk, eggs and cheese."

Edith took this without comment, accepting the well-sweetened coffee and sipping gratefully at the hot brew.

"I've made scones, Miss Ede, for later, but I put in some cheese straws along with them and they're still warm from the oven."

Knowing her uncle would be quoted at her if she refused, Edith took the plate on which the housekeeper had placed a couple of the pastries, and laid it on her lap with a word of thanks. Mrs Tuffin did not bustle out until she had pressed cheese straws upon his lordship as well. When they were alone again, he set them down on the tray uneaten.

"You had best at least taste them, my lord, or you will offend Mrs Tuffin."

He threw up his eyes and picked one off the plate. "If you insist."

"Well, I don't see why I should be the only one to suffer."

Amusement gleamed in his eyes. "I am not recovering from an illness, Miss Westacott." He bit into the pastry and his brows rose. "Tasty indeed. Your uncle is to be congratulated."

Edith had to laugh. "Yes, she is an excellent cook. I wish I might do justice to her efforts."

"You will, in time."

She sipped her coffee, regarding him over the rim of her cup as he lifted his own to his lips. "Are you a soothsayer, sir?"

He choked, and her conscience pricked. She waited until the coughing subsided.

"That was ill done of me."

But Lord Hetherington was laughing. "Horrible girl! How could you exercise your wit at my expense just then?"

Laughter bubbled in her and she could not hold it back. "I will say not another word until you've finished drinking."

"Too kind. For your information, ma'am, I have some experience of the effects of severe illness on the body." She looked a question and he shook his head. "Not myself, no, but I've seen men debilitated by fevers, dysentery and wounds. And nursed them, come to that."

Her interest aroused, Edith watched him take another draft of his coffee. "The Army appears to equip a man for all manner of emergencies. Have you seen a deal of action?"

"Intermittently over the years. I've enjoyed it when it came."

She opened her eyes at him. "A fighter, sir? I fear you'll have scant opportunity to indulge your preference in Itchington."

Lord Hetherington surveyed her with a kindling eye. "On the contrary, if you continue in the village."

A chuckle escaped her. "You must blame my profession, my lord. I learned to use my tongue so that I might spare the rod."

"A disciplinarian, ma'am? I do not envy your pupils."

"Yes, I deserved that."

His laugh warmed her unexpectedly. Edith suppressed the feeling, taking refuge in sipping her coffee. He did likewise, glancing away from her, almost as if he noticed her reaction. She hunted for an innocuous subject and fell back upon his earlier comment.

"Pray tell me what is enjoyable in battling your fellow man in the field." She caught his glance and put out a hand. "Oh, I am not teasing you, sir, I am interested."

His brows rose. "I can't think why."

"Because I am evidently missing something. I had thought it was all gunfire and smoke and screaming men."

He winced. "That too, and I don't pretend to pleasure in that. But it's not pleasure. How can I explain? Yes, I can, though. It is what one might call fire in the belly."

The change in him was startling. His eyes, alight with that fire, she supposed, were bright with echoes of his thoughts as he spoke.

"It's a feeling like no other — a roaring giant inside me who can conquer the world."

Mesmerised, Edith regarded him with her cup stilled halfway to her mouth. He caught her glance and at once looked conscious, the tanned skin darkening.

"I beg your pardon. It's hardly a fitting subject for female ears."

Edith let out an irritated breath. "Don't spoil it. And I asked you, remember."

"Yes, but I had no business to speak of such things. I don't know why I did so. I never have before. You are a terrible influence, Miss Westacott."

Edith found herself relishing the scold. Why, she could not imagine, but it pleased her that he had been betrayed into speaking freely. She answered in kind.

"Well, I am glad of that, for I am now enlightened as to why the village males insist upon battling on the green any time they are in their cups."

He burst out laughing. "You are utterly without proper feminine conduct, Miss Westacott. I wonder at your being permitted anywhere near young female minds."

She struggled with the immediate shaft that went through her, chiding herself for being over-sensitive. Lord Hetherington could not know, would not deliberately taunt her. To her intense relief, before he had a chance to notice the change in her, the door opened and her uncle came in.

"Lord Hetherington! Goodness me, sir, I am sorry to have kept you waiting."

His lordship had risen. "Not at all, sir. I have been well entertained."

"By Edith? I am so pleased. Not that it's quite proper to be with her unchaperoned, but we won't regard that."

Lord Hetherington looked dismayed, glancing at Edith. "Ought I to have gone when the ladies left?"

"By no means," she said, chagrined. "I am not a girl, Uncle Lionel. I'm a schoolmistress. There can be no impropriety."

Her uncle came to the day-bed and patted her shoulder. "My dear, I should never accuse you of impropriety. Nor could I suppose Lord Hetherington to be guilty of importuning you in any way, not after his kindness the other day." He turned from her to offer his hand to the guest. "Mrs Tuffin says you wished to see me, my lord?"

"I did, sir, and you may rest assured Miss Westacott has nothing to fear from me."

Which was as much as to say that her shrinking fears of his being even slightly attracted to her were groundless. Why the realisation should cause a drop in spirits Edith could not fathom. She ought to be glad. Then her attention was drawn to what Lord Hetherington was saying.

"I have been remiss, Mr Westacott, but I hope you will forgive the lapse for I had no notion my estates encompassed this village. Nor that the vicarage is in my gift."

Her uncle beamed through his spectacles. "That explains it, my lord. I did wonder at the time. But indeed, indeed, you owe me no apologies. The boot, my lord, is on the other leg and I must certainly have called upon you had I not been preoccupied with my poor Ede here."

She caught Lord Hetherington's glance as he looked across.

"Our two arrivals coincided then?"

Her uncle took the question. "No, indeed, sir. We none of us in the village heard of your coming until I met with Mr Eddows three weeks ago, by which time I had my niece on my hands. The poor girl was in a dreadful way, and I confess my attention was concentrated upon her needs."

"As it well ought to have been, sir. I am happy to know you did not spare me a thought under the circumstances."

Edith could endure no more discussion of her illness. "Pray why did you creep into the place in secrecy, my lord? Did you arrive in the dead of night and bury yourself in your castle?"

Her uncle tutted. "Ede, my dear, what in the world are you saying?"

She set her teeth, trying for patience. "Oh, Lord Hetherington will not take it amiss. I am sure he is growing used to my sallies."

"I am indeed." A minatory glance was cast her way. "I shall, however, refrain from taking you up, Miss Westacott, until a later occasion."

Her lips twitched. "And you a soldier, sir? Am I to call you coward?"

"Ede!"

Lord Hetherington ignored the intervention, his eyes acknowledging a hit. "By no means. But a good soldier knows when to retreat." She laughed as he turned to her uncle. "Don't look so dismayed, sir. Your niece's banter is refreshing. May we retire to another room?"

Her uncle became flustered. "Yes, yes, indeed. My study, sir, if you will. But it's most odd in you. Gracious me, yes, most odd."

He ushered his guest towards the door, where his lordship turned his head.

"*Au revoir*, Miss Westacott. I look forward to our next bout."

"Gracious me, my lord! Most odd."

The conspiratorial look Lord Hetherington threw at her as he left proved too much for her gravity, and she was glad the door shut behind the two gentlemen as she gave way to laughter.

It did not last. Too soon the trouble in her mind and heart returned to plague her. She recalled Lord Hetherington's saying he found her refreshing. Or her banter at least. She might say the same of him, since he provided her with a diversion from the darkness of her thoughts.

Her uncle was right, for he was an odd creature. Oh, not in sparring with her, for she must take the blame for provoking him in that. But from what she'd learned of him, he was more frustrated than honoured to have been raised to his new estate. Was it the loss of his military career? He was clearly a man more than capable of taking on a difficult challenge. A sense of responsibility evidently kept him from repudiating the inheritance. She must suppose it was possible to do that, to let it go to the next in line. This he had not done, taking up what he felt to be a burden and making the best of it.

Though he was not doing that, was he? Like herself, he was chock-full of disappointment, resenting his situation and hating the necessity to endure. How odd. Was that why he was drawn to her, as she was to him?

No, stop that at once, Edith Westacott! She might allow herself the indulgence of bandying words — exercising her wit at his expense, as he'd put it — but that was, must be, the sum of it.

Instead, let her turn her mind to the future. She should begin her scheme of scanning the newspaper advertisements. It ought not to tax her ingenuity to do so without Uncle Lionel's realising what she was at. It was bound to take time to find a suitable post. Better she started now than wait until her Nemesis caught up with her.

It would be too late then to escape.

Chapter Five

Apart from a brief greeting on the intervening Sunday when Niall felt it incumbent upon him to attend the Reverend Westacott's morning service, he did not encounter Miss Westacott for some days. Matters at the Court had become pressing and he had no attention to spare for doing the pretty, excusing himself from an invitation to dine again at the Manor.

He had risen from the chair before the desk in the library, which he had made his headquarters, and was regarding his man of business with his temper on a tight rein.

"You told me, Scoones, that probate was in train and it needed only my signature."

The lawyer, a spare creature with a perpetual sniff, became apologetic. "True, my lord, but these things take their own time."

"I have no time, Scoones." He crossed back to the desk and picked up the polite letter he'd received two days ago, holding it up. "My bankers inform me I am in danger of outrunning the constable. My personal bankers, Scoones."

Another sniff preceded the fellow's response. "It is unfortunate your lordship has been obliged to draw upon personal funds, but —"

"Unfortunate? Sir, I no longer have a salary and the profits from the sale of my commission have dwindled to next to nothing."

The lawyer cleared his throat. "Your lordship's bankers are aware, however, of your lordship's having taken possession of the estate."

His anger mounting, Niall glared at the fellow. "I'm not concerned with my bankers. Do you expect the local tradesmen to survive on air? And Eddows was unable to pay the servants at the last quarter. That, sir, is unacceptable."

The inevitable sniff made him want to throttle the man.

"Once probate is granted, my lord —"

"Don't quote me that platitude again, Scoones. I'm familiar with the dilatory tactics of lawyers and I tell you now I won't stand for it."

"The matter is out of my hands, my lord. I have done my part."

"Then put pressure to bear on the hands who have it, sir. Good God, if we'd waited on this sort of red tape in India, we'd have been overrun by the Marathas!" Niall heard a muffled laugh from his agent, silent in the background where he stood by one of the tall bookcases, and glanced at him. "How badly are we dipped, did you say, Eddows? Tell him, if you please."

The sum named caused the lawyer to wince and sniff again. "A trifle, my lord, once you have access to the Hetherington funds."

"I dare say, but I don't care to be behindhand with the world. Nor, I may add, does Eddows. He's done wonders, holding the place together, even I can see that. But it will not do, Scoones."

The man bowed slightly. "I will do what I may to hurry things along, my lord."

"See you do, or I'll find a man who will."

The threat caused a red stain to rise into the lawyer's cheeks and his features tightened. "Was there anything else, my lord?"

Niall drew in his horns with difficulty, again looking to Eddows. "Where did we put that pile of papers I need Scoones to check through?"

"In the second drawer, my lord," said his agent, coming to the desk and withdrawing a bulging file from the specified drawer. He offered it to Niall, who waved it towards the lawyer.

"Take these with you, if you please, but don't waste time on them. Probate is our first concern."

The lawyer took the file with another sniff. "My clerks may manage these, my lord. I will likely have to journey to the capital if I am to expedite matters."

"Then do so and chalk it up to me."

Scoones bowed himself out, Eddows in attendance, and Niall was glad to see the back of him.

He'd been appalled to discover the state of the finances and had written to Scoones as soon as Eddows put him in the picture. When he'd met the lawyer at his office in Warwick, Scoones had told him probate would not be delayed since the necessary papers had been put in train once they'd found the heir. The Law's notions of delay and his were evidently vastly divergent.

Niall sighed in defeat, turning to look at the view beyond the window, which ought to gladden the heart of any landowner. Set in a valley of woodlands, the vista encompassed well-kept lawns dotted by copses of trees, a distant waterway and cultivated fields. He must be the most ungrateful dog alive.

Eddows came back into the room before he could pursue this thought.

"It occurs to me, my lord, that you might with advantage employ a secretary."

Niall swung on the man. "And pay him in bread and cheese? For God's sake, man, let's not introduce any new expense!"

The agent's lips quirked. "I did not mean quite immediately, my lord."

"Thank God for that! What, if anything, can we do to ease matters until these Godforsaken lawyers manage to settle?" He flung into the chair at his desk, dropping his hands on to the leather blotter and clasping them together.

Eddows took the chair opposite, absently drumming his fingers on the desk, his eyes resting upon the ornate inkstand in the Chinese pattern with its inset crystal bottles and pot of ready quills. At length he looked up.

"Are your funds exhausted, my lord?"

"It's not quite as dire as I allowed Scoones to think, but I doubt I can keep us afloat for many weeks."

"Would you consider asking Lord Tazewell for a loan, my lord?"

Startled, Niall eyed him. He'd never allowed himself to fall into debt in his life, beyond a few guineas from a friend once or twice when he had no loose change in his pockets. And he'd paid that back without delay. The thought of incurring the sort of indebtedness this estate would involve was anathema.

"No, Eddows, I would not."

The agent sucked in a breath. "His lordship is a very wealthy young man, my lord. It would not incommode him."

"That may be so, but it makes it no better. We are in enough debt as it is."

"Nothing the estate cannot stand, my lord, once —"

"Probate is granted. Yes, I'm aware of that."

Eddows was silent for a space but Niall doubted the fellow had any more idea than he how funds might be raised should probate be too long delayed.

"There is one way, my lord."

"Indeed?" The agent's speculative gaze intrigued him. "Well, don't keep me in suspense? You're not going to suggest I turn highwayman or some such thing?"

Eddows laughed. "It has been known, my lord, but I should doubt of your principles permitting you to engage in criminal activity."

"You may well doubt it. Come, out with it, man."

"If the worst comes to the worst, my lord, you could offer to sell the village back to Lord Tazewell."

"Good God!"

Niall stared at the man, turning the matter over in his mind. An ingenious notion, which would likely solve all his problems at a stroke. And he had no interest in the village.

An image leapt into his mind. Damnation, yes he had! A very strong interest. If he sold the village, Edith Westacott would no longer be his responsibility. He spoke on the thought. "No. It's genius, Eddows, but no." He saw the agent's puzzlement and amended his response. "Unless I am driven against the ropes."

"I meant it as an extreme measure, my lord. We must hope it will not be necessary."

Niall heard him only vaguely, his attention caught on his own extraordinary feeling of ownership towards Edith Westacott.

Chapter Six

With returning strength, Edith's restlessness plagued her the more, much to her chagrin and dismay. She'd possessed her soul in what patience she could, allowing her uncle and Mrs Tuffin's cosseting regime of rest and food to rule her days.

Although she viewed the diet of extra eggs, milk, pancakes and pastries which supplemented the main meals throughout the day with a jaundiced eye, Edith was forced to acknowledge the benefit. Her skin began to look fresher, gaining a trifle of colour and her flesh was no longer as wasted.

She occupied herself with scanning the newspapers and making a secret note in her pocket book of the details of those advertisements for positions for which she might with advantage apply. Edith told herself that until she was well enough, there was little point in actually making an application, refusing to give room to the fear that lurked beneath.

With her uncle's permission, she took a turn in the back garden each day, unwilling to worry him by going further afield until she could be certain she would not collapse. But she eyed with longing the woods in one direction and the road that led to the Hetherington grounds in the other, which she knew from her childhood to be both extensive and picturesque. The latter would afford the opportunity she craved to lose herself in the privacy of her own thoughts without encountering the ladies from the Manor. That she might instead encounter the new owner of those estates, Edith refused to consider. Lord Hetherington was clearly far too busy to have leisure to wander his own grounds. Nor to go visiting it seemed. Not that she wished to see him. The amusement of bantering with him might have afforded her a little relief from the darkness in which she dwelled. But what she'd really hoped for was an opportunity to ask his permission to roam in his lands.

A foolish thought. He would not give it, would he? Not because he was ungenerous. He wouldn't mind in the least, she was sure of that. But he would be bound to disapprove of her wandering alone, even could she convince him she was well enough, and she did not relish having to explain her need of solitude.

However, Lord Hetherington did not appear, either at the vicarage or at the Manor when she and her uncle at last accepted an invitation to dine there.

Edith had not been looking forward to the treat. The two ladies, unlike a certain gentleman she refused to think about, had not been remiss in coming to see how she did, arriving unannounced on two occasions and remaining with her for more than an hour each time.

Really, she might as well have been back at the school in Bath. She felt, in their presence, more like a matron than her five and twenty years. Although Miss Burloyne, she discovered, was a couple of years older than Lady Tazewell, who was not yet nineteen.

If she hoped for the leaven of Lord Hetherington at the feast — which she would not acknowledge to herself — she was disappointed.

"I'm so glad you could come at last, dear Miss Westacott," gushed her hostess. "And we are to be quite informal, you know, for it is only the two of you, so you may rest upon the day-bed in the drawing room after dinner, if you should feel tired."

"I hardly think I shall need to, Lady Tazewell. I am a good deal recovered."

"Yes, and I am so glad. You are looking so much better, and quite beautiful. Don't you think so, Tom?"

Edith's cheeks warmed as the silly woman's husband, who had been in conversation with her uncle, turned his head to glance at her. She intervened before he could speak. "I wish you won't say anything, Lord Tazewell. It is quite ridiculous that you should be urged to compliment me." With deftness, she turned the subject. "Miss Burloyne, how is your embroidery coming? May I be permitted to see it? Do you think you will finish it in time?"

She'd heard all about the proposed gift on one of the ladies' visits, and had no real interest. She'd seen enough poor efforts at stitchery to last a lifetime. But anything was better than Lady Tazewell's effusions. She meant well, Edith knew, but she had no tact.

The other young lady looked gratified by the attention. "I've made good progress, I think. Would you really like to see it?"

The short answer was no, but Edith felt a little sorry for the girl. And a trifle guilty at using her. "Very much, if you are willing to show it to me."

"Fetch it after dinner, Delia, when we leave the gentlemen to their wine."

"Yes, that will be best, no doubt."

But Edith felt chagrined on the girl's behalf. It was evident she took pride in her work and was eager for praise. Of any kind, perhaps. It might be interesting to try and draw her out, if opportunity offered.

And then Miss Burloyne, quite unconsciously, alienated Edith's sympathies.

"Such a pity Lord Hetherington cannot come tonight. We've not seen him for days. Have you, Miss Westacott? I wondered if he had been again to see how you do after your adventure in the woods."

"No, indeed." Edith realised her tone was repressive and added a rider. "I must suppose he is tied up with his estates, since he is new to the title."

"Oh, yes, it is too bad," chimed in Lady Tazewell. "We had quite counted upon him, but to no avail. I shall scold him dreadfully when we meet at last."

Edith found herself hoping the girl would, since she had no legitimate reason to do so herself. *Ridiculous, Edith Westacott. Stop it at once!* But the spectre of his missing presence would not be dismissed. Especially when it was borne in upon Edith that Miss Burloyne considered her a rival for Lord Hetherington's favours. They were seated side by side at dinner, and Edith might indeed have carried out her plan to draw the girl out had she not shown her interests lay otherwise.

"I am surprised Lord Hetherington has not been to see you again, Miss Westacott. He was clearly concerned for your health."

Edith partook of a mouthful of artichoke pie to give herself an opportunity to think how to answer such a leading question. "As a matter of fact, ma'am, he came that day to see my uncle because he had discovered the vicarage lay in his gift."

"Oh, I see. Still, I am sure he must have wanted to assure himself you were well after his rescue."

Edith felt as if she were under interrogation. Did Miss Burloyne wish to ascertain whether she had an interest in Lord Hetherington? Or was it the reverse?

"I was lucky he was by at the time. These military men are so capable, don't you think?"

The ploy did not succeed.

"I rather thought he was amused by your wit, Miss Westacott." A brittle laugh came. "As were we all, I admit."

Not you, it would seem. But Edith did not say as much. She adopted as airy a tone as she could find. "I believe you exaggerate, Miss Burloyne. I was used to employ my wits to counter schoolgirl impertinence. I dare say it has become a habit."

The girl had the grace to blush, and Edith hoped she would leave the subject alone. She was able to eat in silence for a space, but it did not last.

Miss Burloyne adopted a low tone, her gaze fixed upon her plate. "You can have no notion, Miss Westacott, as confident as you are, of the pangs of constant failure."

Startled, Edith glanced at her. "I beg your pardon?"

Miss Burloyne looked round. All trace of the giggling schoolgirl was gone. A vulnerable, unhappy young woman had taken her place.

Edith's heart melted and she leaned in, speaking low. "You are mistaken. Contrive to come and see me again. Alone, if you can manage it."

The woman did not speak, only eyeing Edith as if she sought to determine whether she might be trusted. Then she gave a bright smile and adopted her erstwhile thin imitation of Lady Tazewell's vivacity.

"Jocasta tells me we are to visit Lord Tazewell's parents shortly, Miss Westacott. Have you met them?"

Disconcerted by the change, and half wondering if she had imagined the earlier exchange, Edith answered without thinking. "When I was a child, yes, now and then. They were not often here. One of Lord Tazewell's aunts was in residence at that time."

Lord Tazewell, overhearing, remarked upon his aunt's character and the conversation became general. No further mention was made of Lord Hetherington, but Edith was uncomfortably aware of his image stubbornly persisting in her mind for the remainder of the evening.

She'd been relieved not to receive a further invitation, and hoped the promised visit to Lord Tazewell's parents would occur before Miss Burloyne had an opportunity to take her up on that ill-considered invitation of her own. So far there had been no sign of the girl and Edith was relieved. There could be no doubt Miss Burloyne had thought to set her cap at Lord Hetherington. Edith was uncomfortably aware both of dismay and a sneaking suspicion that she had put a bar in the girl's way, however inadvertently. Although there was no saying Lord Hetherington would succumb to Miss Burloyne's lures, even if he was hanging out for a wife. One thing was certain. He would not find one in the vicar's niece.

The feeling of oppression, never absent for long, returned full force. Edith looked up from the newspaper, which was spread out on the bureau where she sat in the family room at the back of the house, and stared out into the garden.

How long had she been sitting here pretending to read, her mind far away? It felt an age. The day had dragged and her restlessness refused to be contained.

She rose from her chair and left the room, heading for the back door. It was open, and Edith saw a shadow fall across the flags of the porch beyond.

A flurry disturbed her heartbeat and she hesitated. Someone was out there.

Could it be Mrs Tuffin? No, she was in the kitchen. Besides, it was too long a shadow for the bustling housekeeper. Her uncle kept no manservant, preferring to give employment to the men of the village as needed, just as Mrs Tuffin had girls in to clean and scrub.

The shadow vanished, and Edith went with cautious steps to the door and peered out. She caught a glimpse of someone slipping around the corner of the house and followed, her heartbeat accelerating.

By the time she gained that side, whoever it was had gone. Edith half ran to the low wall that enclosed the property and looked across the green. Apart from the usual idlers outside the tavern and the delivery boy from Ash's shop crossing with a basket, the scene was as peaceful as it ever was, with no sign of a stranger.

By no means reassured, Edith remained by the wall, leaning one hand on the stone surface, the nightmare resurfacing. Had he come? Had he traced her whereabouts?

An ugly thought crept into her mind, freezing her blood. While she sat rapt in contemplation, her mind far away, had those predatory eyes been watching her through the window, spying upon her?

A shiver ran through her and her heart cried out in protest. Would she never be safe? Even here did he dare to pursue her, in the sanctuary of her uncle's home? Was it not enough that he had ruined her standing with Mrs Vinson and forced her exit from the Academy?

The fear gave way to anger and Edith strode to the back gate, unlatched it and went with swift steps onto the green, her gaze flicking this way and that. There was no sign of the man she called her Nemesis. Rightly, if he had truly tracked her here.

If he'd been here, he had successfully hidden himself. Had she imagined it? Was this her overwrought nerves playing her false?

She drew deep breaths, forcing herself to calm, unable to help a searching regard at as much of the vicarage as she could see from the middle of the green. Her eyes went to the steeple a little way along the lane. Should she try the church?

No, stop it, Edith Westacott! If it was he and he was determined to hide, she would not find him. And the church at this time of day would be empty. Foolish to put herself in a position where she would be altogether vulnerable.

She must have been mistaken. An irritation of the nerves. What had she seen after all but a shadow? No sound, no sight of the hated figure, the detested face. She could not even now be sure she'd seen someone slip around the corner of the house. It must be her unnatural fear preying upon her to produce the creeping familiarity of his nearness.

"Miss Westacott!"

Her heart leapt with shock and she spun round. A very different man was striding towards her across the green from the direction of the tavern. Edith all but fainted again, the relief was so intense.

"Lord Hetherington, how you startled me!"

He was frowning heavily as he reached her. "I appear to have shocked you rather. What is it?"

Still dazed, she stared at him. "What is what?"

"I find you out here, without even a hat, staring about you and looking shaken and you can ask that? What has occurred?"

Too distrait for discretion, Edith blurted it out. "I thought I saw him. In the back garden. I must have been wrong, for I've looked and looked and…" Realising where her words were tending, she faded out.

"Who did you see? What man is this you fear?"

She took a step back, closing into herself. "I didn't say I feared him."

"You had no need to say so. I can see it in your eyes."

Struggling with her inner demons, Edith tried for a lightness she did not feel. "You are imagining things, my lord."

His gaze hardened. "Don't lie to me. If you wish to keep your secrets, so be it, but don't insult my intelligence."

The harsh tone both hurt and angered her. "Then let us say I am suffering from an over-active imagination. I'm sure you would say so did you know how little evidence I have."

His brows rose. "I know you to be a woman of common sense, ma'am. If you felt something threatened you, I would be more inclined to search for what it might be than to accuse you of imagining things."

Her ruffled feathers smoothed down. "Thank you for that, at least."

The crease reappeared between his brows. "Do you feel threatened?"

She drew a shaky breath. "No more than I have done for some time now."

He was silent, regarding her in a manner that made her both conscious and uncomfortably aware of prevaricating. Why she should feel it so was a mystery. She owed no allegiance to the man, nor had he any right to probe into her private affairs.

He seemed to realise this, for he argued no further, but offered his arm. "Let me escort you back to the house at least. If you stand here looking so wildly you will be remarked."

That was all too true. Edith set her hand upon his arm and allowed him to lead her back towards the gate. "You have a knack, my lord, of appearing at just the right moment."

He looked down as she glanced up and his features relaxed. "That's better. You begin to sound more like yourself."

She was obliged to laugh. "Did I truly seem wild out there?"

"Very much so."

He paused as they reached the gate, setting his hand on hers. Edith felt its warmth and a measure of calm returned. "I will not pry, since you are clearly reluctant to confide in me." His mouth twisted. "And why should you indeed? But if you are menaced in any way, I wish you will send to me."

Edith warmed inside, but she could not let it pass without comment. "My official knight errant, Lord Hetherington?"

He smiled. "If you like."

"Well, it is kind in you, but I trust I will not be obliged to call upon you. I believe I have been guilty of jumping at shadows, which is all it was when all is said and done." She moved to open the gate but he forestalled her, his hand on the latch.

"You saw a shadow?"

She gave in. "On the back porch, yes, as I was coming towards the door."

"The door was open?"

"There is nothing unusual in that, especially in this weather."

The day was not overly hot, but July remained clement. Lord Hetherington seemed unimpressed.

"Then I suggest you keep the door closed in future."

He opened the gate and she went through. She waited for him to follow, but he remained on the other side. At the thought of his leaving, Edith felt a cold shiver go through her and acted on instinct.

"Will you not come in for a space? At least let me offer you coffee."

Lord Hetherington looked regretful. "I have business that cannot wait. I would not have stopped at all had I not seen you."

She was both touched and warmed to think he'd interrupted his duties to come to her aid. Smiling, she held out her hand. "Then I must count you a true knight errant, and thank you for coming to my rescue a second time."

To her surprise, he did not disclaim, but took her hand and held it, curling her fingers into his larger one.

"Yes, and I have a strong notion it is not the last. Don't hesitate to call on me. I mean it, Miss Westacott. If this fellow you fear should turn up, send to me at once." With which, he released her hand and strode off across the green, leaving Edith with a warm sensation inside. She had no intention of calling upon him, but it was comforting to feel that he cared.

Chapter Seven

Turning his steps towards the lane that led to the cottages Eddows wanted him to inspect, Niall had little attention to spare for the problems of his tenants. On catching sight of Edith Westacott, he'd left his agent standing with a brief word.

"Go on, Eddows. I'll catch you up."

It had taken only a glance to realise something was wrong, and he was by no means reassured after having restored her to safety. The reverse, if anything. She had recovered her equilibrium within minutes, but the fear in her was palpable.

His mind turning on the man who clearly menaced her rather than what she had seen, Niall replayed in his head the times she'd shied from even a mild compliment. Was this to be set at the fellow's door?

He reached the other side of the green to find Eddows awaiting him, and inwardly cursed at the necessity to master his thoughts and turn them to more mundane matters.

"The cottages are just up this lane, my lord. We are fortunate there has been little rain, for in general it turns into a hasty pudding of mud up here."

"I can see why," Niall said, regarding the rutted lane with disfavour. "Set a repair on your urgent list, Eddows."

"I will do so, my lord, but you may feel it to be unnecessary if these cottages must be condemned, as I suspect will be the case."

With reluctance, Niall consigned Miss Westacott's affairs to the back of his mind while he concentrated upon his own.

The cottages were found to be in a parlous state, but since he had at present no means of rehousing the tenants, he directed Eddows to put in the repairs to the rooves at once.

"If the money proves to be wasted, so be it. But these people must live somewhere while we build anew."

By the time Eddows had dragged him to a nearby farm to confer with its disgruntled owner and he had ridden across several fields to inspect the failing drainage, Niall was too preoccupied with how much needed to be done and the lack of funds to do it to allow room for Miss Westacott and her shadows. When he began upon his solitary dinner, however, it crept back and would not leave him.

He found himself dwelling on the spectre of this unknown man. Why did she fear him? What had he done to her? The obvious answer was so unpalatable Niall wished he might dismiss it. But he could not.

He knew nothing of the life of a schoolmistress, but he did know how vulnerable an unprotected female could be. True, Bath was not a stricken Indian village decimated by battle-weary soldiers in search of provisions or entertainment. But men were men the world over and Niall knew, perhaps better than some of his pampered fellow peers, of what they were capable when in pursuit of a woman.

His mind froze on the images leaping in his imagination. He had no means of knowing whether Edith Westacott had been subjected to sensual brutality, and she would not tell him. How should she indeed? Shame, as much as fear, must prevent her speaking of it. He took up his wine glass and sipped, only half aware that he did so. Of one thing he could be certain. Whoever this man was, he was no welcome lover. Edith was terrified.

Fire leapt in his belly, akin to the feeling he knew before battle, but edged with fury. That anyone should dare to hurt her! Let him come. Niall would know how to answer his insolence.

A crack sounded and liquid spilled over his hand. Niall's mind sprang back to the present and he cursed. He'd snapped the stem of his wine glass.

The butler was already wiping at the stains as he set the broken vessel down, drying the fingers on his napkin. "Beware splinters, my lord."

Niall examined his hand. "Bring one of the candles here, will you?"

Hempsall fetched a silver candelabrum from the centre of the table and set it on the corner nearby. Niall checked his hand in the better light, wondering what had possessed him.

"I can see no damage, Hempsall. Take it away, if you please. And bring me another glass. You may clear the rest."

"Will your lordship not partake of the syllabub?"

Niall was about to reject it with loathing when duty tapped remindingly on the walls. It formed no part of his plans to be offending the cook. Or any of the remaining domestic staff, none of whom had yet been paid for the quarter.

"I'll take a small quantity, thank you. And pray request Mrs Radway to convey my compliments to Cook. An excellent repast, and I must thank her for adhering to my request for simple meals."

Quite aside from the expense, Niall was used to making do with whatever was available to the camp. He was a good trencherman, enjoying his meat, but the array of dishes set out in several courses at the Manor he found both wasteful and far more than was needed to keep body and soul together. Until he was obliged to entertain, he would not indulge such extravagant habits in his new home, any more than he would have done in his various billets.

Having disposed of the syllabub, he allowed himself the indulgence of sitting over his wine and pondering on Miss Edith Westacott.

She evidently wished it to be understood that illness had driven her from her post at the school in Bath. But today's episode put a different complexion on the matter. It had not before occurred to Niall, but now it struck him as obvious it could not be that. Why would she leave her means of livelihood and return to her childhood home when common sense dictated she could as well recover where she was? The illness — was it fever? She had never revealed its nature. Yet even if the illness had left her too debilitated to teach, a sojourn at home would be only temporary. Then why would she not say so? No, there was more to it. And this man she feared was involved.

Not only had he importuned her somehow — Niall prayed it was not in the worst way — but he had been instrumental in her decision to abandon her only means of livelihood. From the little he knew of her, Niall did not suppose she would be content to live at her uncle's expense. A woman of independence, was Edith Westacott. He admired her for it. He admired her spirit, her courage and her wit. In fact, he admired her a good deal too much. He liked her too much, if truth be told.

And she? He could not flatter himself she liked him above the ordinary. Recalling her sallies and the shared laughter, Niall allowed himself to think she at least enjoyed his company. But when he'd offered his aid, she'd turned it off with a jest about his knight errantry. He had not won her trust. Then that must be his goal. To which end, recalling their earlier encounters, he could not by any means allow her to see his admiration. The slightest hint at gallantry would cause her to poker up.

Very well, Miss Westacott. If she had no use for a cavalier, a knight errant it should be.

Chapter Eight

Miss Burloyne's visit was well-timed. Only a short while ago, Edith would have found it irksome to have her ill-thought invitation taken up at all. Now, with her nerves jumping for the last couple of days, she found it a welcome diversion.

The girl had managed, by a ruse, to escape her hostess' company.

"Jocasta is in a pother, supervising the packing, and I do need more threads. Not that Mrs Ash across the way has precisely the shades I am using, but they will do."

"Did you buy some, then?"

"Yes, for Jocasta is bound to wish to see my purchases."

Edith had to laugh. "Well, I am glad to see you. When do you go?"

"Tomorrow. And I will be returning to my own home after that, so it was now or never."

Edith guided Miss Burloyne towards the back family room. "Come, we will be more private here. I will ask Mrs Tuffin for coffee. Unless you prefer tea?"

Miss Burloyne had no preference, and Edith settled her in a comfortable chair near one of the windows and slipped out to the kitchen. When she returned, she found Delia Burloyne in tears.

"Good heavens, is it as bad as that?" Without hesitation, she took the chair beside the girl and patted her shoulder. "Come now, dry your eyes and tell me what troubles you."

Miss Burloyne sniffed and applied a pocket handkerchief to her wet cheeks. "I'm going to end an old maid."

The husky utterance of despair almost overset Edith's gravity. She managed to keep her countenance, however, and applied herself to the task of soothing the girl.

"I cannot think that likely. You are young yet."

"I'm twenty. And I've been out for three years already and Mama says I must give place to my sister next Season."

It might seem a trivial matter to Edith, but she had not taught at Mrs Vinson's Academy for years without coming to understand the importance of a genteel girl disposing of herself in matrimony.

"But you will still be attending yourself, surely?"

"Yes, but everyone will know I've been relegated and no gentleman will look at me when Sophia is by."

Edith understood at once. "Is she very beautiful?"

Miss Burloyne sighed. "Yes, and I don't envy her that. At least, I do whenever I am obliged to look in the mirror, but not otherwise. And of course she will contract an alliance in her first season like Jocasta."

"In which case you will once again be the available female in the family," Edith pointed out.

"I'll be past praying for by then. Everyone will range me with the dowagers."

That proved too much for Edith and she burst out laughing. Miss Burloyne's look of chagrin sobered her and she took one of the girl's hands.

"Oh, don't be offended, my dear, but it is too ridiculous."

A faint rueful smile curved the girl's mouth. "Oh, well, perhaps it isn't as bad as that."

"By no means."

She was ready with a morsel of advice, but Mrs Tuffin came in with the coffee, putting an end to the discussion until it had been dispensed. She allowed Miss Burloyne to drink in silence for a moment, noting that the coffee was having a calming effect.

"Miss Burloyne," she began, and then stopped, shaking her head. "No, Delia — if I may? — do you wish to know what I really think?"

"Yes, but first I must ask you something."

A note of nervousness alerted Edith and she could not help stiffening. "What is it?"

Delia set down her cup and gave Edith a straight look. "Do you return Lord Hetherington's regard?"

Shocked, Edith stared at her. "I have no notion of his cherishing any regard for me."

"Oh, it's obvious. I've seen enough gentlemen turn from me to moon over another female to know it when I see it."

Edith wanted to refute the observation, but honesty compelled her to admit that Lord Hetherington's interest lay with herself rather than Delia Burloyne. She did not flatter herself he was attached, but did a man offer protection to a woman to whom he was not in the least attracted? The implication could not be borne and she broke into impetuous speech.

"Whether or not there is liking between us is immaterial. Nothing will come of it, for my situation forbids any such entanglement."

Delia was sipping her coffee, regarding Edith over the rim. She lowered the cup at this. "Why should it? If he likes you enough, he will not balk at your being the vicar's niece."

"The matter is not open for debate," Edith said, her tone repressive. "And we were discussing your prospects, not mine."

"But do you like him?"

The girl's persistence rubbed Edith's inner wounds, and she had all to do not to burst out against her. But that would not do at all, and she found a compromise.

"Lord Hetherington is an interesting man, and perhaps we share a sense of humour. But I beg you won't let your imagination run away with you on my account."

Delia sighed and took another sip from her cup. "Well, I won't even try since he clearly wouldn't look at me when you are by."

Edith seized on this. "But that is exactly where I believe you are doing yourself no favours, Delia. Don't try so hard. Indeed, you would do better not to try at all."

"I have to. I had to from the start. I didn't take."

"So I gather. But you will not endear yourself to a prospective suitor if you are seen to be desperate, my dear."

"Yes, but I am desperate," argued Delia, stating the obvious.

"You need not show it. Feign indifference and disinterest, and you will see how quickly you will gain suitors."

But Delia seemed determined to think poorly of her chances. "No, I won't. I'm too plain and too dull and my fortune is but moderate."

Edith became tart. "Pray don't recite me a catalogue of your failings. Not every female can be a belle, you know. And not every gentleman wishes for one."

"Then why do they swarm around the beauties like a parcel of moths?"

"I daresay they do, but that does not mean they will necessarily offer for them."

Setting down her cup, Delia smiled at last. "Well, one thing is certain. They couldn't all marry the same female."

"Exactly so. I suggest you stop trying to interest every eligible man who comes in your way. Be yourself, Delia. Don't try to emulate your friend Jocasta or anyone else."

A flush crept up the girl's cheek. "You noticed."

Edith patted her hand. "When you behave naturally you show your own attributes. Talk of things that interest you and stop trying to please."

"You think that will work?"

Edith took a mouthful of her coffee. "Well, it must be worth a try, must it not? After all, it hasn't worked so far to try to be someone different."

A gurgle escaped the girl, a far more natural sound than the giggle she generally adopted. "Well, that's true enough."

"Do you know what I think, Delia?"

An eager look came into the girl's eyes. "No, what?"

"You have not yet met the man who will fall head over ears in love with you."

"Do you think so indeed?"

The hopeful note was reminiscent of so many she'd heard in the tone of a distressed pupil she'd helped, that Edith felt all the poignancy of her own loss.

"I would not otherwise say it. Your prince will likely come upon you when you least expect it."

Delia bubbled with laughter. "Oh, you have made me feel better, Miss Westacott!"

"Edith, please. Go and enjoy your sojourn with Lord Tazewell's parents and stop worrying."

Delia set down her cup and saucer. "I will do my best. And I thank you." She leaned towards Edith and clasped her arms about her.

"Ede, my dear, are you at leisure?"

Edith emerged from the girl's enveloping hug to find her uncle hovering in the doorway. She got up. "Indeed, Uncle Lionel. Miss Burloyne is just going. You've met my uncle, Delia?"

"Of course, yes. At church. How do you do, sir?"

"Very well indeed, my dear, I thank you. But you must allow me to drag my niece away, for she has a visitor who has travelled many miles to see how she does."

Edith's rise of surprise was overshadowed by shock as a man's face appeared over her uncle's shoulder. A face too well-known to mistake.

It had been no shadow. It was indeed he!

Her mind rioting in as violent a manner as her thumping heart, Edith rode through the next few minutes like an automaton, a litany repeating on her nerves.

He had come. He was here. It was he.

Before she could gather her wits, Delia Burloyne was gone and her legs had somehow carried her through the hall to the front parlour, the thick menacing shadow following behind like a hawk hovering over its prey.

Her uncle's voice penetrated the maelstrom, asking the devil if he had found himself adequate accommodation.

God in heaven, don't ask him to stay here!

"I have found the most charming inn but a half mile away, my dear Reverend."

The hated voice, purring with triumph, drew Edith like a magnet. She had kept her eyes lowered but now she raised them, glancing across from the chaise longue upon which she must have placed herself without thinking. He had taken the chair in front of her uncle's cabinet of curiosities and lounged there, wholly at his ease.

"Ah, you mean The Fox and Goose in Long Itchington? Yes, a pretty place, and you will be well served by Louch and his wife. She is an excellent cook."

"So I have discovered." His glance swept Edith in the manner that had ever caused her to feel as if he stripped her where she sat. "And how are you, Miss Westacott? You look much better than when we were last privileged to see you."

We? What, did he couple himself with her erstwhile employer who had found him in her room the last time she'd seen his hateful countenance?

"I am a good deal more myself, Lord Kilshaw."

And better able to counter his every move. Edith hoped her repressive tone might tell him as much.

Her uncle, throwing her a look in which question and censure were blended, cut in again. "She is indeed better, my lord, and we are doing our utmost to build up her strength. My housekeeper sees to it that she is given nourishing foods, and I have insisted upon rest and recuperation."

"A regime that is clearly having a superlative effect. You are looking in great beauty, Miss Westacott."

"Thank you."

She could barely bring herself to say it, once more receiving a minatory glance from her uncle, who fidgeted with his spectacles, removing them and putting them back on. With a trifle more than his usual joviality, as if he must compensate for her lack, he embarked upon a conversation that encompassed the rigours of his visitor's journey and the sights to be found hereabouts while he was here.

Hearing it only in the background of her mind, Edith engaged with it only as it encroached upon her tumbling thoughts.

Uncle Lionel, she surmised, saw only the surface features that Edith had once considered handsome. The full lips that could curl in a leering fashion. The dark, long-lashed eyes with their gleam of sensual promise. The lush fall of black hair he had bequeathed to the daughters consigned to the care of Mrs Vinson's Academy. No doubt her uncle thought her arrogant to be disdaining the man's presence in his house. Improvident too, if Lord Kilshaw dared carry his pretences as far as he had tried them on herself.

"I will not deceive you, sir, for although my thoughts have often been with Miss Westacott and her state of health, I have not come far out of my way."

"Indeed, my lord? What brings you to these parts then?"

"I had occasion to visit an acquaintance who lives near Warwick. I am in fact on my way to Brighton, but I could not leave the area without enquiring into Miss Westacott's present state of health."

Liar! If she did not miss her guess, he had used some spurious excuse to find out her whereabouts and followed her here. Dared she challenge him in front of her uncle?

"How did you find me, sir?"

The charm turned on. "But my dear Miss Westacott, I find you returned to your natural loveliness. Have I not already said so?"

Ignoring her uncle's frown, she threw down the gauntlet. "I meant, my lord, how did you know where I am living?"

"Ede, what is this?"

She glanced at her uncle, who had taken a chair near the fireplace. "I had not supposed Lord Kilshaw to be aware of this place, sir."

"My dear Reverend, your niece is in the right of it. I did not even know her illness had obliged her to retire from the

Academy until Mrs Vinson told me. Naturally I asked her where you had gone, Miss Westacott, for you must know my girls miss you dreadfully."

Oh, you smooth-tongued villain! But he had answered her question, for of course he would have used Millie and Isabel to discover what he needed to know. Those two were ripe for any mischief and they adored their father.

"You have daughters at the school, my lord?"

Edith did not trouble to listen to his feigned raptures over the girls. He had used them for his own ends more times than she cared to count. Even to pleading his cause for him, though Edith trusted neither had fully understood his intentions.

"Do you make a long stay, my lord? May we hope for your company at dinner perhaps?"

Lord Kilshaw's face lit and Edith could have cursed. He clearly had not supposed it would be this easy to insinuate himself into her life here.

"My dear Reverend, I should be only too delighted. I have a few days to kill before I must present myself in Brighton. His Highness has made it quite the fashion to spend some weeks of the summer there."

Edith did not have to look at her uncle to realise the mention of royalty must set the seal on his acceptance. Not that he approved of the excesses reportedly indulged in by the Prince of Wales, but he could not fail to be impressed at the notion of Lord Kilshaw keeping such company. Edith could have told him he was deservedly tarred with the same brush as his royal acquaintance, but she felt too ashamed to tell him the truth. How would he support the knowledge that this man was pursuing her to ruin rather than marriage?

Within a few minutes Lord Kilshaw rose, very correctly, to take his leave. He bowed over her hand, squeezing it in a familiar fashion that made her squirm inside.

"May I hope, Miss Westacott, to persuade you to take the air? Tomorrow morning?" Without waiting for her reply, he turned back to the vicar. "I promise I will take the greatest care of her, my dear Reverend. We might go for a drive perhaps? I came in my curricle, you must know. So much faster and more pleasant than a coach in this weather."

Her uncle became flustered, removing his spectacles and beginning to polish them. Edith guessed he was torn between propriety and furthering her interests.

"Yes, I dare say. I mean, perhaps a drive? Your groom would be in attendance, of course."

"My dear sir, I would not for the world subject Miss Westacott to the censure of her neighbours. Naturally my groom will be in attendance. And if you prefer it, Miss Westacott, perhaps a short walk at first, and we may keep within sight of your uncle's house."

Her uncle approved this suggestion, and her Nemesis took his leave, neither of the men taking in that Edith had not agreed to either proposal. Indeed, she'd said nothing, unable to think how to counteract this first move in the face of her uncle's clear delight in his evident supposition that she had a worthy suitor in Lord Kilshaw.

She waited, in an agony of indecision, for her uncle to return from seeing the creature to the door.

He came into the parlour with a brow furrowed in perplexity, his eyeglasses once more in place. "You were not at all welcoming, Ede. What is the matter? Do you dislike his lordship?"

She looked away, shame rising to her bosom. What could she say? If she began upon it, she must follow through with all of it. She shrank from revealing the full story, culpable as she had been in the early part of it. A compromise perhaps?

"There was a time when I liked him very well. At least, I thought so. But no longer, sir."

Her uncle came to sit beside her, possessing himself of one of her hands.

"My dearest Ede, what of that? Can you not like him again? He seems to be smitten with you."

But not for the purpose her uncle supposed. She tried again. "If you must have it, I find him overwhelming, Uncle."

"Overwhelming? Explain, my dear, for I do not understand."

"His attentions … they became too effusive, too — how can I put it? — too close for comfort."

Her uncle seemed amused as he released her hand. "My dear, is that all? I had not thought to find you missish, Ede. I suspect the fellow is in love with you. You find his ardour a little frightening perhaps, and that is understandable."

Terrifying! He had a strength she had no hope of resisting, should he succeed in getting her alone where he might pursue his advantage to her detriment. He had proved as much on that dreadful day. If Mrs Vinson had not come in… Would her uncle even believe that he could attempt to force his desires upon a woman debilitated and weak from illness? That any man of ordinary compassion and sense would do such a thing? She shuddered involuntarily.

"I cannot like him, sir."

Her uncle's frown deepened. "Ede, this is foolishness. If I read him aright, Lord Kilshaw might offer you a glittering future. Would you willingly whistle it down the wind?"

"I doubt he has any such intention, Uncle Lionel."

That much she might say, but it had no effect.

"Then at least allow him the opportunity to prove himself to you. For my part, his coming out of his way to see you argues a strong predilection."

"I did not say he is not attracted to me. To my person at least."

"Which is exactly where these things must start, my dear Ede. Goodness me, if all young females were to reject a fellow because he does not at once declare his affection, where should we be?"

Bursting with too much indignation to be able to speak with any moderation, Edith said nothing.

Her uncle rose, patting her shoulder in much the way she had earlier done to Delia Burloyne, and Edith knew at once that he considered her objections trivial.

"I must be off about my duties. Don't allow prejudice to stand in the way of your good fortune, my dear Ede."

She watched him leave the parlour and winced as she heard him begin whistling a jaunty tune, just as if he had something to celebrate. Edith remained where she was, the vexation draining as the full force of her endangerment returned.

Without warning, the image of Lord Hetherington leapt into her head. If she could not confide in her uncle in this extremity, dared she instead call upon her knight errant?

Chapter Nine

Edith had slept badly, and the cogitations of the night brought no relief. Her first instinct had been to pack her bags and flee. But where? And how? If anything, she was safer here than on the road where he might catch her faster than she could run.

What if she feigned a relapse? Claimed to be too ill to leave her chamber? But for how long could she do so? And she could by no means trust that he would not find a way to enter there.

Edith shivered at the thought, turning in the bed and curling up as if she must protect her person from assault. Anyone of sense would suppose it to be a foolish thought, impossible that a man could enter a private bedchamber and not be detected. Yet he had done so at the Academy with a dozen girls and several teachers on the premises. If one of the youngest pupils had not entered and run to Mrs Vinson, he would have succeeded.

Here, when her uncle was out, she had only Mrs Tuffin, busy in the kitchen. Lord Kilshaw's snooping before he presented himself had shown him the back entrance to the hall was kept unlocked. Unless she remained incarcerated in her own chamber all day long, Edith had no means of stopping his entry there, short of a guard at her chamber door.

That thought led her back to Lord Hetherington. She'd toyed with the notion of sending to him, but she shrank even more from explaining her predicament to a virtual stranger. If she could not tell her uncle, how should she open her lips to a man whose company she found enlivening?

True, he had offered his services. Nay, more. He had more or less commanded her to send to him should her Nemesis turn up in the village. But he did not know to what depths of degradation she had so nearly been dragged. Edith knew she could not bring herself to reveal the full sordid story.

With daylight, her fears abated. She determined to conquer them and confront him herself. She must convince him once and for all that his pursuit was useless. She would never consent to become his mistress.

Thus determined, she forced down as much of the hearty breakfast provided by Mrs Tuffin as she could manage, showing her uncle a dutiful front when he asked if she was willing at least to walk with Lord Kilshaw today.

"Certainly, sir. I will take a turn about the green with him."

"Not the garden?"

"I prefer to be in sight of the villagers, Uncle."

He frowned. "You will set them all talking."

"I'm sure they are already talking. I doubt Lord Kilshaw's arrival went unnoticed."

He laughed at that. "True. Well, you must do as you think best, my dear. I am pleased you are prepared to give the fellow a chance."

Edith took refuge in her coffee, the food she'd eaten turning to lead in her clenching stomach.

"I must go, my dear. It's almost time for choir practice and I must not be late when I insist upon the boys arriving on the dot." He rose and came around to pat her shoulder. "You will tell me all about it over luncheon."

She agreed to it and watched him leave the little dining parlour, jaunty and utterly unconcerned, having no notion of the danger in which she stood. Edith almost called him back, but she closed her lips. Even had she the courage to tell him the truth, there was no time now.

Leaving the remainder of her meal untouched, she followed her uncle out and crossed the hall to the family room, there to pace as she waited, rehearsing what she must say. The peal of the front doorbell froze her blood. She heard Mrs Tuffin's footsteps and the low muttering grumble she invariably indulged in when disturbed at her morning labours.

Struggling to control her fright, Edith grabbed the hat she'd brought down and left in here and went to the mirror over the fireplace. Setting it on her head, she fumbled as she tried to tie the bow with trembling fingers. She heard the rumble of a male voice and Mrs Tuffin's reply.

"I'll see if she's free, my lord."

The bow was lopsided but it would have to do. Edith turned to the door as the housekeeper's footsteps came back up the hall. She appeared in the open aperture.

"It's Lord Hetherington, Miss Ede. He says he wants a word."

Relief sent Edith reeling and she collapsed into the nearest chair, her hand at her bosom which rose and fell with her short breaths.

Mrs Tuffin came tutting over. "Dearie me, Miss Ede, whatever is the matter now?"

Edith threw out a hand. "It's nothing. I will be well presently." She drew a long breath and looked up to find Lord Hetherington standing in the doorway, regarding her with a furrowed brow. "My lord! I was not expecting…"

The housekeeper bustled across. "Come you in, sir. I'll be within call if she needs me."

Lord Hetherington came to stand over her. "I appear to have startled you. What is the matter?"

Edith knew not how to answer. She longed to tell him, convinced in his powerful presence that he was more than capable of dealing with her Nemesis. But it would not do. At any moment Lord Kilshaw would arrive and she would be undone.

"I'm going out, sir. My — my escort will be here shortly."

He drew back. "Escort? I see."

He eyed her for a moment and Edith felt an uncomfortable warmth creeping into her cheeks. She forced herself to speak with a calmness she was far from feeling.

"Did you — did you wish to see me for anything in particular?"

Puzzlement showed in his gaze. "I wished to assure myself you had not been again incommoded."

"Incommoded?" *Stupid!* She knew exactly what he meant. Her brain refused to function properly.

"Miss Westacott, be plain with me. This man you spoke of, has he been here?"

The harsh note penetrated. She looked up and met his eyes. The words formed before she could stop them. "He is coming to take me for a walk."

Lord Hetherington shifted, setting one hand on the mantel and keeping his eyes on her face. "You are not afraid?"

Edith drew a breath. "I believe I can manage him."

"That does not answer me."

"I can't answer you!"

His face changed. "You are afraid! No, don't trouble to deny it, I can see it in your face. Who is he? What does he want from you?"

She shook her head, unable to speak for the sudden prick at her eyes, the thickness in her throat. The doorbell pealed again and she jumped in her seat.

"Damnation! If that's the fellow —"

Edith pushed herself up from the chair, only half aware of reaching out to him, urgency driving her. "You must go! Please go! Leave the back way and go through the gate. He must not see you!"

His hand had grasped hers strongly and the pressure gave her strength.

"Why not? If he menaces you, isn't it better he should know you have a protector?"

"No! I don't wish him to know anything about me more than he does already. I beg of you, my lord, let it alone! If you knew…" Her voice died as once again she heard Mrs Tuffin's muttering as she went to answer the door. "Go! Go, please!"

He released her. "Very well, if you insist. But I am not satisfied, Edith, so don't think it."

A moment later he was gone and she heard the back door open and close. She no longer knew why she'd insisted on him going. Somehow the thought of the two men meeting — the one as thoughtful as the other was villainous — was anathema. She felt tainted by association with Lord Kilshaw, and could not bear Lord Hetherington to see her in his company.

Irrational? Probably. But at least his coming had given her the needed strength. She no longer felt as vulnerable and her determination was fixed. She would herself be rid of the menace. Without further delay, she walked into the hall and held out her hand to the man awaiting her. "How do you do, my lord? We have a lovely day for our walk, do you not think?"

He looked taken aback by her manner and Edith felt emboldened.

"Shall we go?"

He bowed and opened the door for her. She stepped out into the sunshine and trod along the path to the front gate.

"Allow me, Miss Westacott."

His air of gallantry was accompanied by one of those hateful leers. Did he suppose he'd won? He would soon learn his mistake.

Edith took his proffered arm and allowed him to lead her onto the green, wondering if Lord Hetherington had managed to escape out of sight somewhere. The thought that he might still be in the vicinity was comforting in spite of all.

"I had hoped for a better degree of privacy, my dear Edith."

The oily tone made her skin crawl. She moved a little apart from him as she walked. "I did not give you permission to use my name, sir."

"Then give it now. These missish airs do not become you."

His voice had hardened and Edith's false manner of politeness faltered.

"Nothing you wish for me becomes me! I am not what you think me."

He drew her closer and his free fingers squeezed her arm. "I think you inordinately beautiful. You will adorn any house and I have one ready for you."

Indignation welled. "The pretty little house you offered me before? Do you suppose such a prospect can tempt me to sin?"

"A harsh name, my dear, for a life of ease and comfort. You know well that I will lavish upon you anything your heart desires. You will want for nothing, I promise you."

An inward shudder shook her. "And when you tire of me, my lord? What then?"

"You will not find me ungenerous, Edith."

Fury surged up and she glanced at the handsome profile at her side. "You have not even the grace to pretend you could desire me forever."

"I've never pretended with you, my dear, you know that."

"No, I don't know, sir. You led me on for weeks. Only by the veriest accident did I discover that your wife is still alive."

He sighed out deeply as if in sorrow, but Edith was not fooled. She had long ago understood his utter selfishness.

"Alas, my poor Charlotte! Can you truly wonder at my seeking relief otherwhere?"

"The only thing I wonder at, sir, is your disgraceful lack of feeling. Pray don't pretend to devotion to your ailing wife, for I have enough common sense to recognise the truth."

He smiled, no trace of remorse or consciousness in his voice. "My daughters are prattlers. But they adore Miss Westacott."

"And would no doubt be delighted to find me your mistress? How can you, sir? Do you present your innocent girls to every whore who comes in your orbit?"

The sarcastic note had no effect on him whatsoever. "Only to you, my dear Edith. Have I not promised you will supplant my poor Charlotte in everything but name?"

"I wonder you don't rid yourself of her and be done with the problem for good."

"But that would not look well, my dear, and one must keep up appearances."

Her insides curled with disgust. "Why trouble yourself? I cannot imagine, my lord, that the gentlemen with whom you associate are unacquainted with your true character."

He laughed in the mocking way he had, and Edith felt her words were wasted.

"Do you know, my dear, I believe I might keep you forever after all. It is a pity I cannot marry you, for the thought of taming your bold spirit is one that inflames me."

Taming it? Crushing it rather. But Edith knew not what to say. Not even insults deterred him. She had more than once wondered if her recalcitrance was a spur to his desire, and now she could not doubt it. What horrors might she not endure should she succumb? Was the ravishment of her person not the worst of it, as she had supposed?

"What is in your mind, my dear Edith, to keep you so silent? Have you thought better of your determination to resist me?"

The reverse, if anything. If she'd been menaced before, she was now deathly afraid. The sinister implications of her realisation played in her mind. She'd anticipated seduction. She had not bargained for the violence of rape and torture. The image of his attempted violation when she lay helpless and ill came back to her. Edith wrenched her hand from his arm and faced him.

"I've been so blind! I believed you when you spoke words of ardour and yearning. But you are evil, my lord Kilshaw, through and through!"

"But such heat, Miss Westacott? You wrong me, indeed you do. If it were in my power, my intentions towards you would be pure and honourable."

Edith snapped back. "Yes, let us speak of your power, for I will never put myself within its reach. I would die first!"

The handsome features twisted, a sneer growing in the curling mouth. "When did I ever say you had a choice, Miss Westacott?"

She stared at him, only half believing what she heard. "You cannot force me."

"Can I not?"

The quiet confidence was worse than a threat. Despair engulfed her. "But why? Why do you want me so badly? What have I that you cannot find elsewhere?"

He took her hands in his, holding them in a hard grasp, but his tone returned to the sensuality she loathed. "Because you are beautiful, desirable and the challenge is irresistible." The curl revived at his lip. "And though you may call yourself a lady, your position makes you attainable without provoking a scandal. It's a rare combination, my dear."

Edith released herself, turned from him and began to walk again, shock and hurt riding her bosom. Aware of him keeping pace beside her, she sought in vain for words that would not come. She'd vowed to make him realise once and for all that he had no chance with her. Now she could think of nothing with which to convince him. The arrogance of his suppositions, his utter inability to consider anything but his own desires, his own pleasures, both confused and horrified her.

"I do not understand you. How can you persist in the face of my hatred? When you have damned yourself in my eyes forever?"

"Your feelings towards me will change in time."

The complacent note infuriated her, rising above the numbing of the belittlement she felt at his complete disregard for her feelings and wishes.

"They will never change. I loathe you to the depths of my being!"

The mocking laughter sounded in her ears like the note of nightmare. Would nothing make an impression upon him? She felt doomed.

"Miss Westacott!"

That very different voice, coming out of the blue, brought her head up. "Lord Hetherington!"

He was walking towards them across the green. Edith threw a harried glance at her companion and found chagrin in his face. Triumph lit her bosom. Now they would see.

Chapter Ten

Niall eyed the gentleman at Edith's side with a mixture of suspicion and dismay. He had hardly expected the fellow to be one of these comely specimens over whom females were ready to swoon. Nor had he thought to find a man of mature years. This fellow must be forty if he was a day.

He wasted no time. "Will you not introduce me, Miss Westacott?"

Her colour was fluctuating, her dismay obvious and there was a tremor in her voice.

"Lord Kilshaw, Lord Hetherington."

Before Niall could speak, the other gave a slight bow, his manner suave as silk. "Hetherington? Ah, was there not a tragic event in these parts?"

"My cousin and his family." Niall eyed him. "You must forgive me, sir, if I fail to place you. I have only lately returned from the wars and have little acquaintance with my fellow peers."

He received a long look and Niall hoped his military background might give Lord Kilshaw pause. Even recognise he was not an easy man to cross.

But Edith cut in, her eyes signalling a plea. "Lord Kilshaw's estates are near Bath. His daughters were in the Academy where I was teaching, you must know."

Did she wish him to understand there was more behind her words? It could hardly be typical for a father of girls under a school teacher's care to be pursuing their preceptress, even if she had been ill.

A singularly charming smile was bent upon Edith, and Niall had no difficulty in imagining how she might be attracted to such a man.

"And what an excellent teacher you were, my dear Miss Westacott. My girls miss her dreadfully, sir."

Niall met the man's eyes as he turned, confusion wreathing his brain. Was this a prospective suitor? Had he read Edith's reaction wrong? Had she been merely distrait at the thought of his coming? No, it was more than that. She had been in the suspense of fear, not anticipation.

"What brings you to this out of the way place, sir?"

The smile held something of mockery and Niall's senses came alert.

"But Miss Westacott, my dear Hetherington, what else?"

Niall shot a glance at Edith. She looked far from gratified. Her lips were tightly compressed, her cheeks blanching.

"I see." Niall inclined his head. "I am de trop, perhaps?"

"My dear fellow, I should not dream of saying so, but my time is limited and Miss Westacott can spare me only half an hour."

There could be no mistaking his message. Nothing could be further from Niall's wishes than to leave Edith alone in the man's company. Yet he could not help recalling her urgent efforts to ensure the two men did not meet. He'd thwarted her in that. He glanced at her, trying to tell whether she wished him gone. Edith kept her gaze lowered. There was nothing for him to do but retire for now.

"Miss Westacott, your servant." She nodded without looking up. Niall directed a nod at her companion. "Kilshaw. I trust we may meet again before your departure."

The smile came again and Niall was conscious of dislike.

"It is very possible."

What the devil did that mean? He said no more, but turned smartly away and headed for the tavern, aware of the man's eyes following him. He hated leaving the fellow in command of the field when the thread of suspicion was weaving through his brain. Kilshaw was precisely the sort of man around whom females tended to flock. Niall had seen it often enough in personable fellow officers. Never a target himself, he'd been amused to see how women simpered and fluttered in the presence of such fellows. Somewhat in the manner of Miss Burloyne towards him. But Niall knew better than to suppose that his person had such an effect. His acquired title was to blame for that.

But Edith had never shown the slightest interest in his title. Instead, she'd teased and talked her way into his favour. Not that such had been her intention. She shied off from any suggestion of gallantry. Was Kilshaw the reason?

His ruminations were interrupted by the landlord of the Bear, a beefy individual, whose muscular arms and shoulders belied his deferential manner.

"How can I serve you, my lord?"

"I'll take a jug of your best ale, Gifford, if you please."

The fellow was evidently gratified to have his aristocratic landlord choose to patronise his modest inn, which was in general in use by lesser men, which at least gave some point to his expedition. He'd come on purpose to check on Edith Westacott and had anticipated her offering him refreshment at the vicarage.

Niall took a seat by the window in the tap room and was presently served with a foaming tankard. He took a pull and set it down, watching the perambulations of the couple on the green. He could not judge at this distance whether or not Edith relished the attention. It was idle to suppose her apparent fears had an origin in maidenly confusion. And she had not looked as if she was enjoying Kilshaw's company.

On the other hand, if the fellow cared for her and meant to offer for her, who was Niall to interfere? However much it might gall him to stand aside. She'd given no sign of preferring himself, and now he'd seen Lord Kilshaw, he could not imagine how she might. The wretch had everything he had not. Looks, address, grace and an established position in Society. True, he was an older man, already burdened with daughters. But if he was a widower and needed a son, it was not remarkable he would seek a second wife.

What was surprising was that such a man would seek one in the schoolmistress who taught his daughters. Which thought, coupled with Edith's evident distress and fear, did not augur well. No, there was more to this than met the eye.

He saw that the couple were headed back towards the vicarage and took another draught of ale. Let him see what Kilshaw did. If he left, Niall would seize opportunity and tackle Edith. He could at least satisfy himself she stood in no danger. If the fellow's intentions proved to be genuine and honourable, and if Edith was able to return his regard…

The thought died. Niall discovered he could not contemplate with equanimity the notion of Edith being in the least in love with Lord Kilshaw. What that said of his own feelings he refused to examine. Time enough to think of that when he'd garnered sufficient information to be able to work out a tactical strategy.

Edith and Kilshaw had reached the vicarage gate. Niall watched while they appeared to talk over it. And then Edith turned for the house and Kilshaw came away.

To Niall's surprise he headed in a path directly towards the tavern. Had he the intention of refreshing himself? Or was he coming in search of Niall? A rush of the feeling he experienced before battle ran through him. Now they would see.

It did not take Lord Kilshaw many minutes to cross the green and Niall was ready for him when he entered the tap room and glanced around. The moment he caught sight of Niall their eyes met. Kilshaw turned to the hovering landlord.

"Ale, I think, my good man."

And then he had reached the place where Niall was seated. Seizing a chair, he dragged it forward and sat down, gesturing towards the window.

"No doubt you guessed I should come to seek you out."

Niall eyed him. "I didn't. I saw you return Miss Westacott to the vicarage, however."

The other's brows rose over the dark eyes. "Awaiting your moment? Then I haven't wasted my time coming over here."

Was this an opening gambit? Kilshaw was clearly determined on candour. Niall braced as the landlord brought the fellow's tankard over and set it down on the small table between them. Kilshaw nodded and cast a glance about the tap room. He lowered his voice. "I would bespeak a private parlour, but I dare say we are attracting enough attention as it is."

In fact there were few customers, and although the usual country interest had ensured several stares as the stranger entered, these had already returned to the more interesting business of consuming ale and smoking a pipe of tobacco.

"They've grown used to me. I doubt anyone will listen to our conversation."

"Ah, this is your territory, I take it? Then I am in your hands, my dear fellow."

He might well be, should Niall find his throat within reach. Dismissing the savage thought, he took a soothing drink from his tankard, watching as the other followed suit.

"Quite tolerable." Kilshaw set down his jug. "Let us put our cards on the table, my dear sir."

Niall maintained a cool front, but he was not going to help. "Certainly."

The other smiled, but there was no friendliness within it. "I mean to be perfectly frank, Hetherington, between gentlemen."

Niall lost patience. "Cut line, Kilshaw. What do you want with me?"

The brows rose again and the other man tutted. "You military men are so direct. I was trying to be tactful."

"Don't trouble. I can stand a knock or two and I prefer plain speaking."

A look of satisfaction came and Kilshaw's eyes gleamed. "Just as I supposed. Plainly then, Hetherington, if, as I suspect, you have an interest in Miss Westacott, I must inform you that I have the prior claim."

Niall set his teeth. "Indeed? And does Miss Westacott accept that?"

"She will."

"In other words, she does not."

Kilshaw heaved a sigh. "I had hoped not to be obliged to say this, but I perceive you are more *épris* than I thought."

"We will leave my emotions out of this discussion."

Lord Kilshaw spread his hands. "As you wish. But do not blame me if what I must impart may be — shall we say, disconcerting? — to you."

Niall did not answer. He held the man's eyes, every muscle taut as he fought to refrain from setting his fist into the fellow's pretty face. Another sigh came and Kilshaw took a pull of his ale. Niall waited in barely contained impatience.

The dark eyes met his again. "You see, Hetherington, the matter is not open for debate. Miss Westacott has little choice."

Niall's irritation surfaced. "I wish you will not talk such fustian, sir. Of course she has a choice. You can't force an unwilling bride to the altar in these days."

"Bride?"

There was no mistaking the tone. Niall's senses snapped to. "You don't intend marriage then?"

"Have you run mad, Hetherington? What in the world makes you suppose I could mean marriage? For one thing, I am not free. For another, you clearly don't know Miss Westacott for what she is."

Niall's breast rioted with a maelstrom of feeling, uppermost a strong desire to spit the man on the point of his sword. But he was not a soldier for nothing. Poker-faced, he managed a clipped tone. "No doubt you are going to tell me?"

The fellow spread his hands again, but Niall was alive now to the mockery of his play-acting. "My dear Hetherington, did I not say at the outset that I have a prior claim?"

"You mean you seduced her."

He said it with the flat, unemotional tone of disinterest, but it was plain Kilshaw had divined something of his held-in fury.

"She was not unwilling, if that is what you suppose," he said gently, his tone soft. "That, my dear sir, would be rape."

Controlling himself with an effort, Niall eyed the man. Was it the truth? Why then should Edith be so afraid of him? No, she was not willing. If she had been, then it was no longer so. He wanted to give the fellow the lie, but he hesitated. Always best to know your enemy thoroughly before you attacked.

"What do you intend, Kilshaw?"

"With Miss Westacott?" The mocking smile again. "You know the drill, I am persuaded, Hetherington. I have a charming little house and I am prepared to be generous. She is worth it."

Niall ground his teeth. "I don't doubt it."

"Ah, you have been taken with her beauty, have you not? I declare, it will be a pleasure to display her to my intimates." A gentle laugh came. "I must trust my royal crony may not take to her and offer to relieve me of her too soon. No, on the whole, I may do better to refrain from taking her with me to Brighton. She may await me in the pretty little establishment in the metropolis. I cannot think she will be bored there, for she has never been to London."

Revolted, Niall listened with creeping horror. Whatever he had expected, it was not this distressing programme of Edith's introduction into the life of a courtesan. He managed to infuse calm into his tone. "I understand you, I believe."

Lord Kilshaw sat back, complacency in every line of his fine figure. "There now, I knew candour would serve me best. I am so glad I decided to confide in you, Hetherington."

"Yes, but I suspect you have been less than frank with me, sir."

Kilshaw stilled and his brows rose. "How so?"

"Miss Westacott did not strike me as altogether delighted to see you again. I wonder why, sir."

"Maidenly confusion?" Kilshaw's laugh grated on Niall's ears. "Well, let us be honest. She begged me not to follow her here. Naturally she does not wish her uncle to know the path she is treading. But I am not wholly unfeeling, sir. I have allowed the worthy vicar to suppose me a suitor for her hand. You will, I trust, support this pretence. For the sake of Miss Westacott's honour in the village, you know."

He dared speak of her honour? Again Niall wanted to smash his fist into the comely countenance. But he was obliged to deny himself this solace. Until he had spoken with Edith, it suited him best to keep his true feelings in check. And concealed from the callous and philandering Kilshaw.

"I should not dream of distressing the Reverend Westacott."

Let him make what he chose of that. It did not greatly limit what Niall might say or do with regard to Edith's uncle. That must depend upon the truth.

Kilshaw looked perfectly satisfied. No doubt he thought he had effectually silenced a possible rival. Niall watched him drain his tankard and set it down. He threw a couple of coins onto the table and rose.

"My errand is done. I must retrieve my curricle, which I left at the smithy. No doubt we shall meet again."

Niall rose. "You may count on it."

"Yes, since my campaign will likely keep me here some days. I trust to your discretion, my dear fellow."

Niall had no intention of fulfilling that trust and did not choose to reply.

He watched the man leave and sat down again to resume his vigil from the window. Lord Kilshaw went past, walking along the lane towards the blacksmith's forge, which lay just beyond the green. Niall wanted to make sure the fellow did not turn his steps back towards the vicarage. He was quickly out of sight and Niall left his own douceur on the table and walked out of the tavern.

His quarry was still within sight, but he had nearly reached the smithy. A sigh escaped Niall and he realised he had been holding his breath. All that remained was to decide whether or not to go to Edith now. Should he give her time to recover her countenance? Indeed, he felt he needed time himself, to absorb and sift what he'd been told.

To be truthful, he knew not what to believe. Except for one thing. He was convinced of Edith's unwillingness. Whatever had occurred in the past, she did not now wish to resume the liaison. On that he would stake his earldom.

He had drifted along with his thoughts, shifting onto the green, and so he was in an excellent position to see a curricle pulling out of the smithy yard. A groom ran alongside and swung himself up behind as the vehicle turned into the far lane and started off in the direction of Long Itchington village. That it was also the direction towards his own home dictated his decision. He had stabled his horse in the mews behind the tavern and directed one of the boys to take care of it. The animal would by now be sufficiently rested to carry him home. But he did not wish to encounter Kilshaw again.

On the other hand, he had an ardent desire to see Edith, to find out the truth from her own lips. Would she tell him? She'd refused to confide in him before, but he could swear he'd seen a signal in her eyes when he met the two on the green.

He started towards the vicarage, but his eye caught a figure stealing from the back gate. *Edith!* She began to hurry down the lane towards the woods, her manner clearly distrait.

Without hesitation, Niall started after her.

Chapter Eleven

The unpleasantness of the interview with Lord Kilshaw had drained every ounce of Edith's returning confidence. Worse, she'd been mortified by the meeting with Lord Hetherington. That he should see her apparently on terms with that evil-minded creature! What must he think?

She'd been so deeply ashamed, she'd answered Kilshaw at random, hardly taking in his words. Until at last he became irritated.

"My dear Edith, I trust this maidenly confusion you are exhibiting is not on account of this Hetherington fellow?"

The note of jealousy was not lost on her and she cast him a glance of loathing.

"I scarcely know him, but the little I do know is enough to convince me he is a far better man than you."

The mocking laughter was for once absent. "Ah, then you do favour him?"

"I did not say so."

"You did not need to, my dear. But if you imagine I will allow him to take you from me, you are wide of the mark."

A wild sort of laugh escaped her. "There is no talking to you, sir. You are mad!"

His hold on her arm, crooked willy-nilly into his elbow, tightened. "Yes, mad with love for you, my dear."

Edith began to feel hysterical. "Love? This is not love! If you loved me the least little bit you would not importune me in this way."

"Ah, but my love is of a peculiar kind."

"That is the truest thing you've yet said."

"You bring spice to the challenge, my dear Edith, with each little spark of rebellion."

The mockery was back and hope withered in her breast. She could make no impression upon him, no matter what she said. The feeling of entrapment intensified. She fell back upon convention. "My uncle will be home soon. I must go back."

To her relief, he directed their steps towards the vicarage.

"The next time I will beg him to grant me a longer time with you. I anticipate no difficulty in persuading him."

Nor, to Edith's chagrin, did she. Unless she told her uncle the full story, he would persist in his belief of the man's honest intentions. After what had been said this morning, she doubted her ability to open her lips upon the subject. Would Uncle Lionel believe such a tale? It was preposterous.

She was surprised when Lord Kilshaw released her at the gate.

"I shall say *au revoir*, my dear. Until tomorrow? One more outing and then I shall ask the goodly vicar for your hand."

Edith had gone through the gate and she turned to look at him. "Are you proposing to carry this farce as far as going through a marriage ceremony?"

"Good God, no! What in the world gave you so ludicrous a notion? No, no. Our ardour will prove too strong to wait and we shall elope. I have it all planned."

Edith stared at him. He must know she would not willingly embark upon such an adventure. He meant to carry her off willy-nilly. Once in his power she would be lost indeed.

She made no objection when he kissed her hand with great punctilio, just as if he was a suitor. Truth to tell, she was incapable of objecting.

She re-entered the vicarage and the familiarity of it warmed the soiled edges of her heart a little. But her body trembled in reaction and she made for the parlour, sinking down onto the chaise longue.

Mrs Tuffin found her there and began tutting at once. "Goodness me, Miss Ede, you look perfectly white! Too much for you, I'll be bound, meeting his lordship again and walking on the green. Coffee! You need reviving. I have a pot boiling on the stove. Just you stay there and I'll be back in a twinkling."

She was as good as her word, and Edith drank as she was bid, thankful for the excuse afforded by her debilitated condition. As her symptoms subsided and she was able to feel again, her agitation returned.

Without Lord Kilshaw's menacing presence, she could think with more coherence. Her thoughts were all of escape. She had not truly known how determined he was, though she'd feared he might follow her. His persistence was incomprehensible. She could not understand how a man could desire a woman who recoiled from him.

The things he'd said made her blood run cold. She now believed him capable of every sort of vicious savagery. And the more she rebelled, the more he appeared to revel in the thought of conquest.

Was that it? Were she to feign willingness would he lose interest? No, for he would recognise her pretence. She'd been too vehement in her denials to hope to fool him now with a volte-face.

But what if she allowed him to think her defeated? A condemned man was said to accept his fate. If she was sullen, but accepting? Would it lull him sufficiently to relax his guard? And then what? How was she to escape from him? Where was she to go? He would run her to earth in a matter of hours or days.

Edith began to feel hunted. She could not be still. Even the house became stifling. Unsafe since her uncle could not be brought to recognise her danger. She must get out!

Rising, she put a hand to her head and discovered she had not even thought to remove her hat. So much the better. She was through the hall and out of the back door before she could even think of the wisdom of going out alone. It occurred to her as she reached the back gate, but she dismissed the risk. Even were Lord Kilshaw still in the village, the likelihood was he would not see her slip away into the woods. Besides, why should he remain here? She was thankful he was staying in Long Itchington nearby instead of Itchington Bishops, which at least gave her a respite.

She headed for the woods, feeling immediately freer as she hit the path and the trees closed in around her. The feeling proved spurious, however, for her inner demons continued to torment her. Try as she would to think how to get away, she could only hold to the thought of doing so. Her mind presented her with the image of that mocking face and snatches of his hateful words replayed in her head.

"*...when did I ever say you had a choice? ... the challenge is irresistible...*"

The sound of rapid footsteps behind her penetrated. Edith glanced back and saw the figure of a man. A sob escaped her and panic took her. She began to run, crashing off the path and into the trees, heedless of the twigs that caught at her clothing.

"Edith, stop! It's I, Hetherington!"

The voice snapped in her attention and she stumbled to a halt, breathing hard, a hand to her bosom, tears trickling down her cheeks.

Next moment, she was held by two strong hands that kept her steady and she looked up into the swarthy countenance. So different from the other! So much less handsome! And so much more welcome to her eyes.

"Miss Westacott — Edith!"

She gasped in a sobbing breath, and out of her mouth fell the most non sequitur thing she might have said. "I don't even know your name."

A grin split his face. "It's Niall."

"Niall." She met his eyes. "Thank you."

"For what? Giving you a fright?"

"For being you and not him."

His face changed. "I knew it! You don't care for him, do you?"

Edith shuddered. "I hate him!"

"Then why in God's name did you encourage his advances?"

She felt as if a bucket of water had been thrown in her face. She stepped back, out of his hold, dashing a hand across her wet cheeks to wipe away the trace of tears. All desire to weep had left her, replaced by a sensation of hurt that went deeper than her indignation.

"You take too much for granted, sir."

Niall's features went taut. "Do I? Then tell me your side of it."

Shock swept through her. "My side?" Realisation hit. "He's been talking to you!"

"To some purpose."

The grim note echoed in her core and she went cold inside. What had he been told? Instinct urged her to demand to know, but a horrid feeling of betrayal made her clamp down upon the question. Her legs trembled under her and she glanced about for somewhere to sit down.

Niall must have realised, for he grasped her again, setting a hand about her shoulders.

"Steady!"

Edith wanted to throw him off but she needed his support. She allowed him to guide her to a fallen trunk and sank down upon it. He stood over her for a moment and Edith felt unaccountably menaced. She could not prevent an irascible note from creeping into her voice. "Pray don't stand there like a hawk! It's too reminiscent of what I've been through today."

"I beg your pardon."

His tone was stiff, but he threw one leg over the trunk and perched a short distance away from her, close enough to touch if she reached out. He did not speak and Edith welcomed the silence, closing her eyes and letting the gradual infiltration of woodland sounds soothe her lacerated nerves: an intermittent bird, a rustle in the undergrowth and the pleasant hush of leaves as the wind brushed through the trees.

Presently she opened her eyes and found Niall watching her. The exigencies of her situation came back, coupled with a sense of humiliation.

"Why did you follow me?"

She heard the bitter note in her own voice with dismay, but there was no recalling it now.

Niall answered in that same grim tone. "Because I don't want to believe what that fellow saw fit to reveal."

Edith raised her eyes to look across at him. "But you can't dismiss it, can you?"

His lips compressed and he looked away. A hole opened up somewhere in the region of Edith's heart, and the thread of hope she hadn't even known was there slithered away. Somehow she secured control of her voice, adopting the light manner that served to keep the world away.

"Then you are well served for indulging in the sin of curiosity, sir."

It was not entirely successful and she hoped he did not detect the underlying tremor.

"You won't drive me away by that means, Miss Westacott. I'm a soldier. Reverses are part of life. One ties a knot and goes on."

Edith knew not what to make of this. She could not look at him without feeling the comparison between the two men. Impulse caught her tongue. "How unlucky it is that I did not meet you first!"

An odd lopsided smile twisted his mouth. "Why should that make a difference?"

She drew a quick breath and let it go. "I don't know. I spoke without thinking." She sighed. "I regret I am far from rational at the moment."

"I don't wonder at it."

Edith wanted to weep. "I wish you will not be so understanding. It only makes it worse."

A laugh escaped him and she heard exasperation within it.

"What must I do, Miss Westacott? No, Edith. I know you to be both afraid and distressed, and now I've met your — what shall I call him? — your —"

"He is not my anything, sir! What he wishes to be is another matter, but I will not endure him to be coupled with me in any way."

"Yet he will have it you have already coupled with him, if I may be so crude."

Shock stopped her tongue. Had she not guessed the villain had traduced her? And Niall could not think her innocent without denial on her part. She passed from shock to fury in a second, pushing herself up from the fallen log to confront him.

"Oh, how like a man! Is this your knight errantry, sir? You offer me protection and fall at the first hurdle?"

He was on his feet, matching her for anger. "Have I walked away? Have I refused my help?"

"I don't want your help! Your mind is already poisoned against me."

"Edith, stop this!"

He made to grasp her shoulders, but she flung off his hands.

"Don't touch me! Have I not had enough to bear without you bullying me in addition to him?"

He threw his hands in the air in a gesture of submission. "I'm not threatening you. I'm trying to help."

"Then don't!"

"I'm not leaving you to tackle that monster alone, so don't think it."

The fury left her as suddenly as it had come. "Forgive me. He has set me all on end."

She put her hands to her face and found her cheeks wet. She wiped them in an absent manner, half aware of the softening in Niall's face. He did not speak and Edith found his silence oppressive.

"At least you recognise him for what he is." Niall's mouth compressed again and a horrid notion sprang into her mind. "What are you not saying? What did he tell you?"

He shook his head. "I won't repeat it. Suffice to say that I have every idea of the danger in which you stand and you may count on my support."

It was generous and Edith knew it. But somehow lacking. Whether or not he believed ill of her, he was ready to stand her knight. She ought to be grateful for so much, but a niggle in her breast wanted more and she did not understand why. It behoved her to answer him nevertheless.

"Thank you. I'm not sure if there is anything you can do."

"Whatever you want of me, Edith. Whatever will keep you safe. You have only to name it."

She was touched, but she could not withstand the urge to levity. "Well, you can hardly stand guard outside my bedchamber."

His lips twisted in amusement. "No, I concede that."

The faint light in her died. "I don't know, Niall. He plans to ask my uncle for a longer time with me."

"Then refuse."

"I cannot, unless I tell Uncle Lionel the truth. And don't ask me to do that for I doubt I could summon either the courage or the words."

His brows drew together. "Edith, you have to stand firm."

"Oh, I've tried. He will brook no denial, no refusal. He is determined to have me, by whatever means. Don't ask me why, for I don't know. The more I rebel, the more ruthless he becomes. There is no moving him, Niall. You can have no notion of the lengths…"

Her voice died as she realised what she'd been about to reveal. The shame and humiliation revived as she remembered to whom she was speaking. Had the villain turned even that episode against her? It would be hard to prove otherwise if he had.

"Was there a time when you favoured him?"

There was an edge to the words and Edith looked up, startled and all at once certain Niall's interest went deeper than mere attraction. Her pulse kicked in her veins. It became vital to give him the truth.

"At first. But briefly. He turned my head with flattery. He has address when he chooses … or he had." She faltered, the words coming in jerks and stutters as she forced them out. "I didn't encourage him — I tried to remain aloof. It wasn't …

appropriate. A teacher at the school and the father of two of the girls. Oh, he was persuasive. Plausible. And then…"

She drew in a breath as the memory hit her, the raw cut of disillusionment and realisation.

"And then?"

The prompt was gentle enough but the edge still underneath spoke of anger. Edith glanced at Niall's face, wondering if it was directed at her or at her Nemesis.

"I found out his wife is alive. Ailing, but alive. He'd lied — by implication more than words. His girls, in innocence, let fall the truth." The humiliation pricked all over again and the underlying rage spilled out. "I should have known. I should not have let myself be led to suppose a man of his stature in Society would deign to think of marriage with a female in my situation. I should have guessed his intention towards me."

"Why should you?" The harsh tone brought her up short. "You may be a schoolmistress but you're of genteel birth."

She gave a hysterical laugh. "Do you suppose he cared for that?"

"I know he did not and does not now, but you need not berate yourself for being taken in."

She drew a shuddering breath. "But I do. For the moment I told him I knew — and I did not spare my tongue, you may be sure — he laughed in my face. As if I cherished aspirations above my station. Oh, you cannot imagine the depths of my humiliation. From then, I must suppose, it became a game with him, an obsession that cost me my health and my livelihood."

She stopped with a gasp. She had not meant to say as much. Feeling abruptly weak at the knees, she moved back to the fallen trunk and sat down heavily upon it.

Niall was silent so long, she felt compelled to look up, to discover his thoughts. His expression gave little away. Beyond a certain tautness at the line of his jaw and a heavy frown, Edith could not judge his mood.

The frown cleared as he caught her gaze. "I see now why you shied away from even the mildest compliment. You have reason enough to be wary."

She eyed him. What precisely had Lord Kilshaw told him? That he had led him to believe her a fallen woman she could not doubt. There was no condemnation in Niall's features, but what of that? He was a kind enough man to feel for her in this predicament, but that did not mean he could overlook it if he believed she was, in vulgar parlance, damaged goods.

Without knowing why, Edith felt it to be of vital importance that Niall should believe in her innocence without requiring her to protest it. The doubt would stand between them, destroying any chance of…

The thought died before she could give it room in her mind. *Enough, Edith.* That road could lead nowhere.

Besides, until — if — she could rid herself of her Nemesis once and for all, she had no hope of any sort of future than to do away with herself. A sinful notion, but what else was left if he succeeded?

"What do you mean to do, Edith?"

They were back to that. As if she knew! "I have no notion. What can I do?"

"Tell your uncle the truth." He threw up a hand. "I don't mean you should expose yourself to his censure by revealing all. But you can at least tell him that the fellow is married already."

Yes, she could. Why had she not thought of that? But the sudden light of hope was succeeded by immediate recollection.

"It won't serve. If my uncle refuses permission for him to see me again, he will find means to abduct me."

"Then we must guard you."

Despair gripped her. "How, Niall? Am I to remain a prisoner in the house? Skulking in my room in fear every time I hear a step outside?"

He was frowning down at her. "No, that won't do. And I can't be always at hand. I'll have to post guards in the village."

"Dear God, it's like a siege!"

"Something like. Leave it to me. I'll escort you home now. Tell your uncle as much as you can bear to speak of and I will cogitate and come up with a plan of campaign."

A faint rise of hope entered her breast. He was a soldier, capable and strong. If anyone could save her, Niall could. She took the hand he was holding out and gave him one of her teasing smiles, at last able to feel genuine amusement.

"My true knight errant! Thank you."

He grinned. "You are welcome, my damsel in distress."

The doomed feeling in Edith's heart lifted a little.

Chapter Twelve

The Reverend Westacott's normally cheery features registered shock and dismay. Edith had bearded him in his little library, disturbing his afternoon's work. He had a bible open on his desk, along with a couple of the erudite tomes which he was wont to use when writing his sermons. He was fond, she knew, of pointing the morality of the Church with apt poetry or the satirical works of Addison, Swift and Pope. It went down better, he claimed, if given a literary turn.

He poised, pen in hand, and looked up when she came into the room and Edith's distracted eyes took in the sheet before him, covered in jottings.

"I see you are busy, Uncle Lionel. I am sorry to interrupt you, but this cannot wait."

She had nerved herself to come, and dared not put off the dread moment for fear she could not again summon the courage.

"My dear Ede, whatever is the matter?"

Relieved he'd taken in her condition at once, Edith had blurted out the fell tidings. Her uncle sat unmoving for a long moment. Then he laid aside his pen.

"Not a widower? Are you sure, Ede?"

"I could not be more so, sir. His daughters prattled of their mother as of the present. You may be sure I questioned them closely, for I was as shocked as you are now."

"But if Lord Kilshaw's wife is living, how should he be seeking another? It cannot be so."

Edith swallowed painfully. "It is so, sir, for I taxed him with it."

"You did? When, my dear?"

Her uncle's bewilderment was evident.

"As soon as I understood that his wife was alive. He — he did not deny it. He told me she has been ailing for some time. I understand she is little short of bedridden and — and not expected to survive for many years."

"But this is monstrous!" Her uncle's tone became severe and he rose in his wrath. "To be seeking a replacement when his wife is not even in the grave?"

Edith drew a breath and looked him boldly in the face. "He is not seeking a replacement, sir. The role he intends for me is quite otherwise."

She was both gratified and dismayed to see how his jaw dropped, his eyes fairly popping beneath the spectacles. Oh, she had known how it would be!

"Forgive me, Uncle Lionel. I did not wish to distress you with this, but I had no choice."

"Distress me?" He came around the desk and seized her hands, holding them in a sustaining grip. "My dear, dearest Ede, you should have told me at once. That he should dare insult you so! I am shocked. More, I am distressed for you, my dear. Is this why you left your post?"

It was worse than he knew, but seeing how badly he took even this piece of news, Edith hoped she need not say it all. "Not entirely, sir, though it was certainly a contributory factor."

The vicar released her hands and threw up his own. "And he actually followed you here? Had the gall to allow me to think him a genuine suitor? Good heavens!"

If that were all. Worse was to come. Her uncle paced away and then swung back on her.

"Are you certain his wife has not died? Is that perhaps why he came? It is reprehensible, for he should be still in mourning, but if his fondness for you overcame his judgement perhaps?"

A fairy tale! He was clutching at straws. Edith was obliged to quash any such hope.

"No, sir. He makes no secret of his intentions. He reminded me that he has a — a house all ready for me, and intimated he would be generous."

Her uncle's ruddy cheeks suffused with a deeper colour. "Monstrous! Disgraceful!"

"Yes, Uncle, but what am I to do?"

"Do, my dear? You need do nothing. You will not see him again, be sure. I shall send the fellow packing."

Edith had an instant image of her jolly little uncle wagging a finger in the face of the formidable Lord Kilshaw and felt an insane desire to laugh. But a greater danger must be averted.

"Uncle Lionel!"

He came across to her, once more taking her hands and squeezing them, looking into her face with an expression of deep concern.

"My poor Ede! I wish I had not consented to your going out as a schoolmistress. I never liked the notion, as you know, but I confess I hardly expected such an outcome."

Edith disengaged one hand and closed it over his, holding it between both her own. "You've been more than a father to me, sir, and this is no moment for regret. Pray listen to me!"

His eyes clouded. "There is more?"

"Yes — I mean, no. It is only that I fear Lord Kilshaw may well lead you to think he has — oh, lord, how I hate to be obliged to say this! — that he has already succeeded with me."

For the second time, her uncle's jaw dropped. He stared at her for a moment, his hand limp in her grasp. Edith released it and the vicar drew himself up and removed his spectacles. She saw a flash at his eyes.

"You wound me to the heart, Ede. Do you imagine I would believe such a thing of you?"

"He is very persuasive, sir."

"He might be the smoothest tongued orator in the world, my child, but never would I countenance so base a slander. I brought you up and I know your principles are fixed. Nothing — nothing! — could make me believe ill of you, my dearest Ede."

Edith's control slipped and the tears would not be contained. She found herself enveloped in her uncle's pudgy embrace, relief and tenderness warring with a sneaking despair that Niall had not been similarly disposed to believe in her innocence.

Her uncle released her and stood back, popping his eyeglasses back on his nose. "I think we would both be the better for a restorative. I am sure Mrs Tuffin will have coffee on the stove. The good woman knows to be prepared. Go and ask her to serve us in the back parlour, my dear, and I will be with you in a jiffy."

Edith gave him a tremulous smile. "I will do so. But one thing more." She hesitated. She must say this, but felt a little diffident. Would it involve her in too much explanation? Her uncle's instant look of apprehension decided her.

"Don't try to spare me, Ede."

"Oh, no, it is nothing untoward. Just that … Lord Hetherington has pledged me his aid."

"Lord Hetherington? Good heavens! I trust he is not concealing a wife about him too?"

Edith let out a laugh. "Not that I know of, sir. No, of course he is not."

A frown appeared. "Do you tell me he knows of this?"

Edith saw that only candour would serve her now. "Lord Kilshaw was kind enough to inform him, since he apparently took him for a rival in my affections."

The vicar threw up a hand. "You need say no more. I have the fellow's measure now."

The suppressed anger in her uncle's voice distressed her.

"I only wanted you to know because — because if anything were to happen to me, you may call upon him."

"But what in the world could happen to you, my dear Ede? No, no, you need be perfectly at ease. Once he has heard what I intend to say to him, Lord Kilshaw will not importune you further."

His confidence was touching, if misplaced. But Edith could say no more without imparting the entirety of the villain's conversation, and that she would not do. Her uncle was sufficiently discomforted already.

She left him and headed for the kitchen, feeling somewhat deflated, if relieved at the outcome of the dreaded interview. The feeling did not last, however, as she began to fret over what Lord Kilshaw might do once he realised she had thwarted his design of hoaxing the vicar. Her uncle, speaking of ordinary things over the coffee they shared in the comfort of the family room, had no real idea of the determination driving her Nemesis.

Uncle Lionel supposed he would retreat, chastened, like one of his parishioners after he'd been obliged to deliver a scold. But then the villagers adored him, just as she had learned to do. He was a fond and judicious guide to his flock, invariably understanding, always kind, and inclined to believe in the goodness of his fellow man. This simple trust was apt to make them feel worse for having transgressed and acted as a better deterrent than any threat of brimstone and fire in the afterlife.

Which was why Edith had been so reluctant to disillusion him when he'd accepted Lord Kilshaw in the light in which he presented himself. She was obliged to admit she had underestimated Uncle Lionel's large gift of compassion and his fierce loyalty. While it could not but touch her to the heart, his assurances failed to appease the demon of apprehension. He had no concept of the depths of degradation down to which her Nemesis wished to drag her. And Edith would not enlighten him.

She remained in her bedchamber when her uncle received Lord Kilshaw in the parlour upon the following morning. Expecting loud voices and an argument, she listened at her own door. But beyond a murmur of voices, nothing untoward occurred.

Presently she heard the front door open and close. Leaving her bedchamber, she crept along the passage and, kneeling on the window seat, peeped out of the casement that overlooked the front garden.

Lord Kilshaw had just gone through the gate and was striding off to where his curricle awaited him a short way down the lane, a groom at the horses' heads. Then he had not intended to attempt to get her alone on this occasion. She watched him jump up into the vehicle and take the reins. The curricle began to move and the groom swung himself up behind. Edith watched it out of sight and then ran down the stairs.

Her uncle was still in the parlour. He greeted her with a smile. "All is well, my dear Ede."

"Was he angry? Did he try to poison you against me?"

"Nothing of the sort. I must admit I was surprised, and felt a little sorry for the fellow, despite his reprehensible conduct."

Edith's heart sank. The conniving dissembler! "What did he say to you?"

"He admitted his fault at once. He confessed he knew he had no right to pursue you and claimed to be driven by his intense regard for you."

A sick feeling entered Edith's stomach. Regard? He had no more regard for her than a snake!

"You may be sure I set him straight. I advised him to return to his wife, who clearly needs his support, and instructed him to put all thought of you from his mind."

"And he accepted it?" Edith tried to keep the scepticism from her voice and her uncle seemed not to pick up on it.

"To be sure, my dear. He knew the game was up. He promised he would not trouble you again."

The villain had played her uncle like a violin. She could hear him saying it, hiding his wolfish intent behind a penitent air. Oh, he was the devil incarnate!

"I told you he was plausible, sir."

A frown creased his forehead. "You don't believe him sincere?"

"No, I do not."

Her uncle sighed. "Well, perhaps you are right. Let us give him the benefit of the doubt. If he does not leave the area within the day, I shall take it upon myself to hasten his departure."

Edith said no more. Her uncle was too trusting. Lord Kilshaw had no intention of leaving without her.

For a while she toyed with the notion of sending to Lord Hetherington, but she refrained, having no real expectation of his being able to secure her safety. But by the end of the day she saw there were at least three stout men, armed with staves, loitering at different points of the green. Were these Niall's guards?

For the first time in days, Edith allowed herself to hope.

Chapter Thirteen

Try as he would Niall could not keep his attention focused on the matters demanding it. While Edith remained in danger, his mind played constantly on the possible ways Kilshaw might use to secure her to himself. That, and any further means he could employ to keep her safe.

He'd taken such measures as he might without raising alarm in the village, confiding only in Eddows who knew the men of the estate. He had told him as little as possible, but did not doubt his agent was able to read between the lines.

"It would be less conspicuous, my lord, if you were to alert certain men already resident in Itchington Bishops. I know of three or four who might suit."

"Can we rely upon their discretion?"

"Oh, I think so, my lord. You will find few men unwilling to do whatever they may for the Reverend Westacott, and Miss Westacott is his niece."

Niall's brows rose. "He is highly esteemed?"

"Esteemed, admired and an object of devotion, my lord. Our vicar has a generous heart."

This intelligence encouraged Niall to feel more optimistic. If his parishioners had Westacott's interests at heart, so much the better.

"This is excellent, Eddows. Let us go and rout them out together."

His agent's lips pursed. "If I may make the suggestion, my lord, I dare say it would be better if you did not appear in the matter yourself."

"Why?"

"I imagine you don't wish to excite gossip in the village?"

"Damnation! Yes, of course you are right. That's the last thing I want. I dare say Lord Kilshaw's presence and his visits to the vicarage have not gone unnoticed."

"Nor his seeking you out at the tavern, my lord."

This admission caused Niall to let out an exasperated snort. "You mean you already know all about it?"

A prim little smile appeared on the fellow's mouth. "I am indebted to your lordship for a more accurate account."

"Good God, it's worse than the camp whisperers!"

"Villages, my lord, are in general hotbeds of gossip, since daily life is invariably dull. Anything that disturbs the general run must be of interest to your neighbours."

Niall had to laugh. "In that case, I must suppose myself to have been closely scrutinised?"

"Only for the first weeks, my lord. They have become accustomed to you."

"And I've given them food enough for gossip already, I suppose," Niall said on a grim note, recalling his various encounters with Edith and the ladies from Tazewell Manor.

His agent chose not to answer this, which was answer enough. Well, it could not be helped. He was not going to risk Edith's safety for fear of his movements affording interest to the curious.

"Summon the men to me here, Eddows. I prefer to interview them myself and ensure they understand what I need from them."

"Yes, I think that is wise, my lord, for it will be supposed you wish to employ them on estate business."

The arrangement was put in hand within the day, much to Niall's satisfaction. The four fellows chosen by Eddows were stout young farm workers well known in the village, all of whom had apparently proved their pugilistic prowess in battles against the neighbouring and rival village of Long Itchington. To which Niall now turned his attention.

"Lord Kilshaw is staying at The Fox and Goose in Long Itchington, Eddows. I would wish to put a man there who may take note of his movements."

They were riding towards one of the outlying farms upon the following morning, and Niall's mind was more at rest for knowing the men he'd briefed would be at their posts.

His agent looked across. "It is in hand, my lord. I took the liberty of setting my son to the task."

"Good God, what would I do without you, Eddows? An excellent beginning to his career in my service. He won't mind kicking his heels?"

A rare grin came from the agent. "Peter had no objection to spending his days idling in a tavern."

Niall burst out laughing. "I trust he may remain sober enough to keep his eye on our quarry."

"No fear of that, my lord. He reports that Lord Kilshaw drove towards Itchington Bishops yesterday morning and returned within the hour."

Cold gripped Niall's breast. "With Miss Westacott?"

"He was alone, my lord. And in a foul temper."

Then Edith must have told her uncle the truth. Relief swept through Niall and as quickly dissipated. No more than Edith did he believe Kilshaw meant to abandon his purpose. But at least he must have been denied access to the vicarage. That he was angered when he went back to The Fox and Goose suggested as much.

"And he has not made any move since?"

"No, my lord, he is still there."

Plotting, no doubt. Restless, Niall unconsciously urged his horse to a faster pace. What was he doing wasting his time in this fashion when that villain was weaving schemes in his den?

"My lord!" Niall looked back and saw that Eddows had reined in. "You are going the wrong way!"

Pulling up, Niall turned his horse and trotted him towards the agent. On the spur of the moment, he made up his mind. "Are they expecting us, Eddows?"

"No, my lord." The agent eyed him. "You wish to abandon the scheme?"

"I should not, I know, but I'm finding it hard to concentrate."

"Why don't we ride instead into Itchington Bishops, my lord? You may satisfy yourself that Miss Westacott is safe and I can make a couple of calls in the village."

"You're a good fellow, Eddows."

The agent led the way back a short distance to a crossroads and took a narrow lane, signposted to Itchington, from which Niall could soon see the church spire in the distance. He parted from his agent outside the smithy where he left his horse and crossed the green to the vicarage, noting the strategic placement of his guards. He nodded at the one closest and clicked open the gate. He was halfway up the path when the door opened and the Reverend Westacott's cheery countenance appeared.

"My lord Hetherington! Come in, sir, come in."

Niall wasted few words in greeting, moving directly to his purpose. "How is Miss Westacott? I gather she has enlightened you as to Lord Kilshaw's true character?"

The vicar tutted as he ushered Niall into the front parlour. "A most reprehensible undertaking. I was never more shocked.

My poor Ede to be subjected to such impertinence! It is too bad."

There was no Edith in the parlour and Niall felt his chest go hollow.

"Where is she?"

"She is resting, my lord. If this affair has not set her recovery back, we may count ourselves fortunate."

The reverend gentleman's concern was evidently heartfelt but Niall could not be satisfied.

"When did you last see your niece, sir?"

The vicar stared up at him with popping eyes. "You are not suggesting —? Good heavens! But we were together at breakfast. Surely not, sir? With these fellows you have set about the place?"

Surprised, Niall eyed him. "How did you know I did so?"

"My dear sir, what else was I to think? At first I could not imagine why young Davey and Mark were loitering here instead of labouring where they ought, but a moment's reflection gave me the picture. Besides, my Ede warned me you had pledged yourself to her support, for which I thank you most heartily."

Embarrassed to receive the beaming look of gratitude, Niall at once disclaimed. "It's little enough and I must hope it will serve."

The Reverend Westacott opened expansive arms. "When you have thoroughly covered the ground, sir? They are good lads and I think we may rely upon their vigilance."

That might be so, but Niall could not withstand a discomfiting sensation of apprehension in spite of all. Without a sight of Edith, he felt altogether distrustful of her safety.

"How long has she been in her chamber, if that is where she is?"

He saw from the man's sudden change of expression that his persistence was causing consternation in the vicar.

"Goodness gracious, my lord, what are you implying? It's been an hour, perhaps a little more." The vicar started for the door. "Wait here, sir!"

He did as he was bid, hearing the vicar's step on the stairs and wishing he had the right to run up himself. The thought sent him pacing to the mantel as if he must prevent his feet from making the move, so strong was the urge. Nothing short of marriage could give him that right.

Niall felt as if his head was exploding. Marriage! Why had he not thought of it at once? If he made Edith his wife, Kilshaw could not touch her. No man would dare make away with a fellow peer's spouse for fear of scandal. Besides, if he had her under his eye, in his own home, he could guard her himself. He'd keep her safe. She need never fear anything again. And he would cherish her as she deserved.

To his shock and dismay, Niall found himself trembling. The truth hit him with stunning force. He wanted her! He was as bad as that villain.

The thought had no sooner entered his mind than he dismissed it. No, he was nothing like Kilshaw. Of course he desired Edith. But it went deeper with him. How in the world had he lost his heart, so rapidly and so completely?

The instant the realisation came, Niall sobered on the thought of Edith's feelings. He could not flatter himself she returned his regard. She had shown enjoyment in his company — before the arrival of Kilshaw at least. But was there anything more?

A treacherous voice crept in. In this extremity, did it matter? If it would serve to secure her safety once and for all, it was selfish to be requiring a like feeling on her part as a prerequisite to marriage. Or was that a convenient excuse?

"Lord Hetherington?"

He swung round, warmth flooding into his face as he caught sight of Edith standing in the parlour doorway.

"Miss Westacott!"

She was here. She had not been spirited away. Niall wanted to cross the room and sweep her into his arms and hold her safe. But the vicar was bobbing about behind her, and in any event he had no right to enfold her in any sort of embrace.

Her smile, as she moved into the room, cut a swathe in his chest.

"I have to thank you, sir, for my guards." A gesture towards the window encompassed the men he'd set in place. "My uncle says you will not be satisfied without a sight of me."

Niall drew a taut breath. "I did not mean for you to get up from your bed." He took a step towards her and gestured at the chaise longue. "Won't you lie here instead?"

"Yes, Ede, do you take your ease," bustled the vicar, coming in behind her. "His lordship may remain with you while I run a few errands — if that suits with you, my lord?"

Niall nodded, his eyes on Edith as she took a seat on the chaise. "I am quite at leisure, sir."

Edith's brows rose. "What, when you rode in with Mr Eddows? He will be wild with me for keeping you."

"Not at all. We abandoned our plans for the day so that I might come to see for myself that all was well with you."

He took in that she looked a deal more composed than when they'd last met and was glad of it. A faint colour had risen in her cheeks at his words and Niall nourished a tiny hope.

"There now, my dear Ede, you have a fine protector in my place. I will alert Mrs Tuffin on my way out."

He bustled off and Niall caught another smile from Edith.

"I trust you are ready for the coffee and pastries that will make their inevitable appearance."

Niall laughed, his unease in her presence dissipating as he took the chair near the chaise longue. "I dare say I can endure it." He recalled her earlier words and did not hesitate. "How did you know I rode in with Eddows?"

"I saw you through the window."

"You were supposed to be resting."

She shifted her shoulders and Niall saw that she was not as calm as he'd supposed.

"I could not rest for long. But I knew Uncle Lionel would fret if I came down too soon, so I sat in the window seat on the landing and amused myself with watching the amblings of your men." An echo of her teasing tone sounded in her voice. "You do realise the whole village will be wondering what in the world they are up to?"

It caused him a momentary irritation. "I had not thought of that. Well, it can't be helped. Your safety is paramount."

Colour washed her cheeks again and she looked away. "Thank you. You are very good."

It was an embarrassed murmur and Niall could not prevent the words from leaving his lips. "Don't look so conscious. Don't you think you are deserving of such consideration?"

Her eyes met his, darkness in them. "When you have every reason to believe otherwise?"

Niall reached out and grasped one of her hands, holding it hard and leaning towards her. "I don't care, Edith. I won't importune you with question and suspicion. Even had I the right — and I wish I had! — I would not so burden you."

She looked as if she would have spoken, but the sound of footsteps and a rattling tray made her snatch her hand away.

Niall pulled back, jumping to his feet as Mrs Tuffin entered the room.

"Here we go, Miss Ede, and I've brought in a plate of almond cheesecakes straight from the oven to eat along with your coffee. Good morning, my lord, and I hope you've brought a good appetite with you."

Niall's eyes met Edith's dancing ones, and he had to exercise restraint to stop from bursting into laughter. Instead he addressed the housekeeper. "Thank you, Mrs Tuffin, and I'll be delighted to sample your cheesecakes."

He made way for her to set the tray down on the table behind the chaise longue and waited while she busied herself with pouring coffee and plying Edith with a plate of the cheesecakes. She pressed a plate upon Niall.

"You'll take a couple, I hope, my lord?"

Niall thanked her suitably, placing two cheesecakes on his plate. But the moment Mrs Tuffin left the room, he set it aside, leaning in towards Edith again.

"I meant what I said."

She was lifting her cup to her lips, but at this he saw her hand waver, the liquid inside in danger of spilling. On instinct, Niall reached out to support it, his fingers covering hers.

Her eyes met his, her colour fluctuating, the cup poised between them. The words leapt from his lips. "Marry me, Edith!"

Her expression changed and Niall became conscious of the uneven rhythm of his heartbeat as he recognised shock, then bewilderment.

"Have you run mad?"

"No."

With care, he removed the cup from her now nerveless fingers, set it into its saucer and laid the whole aside on the tray. Aware that she watched his movements, Niall met her gaze, struggling to overcome the discomfort he had himself engendered.

He reached towards her hand again, but Edith pulled it away, curling her fingers into fists. Niall withdrew the gesture at once, sitting back as he recalled her sensitivity.

"Forgive me. I had not intended to say it. At least not right now."

"Or at all."

Her cheeks were taut and a spark at her eye warned him to be careful.

"Edith, it slipped out. I've not had time to think it through, for it only just occurred to me when your uncle went up to find you."

A disbelieving laugh escaped her, but there was nothing of amusement in it. "Slipped out? Are you in the habit then of popping the question at random?"

"Of course not, don't be ridiculous."

"I'm ridiculous? What is it, Niall? A burst of chivalry?"

"Yes, in a way," he said, goaded.

Her lip curled. "Ah, I see. You will marry me to keep me from Lord Kilshaw's clutches? How magnanimous!"

Fury leapt into his chest. "It's not magnanimous. It's expedient, if you like. But it so happens I've fallen in love with you."

Edith gasped and put a hand to her mouth, her eyes widening. She dropped the hand, looked away from him and back again.

He wished she would say something, even if it proved to be the rejection he expected. It was obvious she did not return his regard. He'd not meant to throw it at her in that fashion.

"I've shocked you. Would it surprise you to learn that I've shocked myself just as much?"

She gave a little laugh, and Niall was touched to see a sheen at her eyes. But her voice, though husky, held all the old teasing quality that had first attracted him.

"That will teach you to think before you speak."

Reaching for her cup and saucer, he gave them to her. "Here. It might revive you enough to be able to consider my offer in a more maidenly fashion."

She smiled, setting the saucer in her lap again. "Was I rude? Yes, I was."

He watched her sip at the cup, evidently turning things over in her mind. Absently reaching for his own coffee, he took a sustaining draught of the hot black liquid and set the cup down to find Edith regarding him with a lurking twinkle.

"No one would suppose our discussion momentous, watching us both. I really think you ought to be indulging in some extravagant behaviour, Niall."

He had to smile. "Extravagant behaviour is not in my repertoire, Ede. Do you think you might manage without?"

Her eyes warmed and her cheeks took on a delicate colour. "I believe you were speaking the truth."

"Did you doubt me?"

"Frankly, yes."

"You have reason enough." He eyed her. "What did I say to convince you?"

Her smile was balm. "You called me Ede."

He thought back. "Did I?"

"If you don't remember that makes it more convincing."

That she believed him sincere was a step forward, but it did not assuage his discomfort.

"You haven't answered me."

At once she exhibited consternation, fidgeting with her cup, moving it in the saucer. She looked up. "Niall, I don't know."

He winced inwardly. "I would not hurry you in other circumstances."

Her brows rose. "You can hardly hurry me now. Even if I agreed, you can't marry me out of hand, you know."

"But you're of age, Edith."

"The banns must still be read for the requisite three weeks. Unless you applied for a licence." The tease appeared in her eyes again. "Or did you have it in mind to carry me off to Gretna?"

He had to laugh. "Better me than Kilshaw."

Her face clouded and Niall regretted having brought up the name. Her voice grated when she spoke.

"He has no thought of Gretna Green, or any other legitimate joining."

Impatience rode Niall. "Which is just why I am importuning you in this way, Edith. It's scarcely necessary in any event that we are married right away. A betrothal would give me ammunition enough to warn Kilshaw off."

"He would not believe you. He would think it a ruse. Which of course it is."

"No, it isn't. I wish very much to make you my wife."

"Oh, Niall!" Edith set the coffee aside on the tray and turned towards him. "I am truly touched, honoured even, but it won't do."

Hurt entered his breast. "Why won't it do? I can think of only one reason — that you don't care for me."

She shook her head and his heart sank. "It's not by any means the only reason. Be honest, Niall. If his lordship had not come here to plague me, would it even have entered your head to offer for me? No, of course it would not."

"You can't know that. I was attracted to you from the first. I did not show it once I saw how you shied away."

Her eyes flared. "You know why I did so!"

"I'm not blaming you."

Her fingers curled into fists again and Niall realised how her nerves were rubbed despite the apparent cool demeanour. Her tone was low.

"Niall, I am not fit for you."

"Don't you think I might be the judge of that?"

"No!"

Her bosom lifted and fell again. Dear Lord, what a tumult of emotion was there! His heart bled for her.

"Edith —"

"Please leave this, Niall. I cannot answer you. Not now. Not while the exigencies of my situation must influence a decision. Must, I am persuaded, have influenced you to speak at all." He opened his mouth to refute this, but she threw up a hand. "Don't! I beg of you, Niall, don't tempt me to take a step I can't be certain is right."

He seized on this. "Then you are tempted?"

She gave a strangled laugh. "Can you doubt it?" But that was no guarantee of her returning his love. "If Lord Kilshaw can be defeated," she continued, "persuaded to let me alone … or if I can escape him, then let us think of this again."

Niall hesitated, pulled to give in, despite the fact it suited with his need to keep her safe, as well as his desire for her. "You allow me to hope then."

"I could not stop you, could I?"

"True. Very well, Miss Westacott. We will play the game your way."

Her smile was wry and she gestured to the tray. "You had better indulge Mrs Tuffin if you don't wish to come under censure."

The distant manner chilled Niall. He took up the coffee, which had cooled, and nibbled a cheesecake, consoling himself with the reflection that Edith had not, in so many words, refused him. Could he at least conclude she was not altogether indifferent?

Chapter Fourteen

Far from indifferent, Edith sat with a secret tumult in her bosom while she schooled her lips to talk of indifferent things.

"Tell me how your improvements are progressing."

She saw his frown and wondered how she had ever thought his features unattractive. His was a mobile countenance, showing every nuance of change in his thoughts, and the splash of unruly auburn hair called to her fingers to caress and comb it through.

"How did you know I am putting in improvements?"

She could not help the smile. If she followed her inclination she would beam at him, allow her eyes to rove the strong contours of his vibrant features, aglow with life and vigour.

"All the world knows it," she told him, looking instead into the dark brown liquid in her cup which he'd topped up for her.

"Ah. Eddows told me village life is rife with curiosity."

"And you are a curiosity indeed."

The look of faint query, a little mistrustful, appeared in his eyes, as if he was not altogether certain whether to take her seriously.

"How so?"

"A stranger in our midst, a soldier too, complete with battle honours." She gestured at the scar which her fingers itched to stroke and Niall's hand went up, running briefly across it in a conscious way Edith found endearing. "How could it be otherwise? You must be an object of interest as the new lord of the district, of course, but as one quite unknown you represented food for a good deal of speculation."

"Not, I assure you, by any wish of mine."

Her compassion stirred, Edith with difficulty refrained from reaching out to him. "It must be galling to you to be obliged to tend the mundane matters of an estate rather than to plan your next battle."

"I am growing more used to it. There is certainly enough to do to keep me from brooding."

"Tell me."

With an odd look, as if he wondered why she chose the subject, he embarked upon a catalogue of needed repairs and plans put forward by his agent. Edith listened with half an ear, putting in appropriate noises just to keep him talking that she might watch him without seeming to do so. He was close enough for her to drink in the indefinable masculine aroma, so different from the perfumed overlay of that other creature. There was the inevitable horse smell too, stronger when he'd first arrived, but faded now enough to admit the subtle manly scent she now recognised to be associated in her remembrance wholly with Niall.

The shock of his proposal was dissipating, but perturbation remained. She was distraught at being obliged to refuse him, elated at his declaration of love for her, dismayed to think he had still a doubt of her purity though he swore he would not regard it. That Edith could not believe.

He might say so now, in the heat of his discovery of his feelings. Had he not said he had shocked himself? But when he'd had time to reflect, to reason with himself, the doubt was bound to creep back. He said he did not care, but he did. Oh, he did. She'd seen it on the day he met her Nemesis. God knows what the fiend had said! But enough to condemn her, that she could swear to.

"The devil of it is there is no money to do these things. We are still waiting for probate."

Edith came to herself with a start, staring at him. He reddened.

"It sounds absurd to be talking of a lack of funds when one is master of so much property, but so it is."

Pulling her mind into gear, Edith made haste to disclaim. "You are by no means the first peer to find his coffers empty."

"That's the bugbear. They are far from empty, but I can't access them until the lawyers arrive at a settlement."

"Frustrating indeed."

He cocked an eyebrow. "But nothing like as frustrating as it is to me to sit here pretending to talk to you as if I am nothing more than a casual visitor."

Warmth flooded into Edith's face and bosom and she took refuge in her coffee cup, sucking up the liquid so rapidly that she choked and fell into a fit of coughing.

"What the devil?"

The cup and saucer was taken from her fingers and a rough hand administered a judicious series of light slaps to her back until the coughing subsided. Edith wiped at her mouth, glancing at Niall who had taken a seat on the chaise longue beside her.

"Thank you, my knight errant." She managed a faint laugh. "I cannot seem to do the least little thing without requiring your assistance."

He grinned, turning his mouth lopsided. An oddity she found tantalising, adding to his charm. Was that his greatest asset? A charm of which he was wholly unaware? It contrasted so completely with the false air of charm that characterised Lord Kilshaw that Edith's heart lurched.

Niall's murmur took her unawares. "I could wish you might require me for everything in your life."

She caught her breath, trying for a light note over the flurry of her pulse. "That could prove a deal more problematical than you imagine."

His lips twitched. "You forget, Ede. I'm a soldier. I should rise to the challenge."

She delighted in his ability to match her wit. It was the first thing in him that had begun the erosion of her barriers. How he had managed to bring them down so thoroughly Edith would never know.

The reminder of her state of mind served to bring back the uncertainty, and she could not but be relieved to hear the opening of the front door and her uncle's step in the hall. Niall rose at once, clearly not wishing to be discovered in such close proximity. With matters in a state of disarray between them, it was just as well.

The vicar came hurriedly in, talking almost before he was properly in the room. "My dear Ede, if this distressing business had not put it out of my mind."

"Put what out, Uncle?"

"The Lammas Day feast, my dear. Such a to-do we must expect, and there is bound to be a scramble between our fellows and those of Long Itchington. And this year it is our turn to host the festivities."

Niall was looking as bewildered as Edith felt, and she was glad he put the question.

"What festivity is this, sir?"

He removed his eyeglasses, waving them as an accompaniment to his words. "It comes round every summer, my dear sir, and every year I am tempted to refuse to allow it. Only it provides a good deal of entertainment for the locals and it is a rare holiday for them after all."

Enlightenment dawned on Edith. "Oh, you mean the fair on the green. Heavens, it's been so long since I attended one I had forgot all about it. Well, you must certainly attend, Lord Hetherington. It is quite in your line."

Niall's questioning eyes were on her. "But what is it?"

"It is the annual excuse for a battle between the rival neighbouring villagers."

"Ah, yes, I remember Tom telling me something of that."

Her uncle was amused. "Did he do so, my lord? I believe he has joined in on occasion. But I doubt he'll be back in time this year."

"Which leaves you, sir, to take the role of judge and referee," said Edith with relish.

He eyed her askance. "Does it indeed?"

"Yes, and you cannot refuse, you know, or your popularity will take a dive."

"Since I have no popularity as yet, I hardly think that will trouble me."

"Oh, but you are mistaken, my lord," her uncle chimed in. "I have been privileged to hear only murmurs of approval. Your interest in the needs of your tenants is much appreciated."

Edith was charmed to see Niall flush. He was not a man given to flaunting his consequence, unlike Kilshaw. The remembrance caused a slicing shaft inside her and her spirits dropped. For this short time, a precious interlude, she'd almost forgotten.

Her uncle's voice penetrated her absorption, and she realised he was giving Niall a more reasoned description of the proceedings he might expect at the Lammas Fair.

Edith's brief moment of anticipation was over. If Kilshaw's purpose prevailed, she would be far beyond any hope of attending.

Chapter Fifteen

Contrary to Edith's fear and expectation, several days passed with no sign of Lord Kilshaw. She had kept to the house, unwilling to go beyond the back garden where she could see one of Niall's guards patrolling the lane that ran alongside the low wall separating the vicarage from the green and that led towards Tazewell Manor. The days were warm although the sun was often markedly absent, intermittent dank clouds producing drizzle and an occasional sharp shower.

Edith was sorry for the young men detailed to watch out for her safety, obliged to stand about in the wet. Although she noted Niall had organised a system of turnabouts among the four. It apparently allowed for each man to be relieved for an hour at a time, which inevitably took them to the tavern across the green.

There was at least one visible throughout the night, too, as Edith had seen last night when, sleepless with her churning thoughts, she'd got up out of her bed and gone down to the kitchen for a glass of milk, warming it in a pot on the range whose coals retained heat from the long day's burning. Edith had caught a glimpse of a man on patrol through the kitchen window.

At first she gasped with fright, backing from the window in the instant apprehension that her Nemesis had come for her. But the man turned and walked back the way he had come for some twenty paces and then turned again.

Letting her breath go, Edith went back to the range, her thoughts flying to Niall and his military background. Of course he would not leave her vulnerable in the long night hours when Kilshaw could come like a thief to snatch her out of the contrived cocoon of the vicarage.

The thought sent her imagination roving with images: unheard creeping feet entering her bedchamber; hands seizing her while she slept; the hated oiling voice whispering his intentions into her unwilling ear.

Shuddering, Edith pulled her dressing-gown more tightly about her body. A faint sizzling told her the milk was ready. With shaking hands, she poured it into the waiting glass, spilling a few drops. Muttering imprecations, she found a cloth and dabbed at the spill on the flagstones.

Then she hurried back upstairs and into the muffling curtained interior of her bed, sitting up against the banked pillows to sip her milk and wishing Niall were in there with her.

The bold notion sent a flush through her body and Edith shivered with a sensation other than cold.

Stop it, Edith Westacott! What, was she so wanton? The protest rose up without warning. Not wanton, no. She'd thought of Niall from the notion of needing comfort in his presence, that was all. To be able to lean into him and feel his arms come about her, holding her safe. He would keep her so. Oh, he would. One only had to look at him to know how readily he could repel any threat. Then why, idiot woman, did she not accept his offer?

Edith sighed and sipped her milk. As if she need ask herself such a question. Was it not obvious? How to accept him when his proposal sprang out of her danger? A spontaneous scheme to protect her from Lord Kilshaw's villainous one. And when Niall could have no certainty of whether or not he'd lied?

A sneaking voice in the back of her mind urged her to tell Niall the full tale, but Edith shrank from doing so. If she married him, she would have to. Indeed, she could never marry him without. What, live always with the niggle of doubt standing between them? It could not be done. Rather would she risk losing him.

She tipped her glass once more against her lips and found it empty. She'd drunk all the milk without being aware of it. Yet she was no nearer sleep.

Setting the glass aside, she snuggled down, drawing her feet away from the cold at the bottom end of the sheets. And there was another thing. If Niall was in her bed, he'd keep her warm too. Hugging her arms about her, Edith turned on her side and tried to conquer her all too vivid imagination.

She slipped into sleep at last and woke in the morning little refreshed, but with an unprecedented sense of optimism.

Lord Kilshaw had stayed away. It might be he'd been put off by the weather. The rain had likely left at least the country roads muddy and pitted with ruts, which would slow down a carriage. Or had her Nemesis merely discovered how well she was guarded? She would have surely heard if he'd been into the village, but he might have sent a servant to scout for him. Edith indulged the hope he'd been thwarted.

She recalled her lurid imaginings of the night and chided herself. Truly she was being absurd. Yes, he was determined. But common sense must dictate how difficult it would be to carry her off in the circumstances. Aside from her screaming — and she would scream with all the power of her lungs — any such attempt must create a stir in the village. And the village was alerted to expect something unusual, even if it was not known why Niall's men patrolled strategic points of the environment.

She'd faced the fear alone before, but now she had both Niall and her uncle, along with her guards. She went down to breakfast in a much less apprehensive frame of mind.

She found her uncle sitting at the table in the dining parlour, partaking of his customary morning meal of ham, eggs and several slices from a fresh baked loaf of bread. He looked up as Edith entered, glancing over his spectacles and waving an unfolded sheet of paper at her.

"We are bidden to dine at Lowrie Court, my dear Ede. Lord Hetherington says it is high time you were allowed out of seclusion."

A tiny flutter ran through Edith's veins. "Today?"

"This afternoon, my dear. Eddows brought the note and he will come to escort us."

"Mr Eddows? Good heavens, does Niall — I mean, his lordship — suppose I might be in danger upon the journey?"

Her uncle consulted the note. "He is taking no chances, my dear. Both Mark and Owen have been detailed to ride alongside the carriage as well."

"Well, I defy even Lord Kilshaw to snatch me from such a comprehensive entourage."

Her uncle surveyed her with a lurking twinkle. "You appear to be in spirits, my dear Ede. It gives me great pleasure to see you so much more yourself."

She selected a portion of ham from the covered dishes left by Mrs Tuffin. "I do feel much less hunted, Uncle Lionel."

"I am glad of that, my dear. Let us hope that fellow will realise his error and depart. Indeed, I cannot imagine why he has not already done so."

"Perhaps he has."

Although Edith could not quite believe he might have gone. Was he biding his time?

"I have given Mrs Tuffin leave to go to her sister's after breakfast, my dear, since we won't need her services. Of course she refused to go without leaving a cold collation that young Sally may serve us at need."

"I hardly think we will need it."

"No, my dear, but you know what she is, the good woman."

Edith was well aware that the housekeeper cosseted the vicar in every possible way, as she had done since Edith's mother died, leaving her uncle more distressed than she had been herself. Edith had often wondered if he'd cherished an unnaturally deep affection for his brother's wife. He'd certainly taken Edith to his heart as if she was his own daughter.

Her glance idled to the window and she noted the grey skies.

"I hope it may not be raining this afternoon. We'll be obliged to hold umbrellas in the gig."

Her uncle waved his fork in the air. "Did I not say, my dear? His lordship is sending his coach for us, so the rain is of no consequence."

Warmth leapt into Edith's bosom. "What it is to have a soldier at one's back. He thinks of everything."

The vicar nodded, speaking only when he'd swallowed down a mouthful of ham. "He is an excellent fellow. His tenants are beginning to realise his worth. Not that Roland Lowrie was wanting. A good sort of a man he was, and his wife a most pleasant woman. But I do believe this present Lord Hetherington may prove more energetic in his approach to his responsibilities."

Recalling Niall's true attitude towards those same responsibilities, Edith was conscious of a wash of compassion for him. Having had experience of the trap of circumstance, aside from the interference of Lord Kilshaw, she could enter into his sentiments. And he need not have taken up the challenge in the way he had. Many men in his position might well choose to let the tenants go hang, and squeeze out every ounce of profit for themselves. But not Niall.

"He has a well-developed sense of duty," she said aloud.

"We may put that down to his military background, my dear Ede. When it is do or die, I dare say a man learns to act as he must."

Yes, but it was not wholly that, Edith was persuaded. It was not in his character to ignore the needs of others. Look how he had taken her safety under his control. He was under no obligation to do so, although his feelings for her must have swayed him. Indeed, a more selfish man would have left her to her fate once she rejected him. But Niall would never do that, whether she married him or no. In fact, she was almost certain he would come to her rescue if the worst should happen.

Realisation struck her. No wonder she no longer walked with fear stalking her mind. It was less a matter of guards than the belief that Niall would go to any lengths to keep her safe.

The day dragged as a bubble of anticipation built in Edith's breast. Her mind presented her with images of Niall's mobile face in a variety of expressions, every one endearing. The prospect of seeing him made her want to break into song and an unprecedented energy made her wish the time away to the dinner hour.

She changed her everyday muslin for one less proclaiming the schoolmistress, and for the first time in years felt dissatisfied with her wardrobe. Really she had nothing suitable to the occasion. And there was no time to refurbish the spotted muslin chemise gown with new green ribands to the sleeves or a lace ruff. Instead she adorned the plaiting around the neckline with her mother's pearl brooch, touching the delicate beads with a careful finger.

"Ede, are you ready?"

Her uncle's voice calling up the stairs set Edith's heart aflutter. It was time.

Chapter Sixteen

"All the arrangements are in hand, my lord."

His butler's assurance failed to quiet the knot of anxiety in Niall's breast.

"I must suppose Mrs Radway is equal to the task."

"Indeed, my lord, she has managed far more complex entertainments than this."

The indulgent note was not lost on Niall. He refrained from cursing the man. God knew he had little enough experience! His batman had been capable of producing a decent meal from the most meagre rations for a coterie of fellow officers, but this was an entirely different situation. He did not care to set an inferior repast before Edith, even if the dinner was a ploy to interest her in becoming the mistress of Lowrie Court.

Reflecting that he was spared having to include the party from the Manor, who were still absent from the district, Niall dismissed the butler, turning to the mirror over the fireplace to check his cravat was presentable and his disreputable hair at least under control. He could not flatter himself his appearance was of the sort to attract females to him. Miss Burloyne's interest had been purely in his title, he was certain. But Edith was another matter altogether.

She had not the least interest in his coronet. She'd shown scant sign of finding anything in his person to attract her. And she'd refused his offer even in the worst extremity of need.

Although he'd felt an almost irresistible urge to go back to the vicarage time and again, he'd held off. Niall hardly knew himself whether it was in the light of a strategic withdrawal or because he dreaded further rejection, but his thoughts were never far from Edith.

The sound of a carriage alerted him to the arrival of his guests and he cast a critical eye about the drawing room. The mirror over the mantel had been dusted, the somewhat faded straw-coloured cushions turned, the wood on the Chippendale sofa polished and the patterned rug newly swept. The wall-sconces and two candelabra had fresh candles awaiting the dusk and two extra chairs had been brought in and strategically placed. Satisfied, he moved forward to greet Edith and the vicar as his butler announced them.

In the flurry of arrival, he had time only to notice that Edith looked in better bloom than when he'd seen her last. She seemed composed and her smile gave him hope. Was there a trace of intimacy in it?

His agent had entered behind them and Niall, pausing only to usher Edith into a seat beside the small fire he'd caused to be set in the grate, took the opportunity to put in one aspect of his campaign.

"Eddows tells me, Reverend, that you are fond of chess?"

Mr Westacott beamed up at him. "I am indeed, my lord, though I seldom find the opportunity to indulge. There are so few opponents hereabouts."

"Yet Eddows informs me he is itching to take his revenge upon you for your last bout with him."

The vicar's hearty laughter sounded and he looked round at the agent. "Fiend that you are, Eddows! You know very well I had not beaten you for some time. I have been basking in my triumph."

His agent gave the prim smile Niall had come to know well. "Ah, but you will allow, sir, that you have the edge if we are counting."

"Counting? All these years?" Mr Westacott's finger wagged at him. "I know you, my dear Eddows. I dare say you have been keeping score in that pocket book of yours."

"I have," grinned his opponent.

"Then I must beg you to take advantage after dinner," said Niall. "I have unearthed a most delightful set of chessmen, exquisitely carved. I believe they must have come from India, for I have seen similar sets there."

His agent's eyes lit. "You don't mean it, my lord? Good heavens, I have not played with that set since the old lord died. The late Lord Hetherington had no fondness for the game."

Both antagonists were clearly delighted at the prospect and Niall was able to congratulate himself on the success of his tactics. They began at once to discuss their last game and he was able to turn his attention to Edith.

"Masterly, my lord," she said as he reached her, the alluring twinkle in her eye.

He dropped into the chair opposite, feeling the colour creep into his cheeks. "Damnation! I should have guessed you would see through me." He gave her a deprecating look. "Don't fear I am planning to renew my persuasions. It's just that we haven't met for several days and I would welcome the opportunity to discover how you are faring."

"A deal better than I was, thanks to you."

"It is worth the effort, if you feel a little less at risk."

Her voice dropped to a level less likely to be overheard. "A great deal less, though I cannot be altogether sanguine. I can't believe he has abandoned his purpose."

"Nor I." A flitter of something passed across her face, and he was sorry he'd been as blunt. He put out a quick hand, matching her low tone. "Don't fret, Edith. We will not relax our vigilance until we know for certain he is defeated." He saw her breast rise and fall in a rapid manner that showed her agitation, and spoke with deliberate lightness. "Let us forget him for this once and talk only of ourselves. Is it agreed?"

She eyed him in a way he could not interpret for a moment. Then the teasing look appeared. "You assume we may find ourselves a sufficient distraction? Alas, my lord, I fear the tale of my dull life will afford you scant entertainment. We had much better talk of you."

"You are incorrigible. You must know I am keen to discover everything about you."

"Good heavens! Should you not keep me shrouded in mystery? Gentlemen, I am reliably informed — by my students, you must know — lose all interest the moment they are permitted to see behind the public mask."

He chuckled. "Is it so indeed?"

"I assure you. My girls were intent upon cultivating as much mystery as they could and made great use of their fans in this regard. I caught them practising many a time in their parlour."

Niall regarded her with a lurking smile. "I have yet to see you flirting with a fan."

Upon which, she immediately took her fan from her lap and treated him to a display of the most ridiculously overplayed flirtation, making him laugh immoderately.

"Oh, Edith, a man might spend a lifetime in your company and never be bored!"

The fan closed with a snap and she dropped it into her lap, colour rising to her face.

Niall cursed himself and sought in vain for a way to gloss over the moment. He'd not meant to refer to his proposal, even in so oblique a fashion. But having recalled it to his own mind, he could think of nothing else than his ardent desire to marry her.

His butler saved the day, coming in at this moment to announce dinner. Niall was able to resume his duties as host and his consciousness faded.

He stole a look at Edith as she took his arm, and found her customary composure had returned. But her voice was cool.

"I've not been in this house since I was a child, my lord. It looks a great deal less imposing than I remember."

He replied with more ease than he felt. "A trick of the mind."

"Indeed, yes."

They crossed into the dining parlour, which had been thoroughly cleaned and polished for the occasion by the trio of maids he'd had Eddows bring in to help Mrs Radway, despite the lack of funds. They were all village girls, glad of the employment, even though lacking in experience. They made up for it with a show of industry, and Mrs Radway had confided to him that she was inclined to believe they would do. Praise of high order, according to his butler.

Edith was seated at Niall's left hand, the vicar to his right, with Eddows flanking Edith. Niall divided his attention between the two principal guests, but could not prevent himself keeping a surreptitious eye out when his agent took opportunity, as courtesy dictated, to talk with Edith.

He could not help imagining how it would be to have Edith at the lower end of the table in the place for his hostess — his wife. The word sent a flitter through his veins and he had to take refuge in his wine.

The first course, of roast fowls, baked salmon, asparagus and a white mushroom fricassee, together with a dish of buttered crab, was well cooked and sustaining, if lacking in the sort of frivolous extra dishes provided at the Manor. The vicar was a good trencherman and Eddows did justice to the Cook. But

Edith, to Niall's combined concern and dismay, seemed merely to pick at the food.

In a lull, he picked up the nearest dish to hand and proffered it. "Can I tempt you to a little more buttered crab, Miss Westacott? The fowl does not look to be much to your liking."

Her eyes met his and her cheeks flew spots of colour. "Thank you, no. It is an excellent meal, sir, only I'm afraid I still have a poor appetite. You must blame my recent illness."

Niall did not protest, but he was inclined to believe it an excuse. Her appetite was clearly lacking, but as she was in much better bloom than formerly, he declined to accept it was due to her physical condition.

Had she taken his reference too much to heart? Did the thought of marriage with him cause her so much unrest? His spirits dropped a trifle and he was hard put to answer the vicar's random remarks with any degree of sense.

He noted his agent's narrow regard, and was glad when Eddows took it upon himself to enlighten the Reverend Westacott as to the state of his crop fields.

The butler and one of the maids began to remove dishes and replace them with the second course. Niall seized the opportunity to draw Edith's attention, speaking low.

"Have I embarrassed you? If so, I am sorry for it."

She started, as if from a reverie, consternation in her eyes as they flew to his. "No, of course not. Forgive me. My mind was wandering."

Where? But Niall did not ask. He was glad of the friendlier note in her voice, and seized the chance to make up for his earlier error. "I'm relieved you don't despise the fare, for Mrs Radway has been quite anxious."

Edith's warm smile appeared. "She has nothing for which to blush. Besides, my uncle and I are used to much plainer dinners."

"I hope you are moved to praise the syllabub. Mrs Radway tells me it is Cook's speciality."

"Then I will certainly sample it."

She was as good as her word, taking care to finish the helping served into her bowl and murmuring her appreciation as Hempsall removed it. "Pray tell Cook that I have rarely tasted anything as good."

The butler looked gratified, and Niall could not avoid the pleasing thought that she would make the perfect countess. Mrs Radway came herself to escort Edith to the drawing room, leaving the men to their port. Niall took care to assure her they would not be far behind.

When he re-entered the drawing room, the butler had already set up the table for the two older men and placed the board and the box of chessmen ready. He found Edith browsing a set of books in the glass-fronted cabinet at one side of the room and went across as the vicar and Eddows took their places for their game of chess.

"Ah, you've found my cousin's collection of novels, I see."

She turned, an open book in her hands, and looked up. "I take it these belonged to his wife?"

"I imagine so. I understand she used this room for her leisure hours."

Edith glanced about at the somewhat mismatched furnishings and the pretty drapes. "It is a cosy apartment. You have larger ones, no doubt?"

"Yes, but not yet fit for use."

A tiny frown appeared between her brows. "Were things left so badly?"

"Indeed, but no blame attaches to my cousin. I gather the deaths took everyone unawares and the usual precautions for leaving the rooms untended were not taken."

Edith's brows rose as she snapped the book shut. "What you mean is that nobody thought to drape the furniture in Holland covers, nor shutter the windows, and the whole place became dusty and the carpets have begun to fade."

He grinned down at her. "Your housewifely instincts are not at fault. Though I think the shutters were closed in due course."

"But it was months of neglect, I suppose?"

"Yes, for the lawyers had all to do. First they had to track down who was heir, and then it took them an age to locate my whereabouts. The house suffered as well as the estate. Nearly all the servants left and Mrs Radway and Hempsall could hardly manage the place alone."

"Heavens, what a task you have in hand!" She set the book she was still holding back in its place and closed the cabinet doors. "You will need an army to set it all to rights. What a pity you cannot call upon your former company."

He laughed. "They would be utterly useless in a domestic capacity."

"Indeed? I had formed an idea that soldiers were particularly adaptable."

"Not all of them."

Her eyes quizzed him. "Just you? Well, I knew you were a rare specimen, but I had not expected to find you unique."

"If we were not alone, ma'am, I'd take pleasure in showing you just how unique I can be."

"Threat or challenge, my lord?"

"Both!"

She laughed then and Niall rejoiced at the lightness of the sound. He touched her elbow, guiding her in the direction of a sofa placed against the wall, a little removed from the two men now engrossed in their game of chess. Once involved, Niall guessed they would have little attention to spare for anything else, but he was anxious not to be overheard.

"Come and sit down."

She went where he guided her and took a seat, looking up at him in an expectant way that at once made him nervous. He hovered a moment.

"You will not be cold so far from the fire?"

"I am not such a poor creature, sir. Besides, it is a warm night." She went on as he took his place, a little removed so that she might not feel threatened. "I have not been used to having my comfort particularly regarded. Mrs Vinson, my employer you must know, was excessively kind, but her thoughtfulness did not stretch to wasting coals on unnecessary fires in the summer."

Niall wanted to express his intention of paying every possible attention to her comfort for the future, but he was apprehensive of causing her to withdraw again. He chose a random question instead. "What in particular did you teach?"

She let out a sound almost as explosive as a snort. "Everything! I was employed initially to teach French and deportment, but I soon found myself detailed to cover anything needed."

"Were your girls of every age?" Not that he had much interest, but Niall wanted to keep her talking.

"We took girls from seven years old to seventeen. But latterly I was mainly in charge of the older girls." The teasing glint appeared. "It seems I have enough of a managing disposition to be successful with them, where my colleagues were not."

"I cannot imagine how in the world they are coping without you."

He regretted his words at once, for her features clouded and her eyes went dim. *Damnation!* A devil in him, wanting to know, took his tongue.

"What happened, Ede? Was it on account of Kilshaw?"

She stiffened, a spark entering her eye. "I thought we were to have an evening free of his name."

"Yes, I meant it so. I'm sorry. Only I can't help wishing —" He broke off, seeing the deepening of anger — or was it? With difficulty, he refrained from seizing her hand. "Don't heed me! I didn't mean it. It's not important."

Her lips were compressed, but she opened them and a metallic tone emerged through their stiffness. "Yes, but it is, Niall. To me. And clearly to you as well."

He wanted to disclaim, but it would only make things worse. "Let us dismiss the subject."

"By all means."

But there was ice in her voice still. Niall hurried into speech. "I meant to tell you more about the house."

"Did you?"

It was not encouraging, but he persisted. "Or rather, I meant to ask your uncle about it. I'm persuaded he will know its history."

He was operating on instinct, throwing this in as if he'd seriously thought about it. He hadn't. It occurred to him out of desperation. He eyed her, trying to see if this gambit was working.

She was regarding him with a steady gaze, her thoughts unfathomable behind the stiff mask of her face. Talk of mysteries! She was an enigma sometimes. A faint smile dissipated the discomfiting expression.

"An excellent ploy, Niall. I must suppose you have learned such quick thinking on the battlefield."

He could not prevent a rueful laugh escaping. "I might have known you had too much wit to be fooled."

Her lips quirked. "Do tell me all about the history of your house."

"Wretch! I had rather administer a salutary lesson, but I dare say that is out of count."

He warmed to her laughter, not a little relieved.

"Count yourself lucky not to receive one instead. I can give as good as I get, you know."

"I'm fully aware of that," he replied feelingly. "And I think I have already had my lesson from you, several times over."

She bubbled with so much mirth it caught the attention of the chess players. Eddows contented himself with turning his head briefly, but the Reverend Westacott waved a cheery hand.

"I am glad you are enjoying yourself, my dear Ede. It is about time you had a taste of frivolity." With that, he returned to the fray and Niall found Edith twinkling at him.

"There, sir, you are a source of frivolity. I'll wager you never thought to be so while plying your trade in the muddy fields of India."

Niall's heart warmed and the words slipped out before he could stop them. "I do love you, Ede."

To his surprise and delight she did not look away. Her gaze roved his, seeming to seek the truth in his eyes. She looked as if she would have spoken, but the opening of the door sent her gaze away from him and Niall gave an inward curse as he turned to find his butler on the threshold.

"Mr Peter Eddows, my lord. He informs me his errand is urgent."

Chapter Seventeen

Edith did not know whether to be glad or sorry the tête-á-tête had been interrupted. She was finding it increasingly difficult to keep her countenance and maintain her determination to keep Niall at arm's length.

Beset by a riffle of disappointment, she watched the hasty entrance of a fresh-faced young man whose countenance was vaguely familiar. His glance swept the company and fixed upon Niall.

"My lord, he's gone!"

Bewilderment warred with instinct and a pounding started up in Edith's heart. Could he mean Lord Kilshaw?

Mr Eddows was on his feet as Niall strode forward.

"Gone? You mean he's left the place or you've lost him?"

"The devil's in it I don't know, my lord!"

The lad, looking both harassed and dismayed, cast a glance at Eddows, who came up to lay a hand on his shoulder.

"Calm yourself, my boy. Just tell his lordship what happened."

The disturbance in Edith's heart increased. There could be no doubt he was talking of Lord Kilshaw. Young Peter, whom she supposed to be the agent's son, must have been detailed to watch him. And he'd escaped! The young man was obviously upset at his own failure.

"I can't be sure of anything, sir. He dined at his usual time, that I know, for I saw the waiters coming and going to his private parlour."

"At what time?"

The lad's eyes went back to Niall. "Just after four, my lord. I thought — I supposed he was safe ensconced in the parlour and…" He faded out, threw a look at Eddows, who nodded. Swallowing, he resumed. "I took my eye off him for a space. I had occasion to leave the inn and I — I'm sorry for it, my lord, but there's no use deceiving you —"

"Give me a round tale, regardless of mistakes."

Niall's tone remained calm enough but Edith noted the tightness at his jaw.

"Well, it was a mistake, my lord," said the lad, throwing another anxious glance at his parent, "for I got into a — a conversation with — with someone —"

Eddows groaned. "Some pretty chit, you mean? When will you learn, Peter?"

"I'm sorry, Father."

"Never mind that," Niall cut in. "So you were otherwise engaged for a space. Where were you? In the yard?"

Young Eddows, who had been looking chastened at his father's words, now exhibited all too much consternation. "No, my lord, that's just the point. I'd gone out the back, but I met —" He cleared his throat. "I met the girl as I was coming back and, one thing leading to another, we — er —"

He reddened, his gaze flying to the vicar and at last discovering Edith's presence. His colour deepened and Edith was conscious of a reprehensible desire to laugh. He must suppose she would be shocked to realise he had been lured into amatory dalliance.

Eddows was looking both annoyed and resigned, but Niall brushed it aside.

"Yes, very well, but when you returned to your duty, what happened?"

The worst of his confession no doubt now out, the young man began to look a little less hangdog. "I went directly to the spot from where I could watch the parlour door unobserved, my lord, and waited. After a bit, I realised it was quiet in there. Too quiet. And none came in or out for the best part of a half hour."

His father exploded. "Good God, boy! I've spawned an idiot! Did you not think to check at once? Could you not have pumped the waiters?"

Niall threw up a hand to silence his agent. As well, Edith reflected, since young Eddows looked to be about to burst into tears.

"That will do. Time enough for recriminations when we know the whole. I presume you then went on the hunt, Peter?"

"Yes, my lord," said Peter miserably, "but there was no sign of Lord Kilshaw, either in the inn or outside. And then I found his curricle was gone. I ventured to question Louch, the landlord you must know, and he said his lordship had paid his shot. The ostlers couldn't tell me which way he went either." The boy's tone became eager. "I mounted my horse and rode at once to Itchington Bishops to see if he'd driven in that direction, but there was no sign of his curricle, so he must have gone cross-country towards Warwick."

"Not necessarily." Niall moved to the fireplace and drummed his fingers on the mantel. No one spoke, and Edith saw all three men watching him, waiting for his dictum.

Had they been alone, she would have had no hesitation in rising and crossing to him, so full of question was her mind. Question as to Lord Kilshaw's present whereabouts and as to whether he had abandoned his purpose. She could scarcely dare hope for the latter. Would he give in thus easily? He had made no move, shown no disposition to attempt her capture, and now he'd apparently left the district.

Niall turned, his gaze going directly to the young man, who was looking more anxious now than distressed. "Do you have any recollection of the time between your leaving your post and returning to it?"

Colour flooded the boy's face again and he stammered in his response. "Not — not exactly, my lord. But — but I cannot suppose it to have been more than a half hour."

"Time enough. We must suppose he'd already made his arrangements for departure. Had he a valet with him?"

"I don't think so, my lord. To my knowledge there was just a groom."

"Very well then; let us suppose he had packed earlier and ordered his groom to be ready to depart as soon as he'd dined. Clearly you did not see anyone take a portmanteau out to the yard, so he must have had that carried down while you were otherwise occupied."

Did Niall gloss over the dalliance for the boy's sake or because it did not interest him? Edith decided on the latter. It was scarcely germane and there was no way to tell whether or not he disapproved — except presumably insofar as it had affected the lad's vigilance.

"He might accomplish all that in a matter of minutes, my lord," put in Eddows, moving a little in Niall's direction. "I suspect even half an hour is an over-estimate." With which, he cast a glance of censure at his son, who dropped his eyes, looking shame-faced.

"Possibly." Niall became brisk. "What I'm trying to establish is how far Kilshaw might have got before Peter realised his absence. He could well have passed through Itchington Bishops on the road to Tazewell Manor and carried on towards

Kington, which would set him on a path in the direction of the capital. I know he has the intention of joining the Prince's set in Brighton, for he told me so."

Edith could be silent no longer, rising quickly and moving into the fray. "Then you believe he might truly have gone? Have we done the trick? Has he given up?"

The tumult in her bosom had settled, but it rose up again at Niall's frown. "I wish we might make that assumption, but I fear it would be premature."

Her uncle, who had been a silent spectator of the little scene, now bounced out of his chair, moving to accost Niall with a hand to his sleeve.

"What are you thinking, sir? Do you not suppose my poor Ede is safe yet?"

His distress smote Edith to the heart, and she wished fervently she had not been obliged to involve him in this horrible mess.

Niall's smile was forced, she was persuaded. "We will not relax our vigilance, Reverend, be sure."

"Yes, but that does not answer me, my lord."

A sigh escaped him and he flung an apologetic look at Edith. "I'm sorry not to be more sanguine, but merely because the fox has gone to ground does not mean he's ceased to be a menace."

Her uncle's fingers fell from his sleeve and he came across to seize Edith's hands.

"My dear, how does this affect you? Are you as fearful as ever? I cannot wish to see you still so confined in this way."

Edith returned the pressure of his fingers, summoning a smile. "And I am all too dismayed at his lordship being obliged to maintain all these complex arrangements on my behalf."

Releasing his hands, she turned to Niall. "I cannot tell you how grateful I am, nor how sorry."

His mouth went into that lopsided curve. "Don't be. It is an honour to serve you. And your reverend uncle, of course."

She was too relieved, despite his warnings, to be pessimistic. Recalling instances of the girls in her care when in the throes of guilt over a mistake, she turned her attention to the youth, who was clearly suffering agonies, as young persons did in such circumstances.

"Mr Eddows, is it not? Or may I call you Peter?"

His father at once cut in. "Miss Westacott, Peter. Make your bow, boy!"

Flushing again, the young man made haste to obey, but Edith took his hand as his head rose again, smiling at him.

"I think I remember you, Peter. When I was a girl, I envied you and your friends the freedom of your breeches to be able to climb trees and career all over the green on your hobby horses."

Young Peter broke into an embarrassed laugh and his colour deepened. "I remember you too, Miss Westacott. We all thought you were too grown up to notice us."

Edith released his hand. "Well, I have the advantage of you by a few years, I dare say. But you must let me thank you. I gather his lordship assigned you to what must have been a somewhat tedious duty on my behalf."

His colour much heightened again, the lad disclaimed. "It was no trouble, miss — ma'am —" changing his address at an admonishing look from his father "— and I'm only sorry that —"

"No, pray don't be. A misjudgement only. I doubt you will hang for it. You have not broken even one of the commandments, has he, Uncle Lionel?" She turned a pleading look upon the vicar, who responded at once with a cheery smile.

"Heavens, no! A most understandable lapse, my dear boy, and no harm done."

To his credit, Peter refused to accept this. "Yes, but there is, Reverend, for now his lordship has no means of knowing that fellow's movements."

Edith saw a measure of approval enter his father's countenance, and hoped her intervention might lighten the harshness of the scold he was undoubtedly storing up. She was glad when Niall backed her up.

"Don't torture yourself over it, lad. If he intends to make a move, we will know it soon enough. We could hardly expect him to kick his heels indefinitely."

The boy looked gratified, but the episode had broken the comfort of the evening. Her uncle turned to Eddows senior, waving a hand at the abandoned chessboard.

"I fear we must leave this bout unsettled, my dear fellow."

"Ah, an excellent excuse, sir, since I have you on the run."

Her uncle gave his opponent a hearty slap on the back. "You will get your revenge in due course, I don't doubt."

Niall settled the matter. "I shall instruct the servants to leave the pieces intact, gentlemen. You may resume your game upon another occasion."

Her uncle waved his hands. "No, no, my dear fellow, don't do that. You will only give this fiend the opportunity to sneak a look when my back is turned and plan his next move."

This caused a general laugh and the party broke up. Niall called for the carriages and himself set Edith's cloak about her shoulders. He escorted her downstairs to the hall, the others following behind.

"That was a kindly gesture of yours, Edith," he murmured under cover of the conversation continuing between the chess players.

She caught the inference and spoke in the same low tone. "The poor boy was quite overcome, and I could see Mr Eddows was perfectly furious with him."

"So also was I for a moment. But he judged himself more harshly, I agree."

"In my experience, young people place far more importance than is necessary on the errors they make."

"The wisdom of a school teacher?"

"If you had been obliged to soothe as many broken hearts as I, you might say the same."

He cocked an eyebrow. "Speaking of broken hearts, Miss Westacott…"

"Oh, stop!" Her pulse kicked. "I wish you won't harp on it. Especially now."

"Why now so particularly?"

"Because … well, because … you said yourself we cannot be sure he has really gone."

A sober look entered his countenance. "So I am to wait upon his convenience? Very well, Miss Westacott, I will possess my soul in what patience I can muster."

Edith's heartbeat speeded up. "I wish you won't be so absurd! It is not as if I don't…" She faded out, shocked to realise she had been on the verge of committing herself. On the whole, she was glad the butler chose this moment to open the front door and announce that the coach was waiting.

Although Niall handed her up, his farewell held no special meaning and Edith regretted her sharp dismissal. Yet what could she do? Without a resolution, and until he knew the truth, she dared not give her heart into Niall's keeping.

Chapter Eighteen

The heat was stifling. Edith had left her bed-curtains open, unable to tolerate the confinement. It was too reminiscent of the days of waiting for Lord Kilshaw to make a move while he was still at the Fox and Goose, like a spider plotting in the middle of his web.

Despite Niall's warning, Edith felt freer than she had in days. He had made time to visit the vicarage since the fateful dinner three nights ago, sitting with Edith in the front parlour for an hour and heroically partaking of the scones pressed upon him by Mrs Tuffin. He had behaved impeccably. No mention was made of his desires or his feelings towards Edith.

Indeed, she had felt a trifle piqued. She had no right to and she chided herself for her perversity. She had been the one to demand his silence. She should not be offended when he complied with her wishes.

Although, she reflected, as she gazed into the gathering dark of the late summer night, Niall's reticence had allowed her feelings to flower. She could no longer deceive herself. She cared for him. Loved him. Too deeply to be willing to give herself to him while trammelled with the taint of the past. He did not deserve that. He had been more than kind, taking up the gauntlet for her even before his interest was fixed. A true knight errant.

She contemplated the inner vision of his countenance, changing to his moods, and caught her breath on a swelling within as the image widened to encompass his manly figure. How well his buckskins encased those muscled legs. Even beneath the cloth of his frockcoat, one could see the power of his arm, the sinews honed, she must suppose, with wielding a sword.

She had not before recognised the pull of her body towards his, yearning to be held in that potent embrace. Edith groaned, turning over in the bed to bury her face in the pillows and pummel the mattress with both feet and hands. Sighing, she relaxed again, throwing her arms up to hold the mound of her pillows, squeezing them as her mind presented her with the broad chest she would fling her arms about if she could.

Frustrated with herself, she turned again, beating her fists beside her on the bed. *Stop it, Edith Westacott!* Torturing herself would only make it worse.

She took a deep breath and tried to relax, commanding herself to go to sleep. Yet no sooner did she allow her thoughts to drift than back Niall came, invading her mind and smiling in that lopsided fashion which could not but melt her heart all over again.

Giving up all pretence, Edith got up out of her bed, threw a cotton shawl across her shoulders and went to her window. She'd left the drapes only partially drawn and the casement slightly open. Edith threw it wide, breathing of the cooler air and gazing up at the pinpricks of tiny stars just beginning to appear.

Her window overlooked the back garden and a movement drew her eye. She looked down and her heart stopped. Lord Kilshaw was standing there, bold as brass. His face was turned up and he was staring directly at her.

Perforce, Edith met his gaze, uncertain in the fading light if she saw his eyes beyond a glitter in the pale oval of his face.

She was beyond thought, mesmerised, a ball of terror suspended in her chest, freezing her to the spot.

He was here! He had come! He had come for her!

He lifted a hand as if to wave and the spell broke.

With a gasping sob, Edith shunted back from the window, shutting out the sight. Riding on instinct, she turned for the door and sped across the gallery to her uncle's room.

Her fists rose, beating on the door as she cried out. "Uncle Lionel! Uncle Lionel! Wake up, Uncle Lionel!"

With shaking hands, she found the handle and turned it. Even as she shoved it inward, she heard her uncle's voice.

"What's to do? Ede, is that you? What in the world —?"

His head appeared through the curtains, blinking in an owlish fashion, and Edith ran towards the bed.

"Uncle, he has come! He's in the garden! I saw him, standing there and staring up at me."

"Lord Kilshaw? Good heavens, child, you don't mean it?"

The curtains rattled on the rail as he threw them aside, pushing himself out from under the bedcovers.

Distraught, Edith threw up her hands. "He's here, I tell you! I saw him!"

Her uncle was up at last, bouncing towards the door. "Stay here, Ede!"

She stood trembling by the bed, hearing his rapid steps crossing the gallery and pattering into her room. A moment passed while her knees went weak and she sank down onto his bed, feeling the heavy curtains fall about her. Edith thrust them aside.

She heard the slam of the window, footsteps, and a moment later her uncle reappeared.

"No sign of anyone in the garden, my dear."

Edith leapt to her feet. "But he was there! I swear to you I saw him as clear as day!"

"Yes, yes, I don't doubt you, my dear."

They were interrupted.

"What's the matter, sir? What's happened?"

"Ah, Mrs Tuffin, excellent!" Her uncle snatched up his spectacles from his bedside table, crammed them onto his face and waved at the housekeeper as he groped behind the door for his dressing-gown. "Stay with Ede while I investigate, dear lady. She thought she saw Lord Kilshaw in the garden."

"I didn't *think*," Edith almost screamed. "I did see him!"

"What's this, Miss Ede? Now sit you down and calm yourself, do."

"I'm going down."

"Be careful, sir!"

"Don't worry your head, Mrs Tuffin. I intend to arm myself."

Her uncle vanished through the doorway, his dressing-gown thrown over his nightshirt.

Edith was thrust into a chair, the housekeeper, a voluminous shawl half-covering her night attire, tutting over her. Looking up into the concerned plump features, framed in an all-encompassing white cap tied in a bow under the chin, Edith felt a little of the terror giving way to protest.

"I did not imagine it, Mrs Tuffin! I couldn't sleep for the heat and I went to the window, and there he was."

"Well, I don't know how he got into the garden with all them guards my lord Hetherington has set about the place."

"Neither do I, but the fact remains that he did."

Edith discovered her fingers were quivering and she gripped them together, wishing Niall was there. Idiot woman that she was. She'd had the chance to ally herself to him, to make it all but impossible for her Nemesis to menace her, and she'd thrown it away. But as the fear subsided, doubt crept in. Had she imagined it after all? What had her uncle found, if anything?

Impatience claimed her and she got up. "I'm going down."

"Reverend said to stay here!"

Edith brushed past Mrs Tuffin, ignoring the hand put out to stay her. "I don't care. I can't bear the suspense."

She went through the open door, still in her bare feet, and ran down the stairs, Mrs Tuffin lumbering after her, still voicing objections.

"Hot at hand you are, Miss Ede. Always were."

She did not trouble to refute the accusation, only making for the back door, which, to her horror, her uncle had left open. Breaking into a run, she reached it and slammed it shut, turning as Mrs Tuffin came puffing up.

"He might already have sneaked in! We must search the house!"

Gripped by panic, Edith ran from room to room, flinging open one door after another and sweeping a terrified glance about each shadow-filled room, peering into corners as if she thought to find Lord Kilshaw crouching there.

Someone seized her from behind. Edith screamed. An irate voice sounded.

"Heavens to Betsy, don't do that!"

Her heart pounding, she sagged again. "Oh, it's you, Mrs Tuffin! I wish you wouldn't give me such a fright."

"And I wish as you'd stop driving yourself and me into a frenzy, rushing about like one demented!"

Edith leaned against the panelled wall in the hallway. "I thought he might have got in while Uncle was in the garden."

"Well, he hasn't, for I've looked as well as you, if not better. Now come to the kitchen, Miss Ede, and I'll rustle you up a glass of warm milk."

Feeling singularly foolish and trembling in every limb, Edith allowed herself to be hustled into the kitchen and pushed down into a chair. She peered out of the kitchen window, trying to see what her uncle was doing, but it was now too dark to see much beyond shadows.

Mrs Tuffin turned up the lamp she always left burning in the kitchen and lit a couple of single candles, using a spill which took fire when she put it to the embers in the range.

The access of light made the gardens utterly dark and Edith turned her eyes from the window, finding it impossible to see anything at all. She watched Mrs Tuffin bustle about with milk and a pot and tried to settle her mind. Presently the door to the garden was heard to open and close and Edith's nerves lost their edge as she heard the thump of the bolt.

Mrs Tuffin went to the door. "In here, Reverend!"

Her uncle came into the kitchen, and Edith's overwrought senses found relief in a burst of laughter. "Oh, Uncle, you look the veriest tiger!"

He grinned under the nightcap askew on his head, glancing down at his unconventional attire and waving like a baton the stout walking stick with which he had armed himself.

"I am ready to face all comers, my dear Ede." He came to pat her shoulder in the comforting way he had. "Are you feeling a little more the thing, my dear?"

Edith sighed out a heavy breath. "If by that you mean, have I recovered my common sense, the answer is more or less. I take it you found nothing?"

Her uncle shook a regretful head. "No sign of the wretch. Nor anyone. I ventured to go to the back gate to seek out Lord Hetherington's fellow and could not discover him either."

Edith stared at his face, paler than normal in the candlelight. "You mean he left his post? Dear Lord, Niall will be furious!"

Her uncle's eyes widened and Mrs Tuffin turned her head from her work at the range to look at her. Edith blinked at them both.

"But what have I said?"

The vicar cleared his throat. "I had not guessed you were on such terms with his lordship, my dear Ede, as to be making free with his given name."

Heat crept into Edith's cheeks and she berated herself in her mind. *Idiot!* What in the world was she to say now? There was little point in concealment.

"Well, we are a little more friendly than you supposed, Uncle."

"So it would seem." His brows were raised and he was clearly looking for more.

"Nothing is settled, sir," Edith told him, trying not to sound repressive. "And it is just as well, since it is clear Lord Kilshaw has by no means abandoned his purpose."

The vicar lowered his voice. "I will not press you, my dear, but I must beg you to trust me if there is something I ought to know."

She remained silent, hoping the housekeeper's presence would induce him to let the matter rest. To her chagrin, Mrs Tuffin intervened, turning with arms akimbo and addressing herself to the vicar.

"Well, it's a wonder you haven't guessed it, Reverend! What is a body to think when two people go about smelling of April and May? I've ears on two sides of my head and my wits about me like anyone else."

To Edith's relief, her uncle came to her rescue, patting the woman's shoulder. "You have indeed, my dear Mrs Tuffin, and I understand you very well. Now, what is it you have there, milk?" He smiled at Edith as the housekeeper sniffed and turned back to the pot on the range. "What do you say we put a drop of brandy in it, my dear Ede? I could do with a tot myself and I think it would do you the world of good."

Setting aside his stick and without waiting for her agreement, he trotted out of the kitchen, presumably to his study where Edith knew he kept a store of liquor. He was a mild toper himself, but liked to serve worthy visitors.

Mrs Tuffin turned from the range, pot in hand, and poured it into the glass she had ready on the kitchen table.

"If I were you, Miss Ede, I'd settle with his lordship quick," she said in a confiding way as she set the glass before Edith. With a glance over her shoulder, as if to check they were still alone, she leaned in to whisper. "Much more my notion of a manly man than that other finicking smooth-tongued rascal. Just you grab him up before he gets the chance to shab off!"

Astonished and thoroughly ruffled, Edith could not think what to reply.

Fortunately her uncle re-entered the kitchen at this moment, brandishing a small decanter and a couple of glasses. Pulling out the stopper, he held it over Edith's milk.

"Just a drop, Uncle."

"A good dose, my dear Ede. It will help you to sleep."

He poured in a generous measure and Mrs Tuffin leapt forward with a spoon to stir it in. Her uncle poured a tot into each of the glasses he had brought with him and held one out to the housekeeper.

"Here we are, my dear old friend."

The plump cheeks flew colour and she looked gratified. "Well, I don't mind if I do, Reverend, just this once."

Her uncle's eyes twinkled beneath the spectacles. "As if I would leave you out, Mrs Tuffin."

Taking the glass, the housekeeper cleared her throat. "I've been saying, Reverend, as Miss Ede ought to send to his lordship first thing."

"Heavens, yes! I shall write him a note and send it round by one of his fellows. If I can find one of them." He sipped his brandy and wagged a finger. "I cannot understand it. Those boys have been most conscientious up to now."

Edith could not resist. "Perhaps he was lured away by a siren, like poor Peter Eddows."

"I trust not, my dear, for I doubt his lordship would be as forgiving, if that terrible man was indeed in the garden tonight."

Which, reflected Edith with an inward shiver as she sipped the brew made up for her relief, did not augur well. Would Niall also doubt what she'd seen?

Chapter Nineteen

Livid at first, Niall was obliged to hold off ringing a peal over the unfortunate derelict to his given post when he learned the truth.

"He were overcome, me lord. T'weren't nowise his blame."

All four of his appointed guards were present at the parley in a back room at the Bear, appropriated by Niall days since for his use for precisely this purpose.

The culprit, who was sitting on a chair looking hangdog, spoke up. "Someone gi' me a knock, me lord." He raised a hand, gingerly feeling the back of his head.

"You were rendered unconscious?"

Another voice chimed in. "Found 'im a-laying in the lane, me lord. Leastways, he were sat up by then, but Davey couldn't nowise stand at first."

Niall eyed the sufferer. "At what time was this, Owen?"

"When I found 'im? Early this morning, me lord, when I went for to take his place."

"So you'd been out for some hours?"

"Must'a been, me lord. Know I be sick as a dog when I come to meself."

Niall thrust down the sharp words that rose to his tongue. Any soldier under his command would have raised the alarm the moment he came to, regardless of his state. These were village lads with neither training nor experience, he reminded himself. They were doing their best.

"Do you know what time it was when you received the blow, Davey?"

"Can't rightly remember, me lord. T'were near dark, I know that. Only I bain't heard nowt."

"One thing puzzles me. Why didn't the vicar find you? He tells me he searched the lane."

"Davey were up at far end, me lord," volunteered Owen who had found the man. "Must'a been laying hard by the wall, and t'were dark and Reverend would'a missed 'im easy."

Niall let it drop. Far more urgent to adjust his arrangements than indulge in useless recriminations. "Very well. Have a doctor see to your head, Davey, and don't go back on duty until tomorrow."

"I be right enough, me lord, and put about as I be took unawares."

"Nevertheless, you'll rest today. Your vision may be affected, and you won't be as alert as I could wish." The lad looked crestfallen, but Niall did not relent. The ban was necessary, and would serve as a salutary lesson for his lack of vigilance. "No, Davey. You resume duties tomorrow. Now, the rest of you. I want one man inside the vicarage from now on."

All four lads gaped at him. Mark, who had early constituted himself leader and spokesman, entered a caveat.

"Inside, me lord? Reverend willn't be suited wi' that."

"Nor Mrs Tuffin neither," chimed in Jonny. "She'd say as she willn't be suited wi' us clumpin' about and ruinin' her polished floors, me lord."

Amusement lightened Niall's anxiety. "I dare say she will put up with it. And you won't be in her way. The vicar will make no objection. He will be glad of anything that may ensure Miss Westacott's safety."

"Aye, but be we to follow miss about house, me lord?"

"No need for that. You'll be stationed in the hall. It's likely to be tedious for the most part, so you'll take two hour turns, understand?"

All four nodded, though they still looked dubious. Niall thought he detected relief on the features of the injured Davey. Did he suppose the others would fall foul of Mrs Tuffin?

It did not matter. Nothing mattered beyond Edith's safety.

"That's all, men. One of you take first watch in the vicarage, I don't care which." He hid a smile at their reluctant faces. "Draw lots if you have to, but do it quick. Davey, off to the doctor with you. The rest of you, let's have one in the lane and the other this side of the green. Keep moving and keep your eyes peeled. Any sign of our man, and you go directly to the vicarage to warn Reverend Westacott. Have you got that?"

He received a chorus of assent and a collection of unfocused salutes.

"Good lads! I'm relying on you all. Go to it!"

He left them on the words, confident his orders would be speedily carried out. He had not been in command of men for years without learning to distinguish between capabilities one man to another. Eddows had chosen well. Niall counted himself lucky to have discovered the estates to be so ably managed. He would have been lost without his agent's competence.

This setback, however, coming hard on the heels of young Peter's lapse, had set him on edge. His had been the warning voice, but he had no satisfaction in being proved right. Edith had been shaken by her experience of the night, and her peace of mind must be shattered.

He hastened back towards the vicarage, eager to take more time to allay her alarms. He'd had but a brief word with her as yet, his attention taken up by the need to ascertain what had gone wrong and find a better way to secure her safety.

He found her ensconced on the chaise longue in the front parlour, partaking of coffee. She looked drawn, likely from lack of sleep, but she greeted him with a brave quip.

"The conquering hero returns! I do not ask if you have slain the dragon, for I doubt you've had the chance, but you look as if you've been laying about you and felling enemies left and right."

Niall's heart warmed and he leaned down to take the hand she held out to him. "Do I indeed? I regret to be obliged to disappoint you." He scanned her face. "You, on the other hand, look decidedly peaky. Were you much distressed?"

She flushed and withdrew her hand, instead taking up her cup and raising it to her lips. But she spoke with all her customary lightness. "Oh, I was perfectly demented. You would have been ashamed of me. My uncle and Mrs Tuffin did not know what to do with me."

Niall took a seat beside the chaise longue. "I find that hard to believe."

"I assure you. The one ended by plying me with warm milk and the other larded it with brandy. It is a wonder I am not still reeling about the house in a drunken stupor."

He burst into laughter. "You've not lost your wit over it at all events."

A little sigh escaped her and a rueful note crept in. "I wished for you very much, Niall."

He could not speak. He met her eyes, trying to read whether it was his mere presence she'd wanted, as her protector, or if there was true desire for him beneath it.

"I wish I had known," he said at last. "If you'd sent to me last night, I would have come at once."

She eyed him over the rim of her cup. "I know you would. There was no real need, not once Uncle had shown himself in the garden."

Niall frowned, snapping back to the matter at hand. "Do you suppose Kilshaw was still out there somewhere?"

A little shiver shook her and she set down her cup. "He could not have made his escape so swiftly. I ran for Uncle the instant I saw him, and it could not have been many minutes before he reached the garden."

"Time enough for Kilshaw to conceal himself."

Edith's gaze clouded. "Yes, and Uncle left the door open. That was when I lost command of my senses, I'm afraid, for I was convinced he could have slipped inside."

He reached to cover her shaking fingers, holding them fast.

"You are by no means as composed as you would have me think, are you? Shall I ask the vicar to allow me to sleep in the house?"

A trifle of alarm showed in her face and Niall took his hand away, conscious of an unjustified feeling of hurt.

"I am persuaded there's no need. Though it is kind in you to offer."

A breathy quality to her voice puzzled him. If he could only gauge her feelings. Or if she would speak of them. He hesitated to bring up the subject, especially at a time when she was too discomposed to think clearly. It occurred to him to wonder why she'd been left thus alone.

"Where is the Reverend, by the way?"

"In his study. He has someone with him."

"Ah, I see."

"I was half afraid you would dismiss the whole, you know. My uncle and Mrs Tuffin were, I still believe, inclined to think I imagined it."

Niall squashed this without hesitation. "You did not imagine it. My guard in the lane was knocked unconscious."

"Oh, no! But Uncle searched the lane."

"It appears young Davey was lying against the wall near the far end, towards the road leading to Tazewell Manor. The vicar could not have seen him in the dark unless he walked the full length of the lane." She was silent, her eyes fixed upon the dark liquid in her cup. "What are you thinking?"

Her glance met his briefly and roved to the window. Her tone was low. "I had almost persuaded myself I only dreamed it. The nightmare is real." Her gaze came around to his. "He won't give me up. He is obsessed."

The deep despair in her eyes made a hollow open up in Niall's chest. He wanted to catch her up, lift her into his arms and hold her safe forever. But the soldier in him knew the enemy must be defeated before he could hope to win her.

He kept his tone cool. "Kilshaw is a man, Edith, not a fairy tale monster. He is not invincible. Don't let these tactics drive you down."

"Tactics? Then you think he was not planning to make away with me?"

"Hardly. He would not make himself so visible to you if that was his aim."

"Then what in the world was the point of his coming here?"

"To frighten you, Edith. Fear debilitates the enemy. Sabre rattling is a well-known strategy in war. An army won't attack if they can cow their opponents into defeat without wasting ammunition and men."

Her intent stare was disconcerting, but Niall supposed she was merely trying to follow his reasoning.

"He hopes to scare me into submission?"

"Something of the sort. He knows you are being guarded. I must suppose he means to show you that he is not deterred, to make you think, just as you said a moment since, that he will risk all to have you."

"Then how are we to outwit him? Can you outwit him?"

The sceptical note was not lost on Niall. "We let him play his tricks, and we remain vigilant. My expectation is he will attempt a pounce. We will be ready for it."

"How? Without making me a prisoner in my own house, Niall, how?"

He gave her a reassuring smile. "I'm putting a man in the hall. With your uncle's permission, of course. They will turn about every two hours, but one will be here at all times. You have only to call or scream and he will come running."

He saw, with satisfaction, her brow lighten. Her lips quirked.

"I hope I may not shriek at a spider and bring him for nothing."

"What, and you a school teacher? I dare say you have been a match for any number of spiders."

"True. And a few mice as well. I could hardly indulge my own apprehensions with my girls leaping onto their beds and making such a cacophony of protest."

"Good God! You are a brave woman, Ede. I'd rather face the thunder of cannon." He was delighted to see her bubble over with mirth, and rose. "I must speak to the vicar, and then be off."

"So soon?" At once she shook her head. "No, of course, go. My stupid affairs must be cutting into your own."

"Don't even speak of that. You know well I don't begrudge a moment."

Her colour rose, but she spoke lightly. "Perhaps I should instead congratulate myself on providing you with a task a little more in your line than running an estate."

Niall grinned. "You should indeed. I'm gathering a little army here and we will repel all comers."

"I wonder if they know over at Long Itchington? It will certainly make for interest at the Lammas Fair."

"Damnation! I'd forgotten the Fair. When is it again?"

"A week on Saturday."

"Soon enough. I must ask the vicar for a list of what is expected from me." He held out his hand. "Don't fret too much. Send to me if you need me. And don't go out without an escort."

"I should not dare. I shall make use of your inside man."

"Yes, do. Small point in him kicking his heels here if you are out of the house."

He was glad to see her apparently calm again, and was able to leave her with a quieter mind as he went to interrupt the Reverend Westacott.

Chapter Twenty

With a sinking heart, Edith watched Niall leave the room. While he was with her, she could almost believe in a possible deliverance. Without him, she felt both bereft and prey to apprehension. She could not forget that, despite the presence in her erstwhile place of employment of three other teachers, more than twenty girls, the servants and Mrs Vinson herself, Lord Kilshaw had gained entry to her bedchamber where she lay debilitated from fever and vulnerable to his assault.

It did not serve to remind herself that he'd bribed a maid to guide him unseen up the back stair. Who was to say one of Niall's guards might not be suborned by a hefty sum? She had hovered on the brink of mentioning the fear to Niall, but dared not open the subject for the explanations that must inevitably ensue.

With every encouragement to suppose Niall immune to Lord Kilshaw's slanderous tale of his dealings with her, Edith was well able to imagine how he might react to hearing the truth. At worst, it must turn his vaunted love to disgust. At best, suspicion must taint it. Edith could not bear to see the change in his expression, to her detriment.

For want of any other distraction, she sipped her coffee and found it cold. A fretful sigh escaped her, and an unwelcome reflection entered her mind. She had forgotten to offer Niall refreshment. Oh, that devil Nemesis of hers! He had once more made her less than herself, in spite of so many disposed in her favour.

She swung her legs down from the chaise, intending to go to the kitchen with the tray and beg Mrs Tuffin for a fresh pot of coffee. Before she could rise, she heard a step outside the door, which opened and Niall came back into the room, followed by her uncle.

"I've had a notion and your uncle is agreeable, Miss Westacott."

The formal address made her conscious and she glanced at the vicar, whose cheery face was a trifle overlaid with anxiety.

"His lordship thinks it will be of more use to have young Peter Eddows sleep in one of the spare bedchambers, my dear Ede, and I am inclined to agree."

Edith's gaze shifted to Niall. "Instead of your men taking turns in the hall?"

"At night, yes. As the Reverend pointed out, none of you will get any sleep at all if the back door is constantly being opened and shut. I had not considered it, but what should have occurred to me is that if Kilshaw should be watching the place, it will give him too many opportunities to find a way to slip inside."

Edith could not repress a shiver, but she entered a caveat. "But do you trust young Peter after what happened at the Fox and Goose?"

"It will give the poor boy a chance to redeem himself," her uncle cut in. "And his lordship does not mean him to get between sheets."

"Indeed not. The more uncomfortable he is, the less likely he is to drop off. I don't intend he should sleep through his vigil."

She had to laugh. "Poor Peter. We had best keep a pot of coffee on the stove so that he may keep awake."

"Well, if you do, don't go lacing it with brandy."

Her uncle broke into a hearty laugh. "No, indeed, my lord. Fortunately we have no maids upon the premises to tempt him from his duty."

"Even if we had, I can't see Mrs Tuffin allowing him within ten feet of her."

"Very true, my dear Ede. Well, if that is settled, I must return to my student. I am hopeful, if he will apply himself, young Barnabas may please his father and prove himself eligible to justify the expense of 'wasting the ready in sending the cub to Oxford' as Mr Chamberlain puts it." With which, he departed for his study.

Niall raised his brows. "It seems the teaching bone is inherited?"

She was glad of the innocuous subject, and the chance to keep him with her a little longer. "Well, Uncle schooled me after my mother died, so perhaps it was a contributory factor in my choosing a school rather than becoming a governess. Although never having had one myself, I did not feel qualified to take such a post."

He came to the sofa and stood over her. "I no longer wonder at your unusual qualities if you had the benefit of your uncle's erudition."

"He is a very learned man, though you might not think it from his manner."

Niall dropped into the chair he had recently vacated. "He is an excellent man in every way. I cannot think how he permitted you to go off as you did."

Edith did not answer at first. "Will you not have coffee? I was just going to ask Mrs Tuffin for a refill."

"It must be a quick one if I do."

She was disappointed, but did not allow it to show. She got up from the chaise longue, but her intention was forestalled by the entrance into the room of the housekeeper herself.

Edith had to laugh. "I swear you read minds, Mrs Tuffin. I was just coming to ask you for a refill."

Then she realised the housekeeper's face was flushed, her expression fierce as she set her arms akimbo. "Never mind the coffee, Miss Ede. I've got one of those pesky lads at the kitchen door demanding to come and sit in the hall. As if I'd—"

Niall was up, cutting in, his tone apologetic. "Lord, Mrs Tuffin, I do beg your pardon! I meant to make all right with you and I became distracted and forgot."

Her pugnacious attitude abated not one jot as she glared up at him. "Oh, it's your blame is it, my lord? Well, I tell you to your head it won't do!"

The sight of the bustling housekeeper squaring up to the much larger soldier was so comical, Edith had difficulty preserving her countenance. But she felt it prudent to intervene.

"It's for me, Mrs Tuffin. His lordship thinks a man inside is a necessary precaution."

Clearly taken aback, the housekeeper's glance swept from her to Niall and back again.

"Well! If that's the way of it, I suppose I must relent." A finger wagged, much in the manner of her uncle. "But I'll not have him muddying my clean floors, mind! He's to wipe his feet before coming in."

"Of course, Mrs Tuffin," Niall agreed in an unaccustomed meek tone that nearly overset Edith's gravity.

A resigned humph escaped the woman. "I'd best put a mat down."

"The intention is for them to remain in that big chair by the table in the hall, unless they are needed."

The housekeeper's belligerence returned. "They? How many of 'em, sir, if I may make so bold as to ask?"

"Only one at a time, Mrs Tuffin. I told them to take two hour turns."

It was plain this intelligence did nothing to reconcile the housekeeper to the invasion. She muttered something about an army of clumping feet and having to clean up after it.

"I'm sorry to discommode you in this way, Mrs Tuffin, but the men won't be here at night."

"I should think not indeed. The very idea!"

Edith cut in again. "The young Eddows boy will be here instead, Mrs Tuffin, in one of the spare bedchambers." She added, as the housekeeper's mouth opened with a ready protest, "You need not fear you must make up the bed, however, for his lordship wishes him to remain awake."

"He'll do that right enough if he's not between sheets," said Mrs Tuffin sourly. "Likely he'll freeze. I'd best give him one of the old quilts."

Edith glanced at Niall, wondering if this squared with his desire to make poor Peter uncomfortable, but he was looking bland enough. He gave a slight bow.

"Whatever you wish, Mrs Tuffin. I am in your hands."

The housekeeper sniffed. "Well, my lord, I don't mean to be disobliging, and if it's to keep Miss Ede from that nasty creature, it'll be worth a trifle of inconvenience when all's said."

"Thank you, Mrs Tuffin. I was persuaded I might rely upon you."

The obsequious note set Edith's lips twitching, but the housekeeper's ruffled feathers smoothed over. She regarded Niall with a measure of approval.

"And a good thing Miss Ede has your lordship to think for her." She gave a decisive nod and turned her attention to the coffee pot, bustling over to the tray. "I'll bring a fresh pot, Miss Ede. You'll take a cup, my lord, I'm sure." With which, she hefted the tray and left the parlour, ignoring both Niall's words of thanks and Edith's choke of laughter.

"I have never seen you outgunned before, my lord Hetherington."

He grinned. "I was utterly routed. I can now understand why the lads were reluctant when I proposed the scheme."

Smiling, Edith made herself comfortable on the chaise longue again. "She is such a cosy woman as a rule, one is apt to forget how formidable she can be."

"Formidable indeed. It would not surprise me to hear she'd driven off Kilshaw with a broomstick."

Though she doubted her Nemesis could be driven off by anything less than the sword's point, Edith dutifully laughed.

The coffee arrived in short order, but without the usual pastries, Mrs Tuffin stating that she'd no time for fripperies if she was to find a suitable mat for that lout Jonny's feet since he'd already installed himself in the hall.

Since the door was open, the peremptory warning she issued was perfectly audible in the parlour, along with the unfortunate youth's meek response.

Reflecting that the episode had ruined any hope of a continuing tête-á-tête, Edith was less disappointed than she might have been when Niall finished his coffee and rose to leave.

"I really must go if I'm to find young Eddows and let the other lads know they will not be required for the night."

"Of course." She summoned a smile and held out her hand. "Thank you. Mrs Tuffin was right. I don't know what we should do without you."

He surprised her by taking the hand and dropping a light kiss on her fingers before releasing it. "I'll call tomorrow if I may."

"You are welcome at any time."

His eyes scanned her face. "Is that true?"

She felt warmth rise to her cheeks. "Of course."

A muscle twitched in his cheek, but he made no further reference to the matter. "Take care of yourself. And don't fret!"

"I won't. I have the intention of distracting myself with some copying for my uncle. He needs a passage written out for his sermon on Sunday."

He nodded, and with a quick word of farewell, he left her.

Edith heard his voice in the hall, having a brief word with his man there, and then the front door shut behind him. She watched his tall figure walk down the path to the gate, and then he turned down the lane along the vicarage wall, presumably in search of the guard patrolling there, and was lost to sight.

She struggled against the drop in spirits, and a foolish impulse to run after him and beg him to remain with her. She tried to persuade herself it was merely due to the fear of Kilshaw, but a streak of longing for Niall gave her the lie. There was no use deceiving herself, even if she had succeeded in deceiving him into believing she might not care for him enough to give her heart into his keeping. He was a fine man, and he deserved better than she could offer.

Chapter Twenty-one

Contrary to Edith's expectation, the constant presence in the house of one or other of Niall's appointed guardians served to rub her nerves raw. Far from feeling safer, she could not forget for a moment that she was under threat.

She chafed at being confined, and on the one or two occasions when necessity compelled her to venture forth, the presence a couple of feet behind her gave her a horrid feeling of unease. The impulse to dart glances about the green or into dark corners was irresistible. Edith half expected to see Kilshaw lurking at the edge of the row of cottages, or within the lea of the Bear's broad walls as she made for the village shop across the way.

She was hard put to it to remember what she'd come for and dawdled over the trays of gloves and cheap brooches, trying to school her mind to calm while Mrs Ash awaited her pleasure. The woman's curious glances and oblique references to the presence of the young lad at her heels gave her to understand she'd become an object of curiosity in the village. Yet another black mark to be laid at Lord Kilshaw's door.

Remembrance hit and she exclaimed aloud. "Ink!"

Mrs Ash started, gazing at her in a kind of fascinated wonder. "Ink, ma'am?"

"Yes, ink, Mrs Ash, that is what I came for. Chiefly. And if you have any of the good paper suitable for letter writing, I will take a quire of that too."

Relieved to see the woman move to locate these items, Edith glanced towards young Mark, who happened to be on duty on this occasion and had effaced himself by the door while she shopped. He looked as conscious as she felt and Edith could not wonder at it, laid open as he was, as they all were, to the curiosity of the whole village. She dared say her predicament was known from one end of the county to the other.

Stop it, Edith! That must be an exaggeration. Still, it gave her no satisfaction to think how many people might be on the watch for Lord Kilshaw, since it must set her in a poor light. It did not take much imagination to realise why he sought her, and people were apt, she knew, to believe there was no smoke without fire.

Besides, she'd been seen walking on the green with him. Edith could readily picture the construction that might be placed on the whole affair.

She was relieved when Mrs Ash produced a large bottle of ink and a pack of the precious paper. Twenty-five sheets would go a long way.

"Thank you, Mrs Ash. Chalk it up to the vicarage account, if you please."

"As you wish, Miss Westacott. Is there anything else I can serve you with?"

"No, I thank you. Unless you happen to have a cloak of invisibility?"

"A what, ma'am?"

"Never mind. I am merely funning, Mrs Ash."

The paper was parcelled up and Mark leapt forward to take the package and the ink bottle. "I'll carry those for you, miss."

Edith thanked him, the feeling of helpless dependence increasing. What a poor creature she was! Unable even to carry her own purchases. It struck her that if she married Niall, she would be in precisely that sort of position. A countess would hardly be expected to do anything without the assistance of a maid or footman. Absurd. She could not live such a life, too used as she was to fend for herself.

Yet a sneaking little voice at the back of her mind suggested how pleasant it might be to cast at least some of her burdens on Niall's shoulders. It was tempting, especially when she was being given ample opportunity to perceive how broad they were.

But the very fact of his willingness to serve her in any way he could made it impossible for her to accept his offer. Not, at least, until — *if* — her Nemesis was vanquished and Niall was in possession of the truth.

She arrived back at the vicarage in a despondent mood she found hard to shake off. She set herself back to the task she'd undertaken of copying for her uncle, for which purpose she'd acquired more ink, seeing that his supply was running low.

She was working in the back family parlour, seated at the desk which overlooked the rear gardens. It did not help that this was where she'd seen Lord Kilshaw the other night. The least flash of motion catching in the periphery of her vision was apt to bring her head up, her gaze hunting the garden, the rhythm of her pulse increasing.

Twice, it was merely a bird taking flight. Another time a hare raced across the vegetable patch. And once it was only a cat leaping onto the vicarage wall.

Edith cursed her nerves, Lord Kilshaw, her illness, the presence of her guardians and Niall himself on occasion. She almost wished her Nemesis would make the expected pounce and end the suspense which was shredding her common sense and keeping her on the qui vive in a feverish fashion.

She saw Niall briefly at Sunday service, wondering if he only attended for her sake since he'd never been before. Her uncle was both gratified and delighted to see him, and invited him back to the vicarage for a light luncheon.

To Edith's mingled disappointment and relief — for she did not wish him to see how his arrangements for her safety were having a deleterious effect — Niall refused the offer.

"I have two of the local gentry coming to the house."

"Ah, the visits of welcome have begun then?"

Niall looked harassed. "They began weeks back and I have been remiss in reciprocating. I met Mr Chamberlain and General Pearman while riding with Eddows and took the chance then."

"In that case, we must not keep you," said her uncle, shaking hands.

Niall turned to Edith with a searching look. "How do you go on? I'm sorry I have not kept my promise to call."

"You've been busy, I don't doubt. Pray don't trouble your head over me any further. So far all is well."

Her uncle having moved on to talk to a couple of waiting parishioners, they were momentarily alone. Niall moved a trifle closer and lowered his voice. "You don't look as relaxed as I could wish."

She managed a tight smile. "I will do."

His eyes scanned her face, his brows drawing together. "I wish I might spend more time here. The case is that probate has at last been granted and Eddows and I have been tied to our desks until today, catching up with the finances."

"That is excellent news. You will be able to put in the improvements you spoke of."

"In due time. I've been able to pay my people at last." He put out his hand. "All my instinct is to remain, for I don't much like the look of you, but I have to go."

Edith gave him an arch smile. "Well, I know I am not precisely a beauty, sir, but I scarcely expected you to insult me to my face."

He squeezed her hand before releasing it. "You know perfectly well what I mean, you wretch." His tone dropped to a murmur. "And you are, as I've told you before, extremely beautiful, though you don't choose to use feminine arts to emphasise it."

She felt warmth rise to her cheeks. There was no mistaking the look of admiration in his eyes and Edith's heart soared. Perhaps there was hope after all.

Her lifted mood remained throughout the day and she slept dreamlessly that night, rising on Monday morning in a much more comfortable frame of mind.

Joining her uncle for breakfast, she found him with an empty plate already set aside and drinking a cup of coffee while he perused a letter, evidently taken from a pile beside him.

"Ash kindly collected these from the Posting Office at Warwick, my dear Ede. What with all this business, I have had no chance to go myself and they have accumulated. There is one for you, my dear."

He held out a folded parchment, a seal visible on one side. Puzzled, Edith took it from him and went to take her place at the table. She read the inscription of her name and turned it over to look at the seal.

"How odd. It is not franked and there is no address. Uncle, this cannot have come with the others."

The vicar raised bespectacled eyes. "Well, why don't you open it, my dear Ede?"

Edith looked at the letter in her hand and a horrid presentiment shot through her. The writing was bold and black. She had seen it before, had she not? An image leapt into her mind, of the same bold, black writing in a note brought to the Academy by the two girls, Millie and Isabel.

With a cry, she threw the letter from her and leapt to her feet, staring at it where it lay on the pristine white cloth as if at a coiled snake.

"Ede, what in the world is the matter?"

"It's from him! I recognise his writing."

"Heavens above!" Her uncle was on his feet, moving to snatch up the letter. "Are you certain?"

"I could not be more so. It could not have been among the others, Uncle, don't you see? He has been here! He must have left it himself."

The vicar was staring at the letter, turning it over and over. He started at this and headed for the door. "We will soon find out."

Shaking, Edith dropped into her chair and set her hands to her now throbbing temples, her mind afire. With all the guards, he yet had managed to sneak a letter into the place. Why should he write to her? She dared not indulge the hope it was to tell her he would desist. He would have sent it through the ordinary post if that were the case. No, it must contain some threat.

Well, she would not read it. She would burn it unread. Let him think she'd seen it, whatever it might say.

But even as the thoughts formed, Edith knew she would be unable to refrain from finding out. Niall would be sure to say she ought to do so. In case there was some sort of clue there. Although Kilshaw would scarcely put his evil intent on paper. That must incriminate him. She could take it before a magistrate and have him laid by the heels. Only none would dare lay hands on a man of his stature, friend to the Prince. But at least, if the letter said something of his intention, it might give Niall leverage.

"The mystery is solved, my dear Ede," said her uncle, coming back into the dining parlour.

"Tell me!"

He came to her side, holding up the still sealed note. "Young Davey says it was slipped through the door early this morning, just after he exchanged with the Eddows boy."

Edith gazed at him aghast. "Slipped through the door? By whom?"

"That he did not know."

"Did he not think to look? Didn't he go to the window at least?"

He patted her shoulder in a soothing way. "Yes, my dear, he did. But he saw nothing beyond an urchin strolling along the lane."

Edith's mind jumped. "He bribed a boy to bring it. That means he was in the village."

"Open it, my dear. There is little point in remaining ignorant of what he says — if it is indeed from that man."

Edith gazed at the bold writing again. "There can be no doubt."

"Open it!"

It was the last thing she wished to do. She did not even want to touch it, feeling her fingertips contaminated by being in contact where his fingers might have been.

Yet despite herself, she set her finger under the folded edge and watched the seal break. The paper quivered in her hold as she slowly opened the sheet and cast her gaze over its message.

"I am not far away, my love. Soon we will be together. Look for me every moment. I will not fail."

Edith's stomach churned and she wanted to vomit. A travesty of a love letter! How dared he write in such terms? As if she would welcome the promise contained in his lying words.

Unable to will her tongue to speak, she handed the letter to her uncle. Promise? He did not lie in that, for the veiled intent was there, even in the twisted meaning.

Her uncle read it with a puzzled frown. "What in the world does he mean by this, my dear Ede? I do not pretend to understand it, for it reads like the words of a respected suitor. Can we have mistaken him after all?"

Drawing a tight breath, Edith held back the hot refutation that rose to her tongue. This was not her uncle's fault, and he was doing everything he might to protect her. She spoke with careful restraint. "It is no such thing, Uncle Lionel. It is a veiled threat. He means me to understand that he will not give up. Yet anyone reading it may take it at face value."

His cheery countenance became overlaid with anxiety and Edith felt horribly guilty. On impulse she reached for his free hand and clasped it between both her own.

"Uncle, I wish I had not brought this trouble upon you. I should have gone anywhere else rather than come home."

"Well, thank heavens you did come home, my dear Ede! Waste no time or words on that nonsense, but eat your breakfast like a good girl and I will send at once to his lordship. It is imperative he knows of this."

Faint amusement lightened Edith's gloom. "I dare say he will approve of your reducing me to schoolgirl status in this shabby way, sir."

He patted her in his usual fashion. "You must pardon your old uncle, my dear Ede. I cannot but recall you in the days of your short petticoats. Eat up, do. It will not serve to be starving yourself and you will offend Mrs Tuffin."

With which, he dropped the letter on the table and left the room again, presumably to write a note to Niall. Reflecting that it was as well he'd almost finished his repast, Edith snatched up the letter and read it again.

Vile man! Had Niall gauged his purpose? Was this another ploy to frighten her into submission?

She straightened her shoulders and put the thing away from her, determined to do her uncle's bidding if she could. Opening the silver chafing dishes set in the middle of the table, she helped herself to a modest portion of baked egg. Taking a warm roll from the pile wrapped in cloth in a basket, she buttered it, her mind running still on the words on the sheet she'd set aside.

She could see a few of the black inked letters in the periphery of her vision, and the temptation to read the letter yet again was strong. Edith took up the sheet and folded it, laying it carefully with the broken seal down so that it remained closed to her gaze.

She lifted the roll to her lips and her stomach revolted. She could not swallow a morsel. Instead, she picked up the silver coffee pot and poured, annoyed to find her hand unsteady. If the villain meant to overset her, he was succeeding.

For what must have been the hundredth time, Edith tried to fathom why a man would persist when the female in the case was so unwilling. What sort of mind had he that he took pleasure, even pride, in torturing her? For it was no less than torture. She shuddered at the thought of what might await her should all Niall's efforts fail.

Without troubling to add either cream or sugar to her cup, she lifted it and sipped. The bitter brew sat well with her mood.

"You have not touched your meal!"

Her uncle was back, eyeing her in concern. Edith gave him an apologetic glance.

"It would choke me."

He said no more, but returned to his seat. "Is that coffee still hot, my dear?"

"Yes, if you don't mean to add cream."

The vicar picked up the hand bell and rang it. "We'll have a fresh pot. I dare say we both need it."

Edith set down her cup. "Did you send to Ni— his lordship?"

Her uncle raised his brows. "My dear Ede, if you wish to speak of him by name, pray don't refrain on my account."

Warmth rose to her cheeks. "Very well, but did you send to him?"

"Our Davey out there has taken it to Mark in the lane, who will ride to Lowrie Court. Ah, Mrs Tuffin, may we have a refill for the coffee, if you please?"

The housekeeper bustled to the table to pick up the pot, casting a minatory eye upon Edith's untouched plate. "Is it not to your liking, Miss Ede? Shall I get you something else?"

"No, thank you, Mrs Tuffin. I'm afraid I have no appetite."

Her uncle cut in. "She's had another fright, my dear Mrs Tuffin."

The housekeeper gasped. "What, that fellow's been here again? And no one saw him?"

While the vicar explained the matter to his housekeeper, whom she knew he trusted implicitly, Edith absently picked up one half of her roll and began to nibble it, her thoughts turning to Niall.

What would he say to this fresh disaster? Should she warn him about the boy being bribed? Had she not guessed how it would be? She might mention the possibility now that Kilshaw had made use of the tactic again, without saying anything of his having done so before.

The horrid suspicion could not but enter her mind that one of the lads Niall trusted might be swayed by a fistful of guineas. What price her safety then? How readily could Kilshaw be admitted into the house. Even assisted to secure her, if the very man who was detailed to come to her rescue should have been bought by the enemy.

Niall was a soldier, an officer. He must have known traitors. Or at least those whose cowardice made them run from the enemy. Such men's loyalty might be readily undermined. She passed the four young lads under review. Her uncle had spoken for them, and Eddows trusted them. But was it certain none would fall?

She no longer felt secure. If indeed she ever had. She could not remember a time when she did not wish she had eyes at the back of her head.

Mrs Tuffin's tread, returning with the fresh-filled coffee pot, dragged her attention back. She found she'd eaten the roll in her abstraction, and her uncle had returned to his correspondence. To all intents and purposes, the panic was over.

She drank the coffee poured for her by the housekeeper, this time sweetened and well creamed. It put heart into her, and she was able to eat a little more and refrain from plaguing the vicar with her megrims.

By the time Niall arrived at the vicarage, Edith's nerves were sizzling. Despite every effort to remain calm, she'd found herself jumping at every sound, turning to look over her shoulder from where she sat at the desk. Several times she could not resist casting a glance at the letter with its broken seal, lying on the mantelpiece where she'd laid it. Much good it had done her to put it as far away as she could without losing sight of it altogether.

She'd copied diligently from the tome her uncle had designated, yet with scant attention to what she was doing.

When the front doorbell sounded, she jumped in her seat. Was it Niall at last?

She set her pen back in the slate inkstand, gazing at the blotched and blotted paper before her. Heavens above, one would think her a backward pupil at Mrs Vinson's Academy! In sudden rage, she snatched up the sheet, screwed it into a ball, and hurled it across the room.

"Is that the letter in question?"

Edith swung about on her chair. "Niall! At last! I thought you would never come."

She rose and went towards him, holding out her hands. He came forward, taking them in his firm hold as he met her.

"I came as soon as I could. What's to do? Where is this letter? Your uncle called it abominable."

Her fingers clung to his, and she had all to do not to throw herself upon his chest and burst into sobs. She managed to command her voice enough to respond.

"It is worse than abominable, Niall. It's a travesty."

Urgency to show him overtook her and she let go of his hands, moving swiftly to the mantel and snatching up the letter. She turned, holding it out. Niall took it and Edith, gripping the edge of the mantel, watched his face as he read it. His lips tightened and he looked up, a spark in his eye.

"A travesty indeed. I am not surprised you are distressed."

"I'm less distressed than troubled, Niall. Did Uncle tell you a boy was bribed to bring it?"

"He made no such assumption, but I gather it was so brought, yes."

"He must have been bribed. He's from the village."

Niall frowned. "But it does not follow he knew what the letter contained. Nor that it must cause havoc in this house."

"Yes, I dare say, but —"

"I can guess what you are thinking, Edith. There is a difference between giving a stray child a coin to deliver a letter and persuading one of my men to act against you. That is what you fear, is it not?"

Dumbly, she nodded, beginning to feel foolish. He was right of course. Her common sense had deserted her. One was a casual act done in all innocence, the other a considered betrayal.

Niall took her hand as her fingers relaxed their grip on the mantel and led her to a chair. "Sit, and I'll tell you what I mean to do."

Overwhelming relief made her break into laughter. "I might have guessed you would have your campaign all worked out."

He smiled as he brought a chair closer and sat down. "So you might. I had time enough to think it through as I rode here."

She gazed at him with a rise of warmth in her bosom. "Even when you had no knowledge of what was in the note?"

"All I needed to know was that Kilshaw had again been in the vicinity. Which means he is close. Eddows is going to ride out of the village in one direction, and I will go in the other."

"To what purpose? He is scarcely going to be found on the road."

"He has to be staying somewhere near. We know he is no longer at Long Itchington, but he cannot be far. We'll make enquiries at every village inn within five or ten miles."

"And if you discover him, what then?"

"Nothing." His brows rose. "Did you suppose I meant to challenge him?"

"No, indeed. If you were to be injured, I could never forgive myself."

"No fear of that." Edith watched with fascination as his jaw tightened and hardness came into his eyes. "If anything, Kilshaw is more likely to suffer an injury."

Brave words, but Edith could not be satisfied. "You can't tell that. You don't know his strengths."

A grim smile curved Niall's mouth. "He does not know mine either."

His confidence excited both admiration and irritation in her, and she could not be satisfied. "I beg you won't expose yourself, Niall. He likely carries pistols. If he saw you, I would not put it past him to take a shot at you. He has no honour."

"Don't fret, Edith. I have his measure. And he won't see me."

Agitation swept through her. "How can you be sure? For all we know, he is concealed in the village at this very moment."

"He will scarcely murder me in full view of the village, Ede, don't be absurd."

She rose, unable to be still, shifting away and back again as she spoke. "You don't know him, Niall. How should you after one meeting? You have no notion of the lengths to which he will go. He has no regard for what people may say or think."

She swung back and found Niall on his feet. "I wish you will take care."

He caught her by the shoulders, his tone fierce. "What aren't you telling me? What happened in Bath?"

Edith wrenched away, backing from him. "Don't ask me! I can't — I won't tell you. Not now. Not yet."

He eyed her with a look of frustration, which slowly died, giving way to consternation. He put out a hand. "I'm sorry, Edith. I never meant to bring it up. Especially now, when you are overset as it is."

But the damage was done. Edith's heart hollowed out. Had she not known it? Had she not predicted all along that it must come to this?

"It is of no use. He has ruined all hope of a happy outcome."

She hardly knew she'd murmured it aloud, but the change in Niall's expression had the power to hurt. His words belied it.

"Don't say that. Don't let him win, Edith. We'll find a way through this, I promise you."

But it was a promise he could not keep. Not if the burn of suspicion remained to poison his affection. She said nothing, for there were no words that would not lead to further argument and more distress.

Niall seemed to wait for her response, and then sighed. "We'll finish this another time. I must do what I may to get ahead of the game."

He turned for the door. Edith could not endure it.

"Niall!"

Halting, he hesitated before looking round, a frown marring his brow.

Edith took several steps towards him and produced a wavering smile. "Thank you for coming."

He nodded, still frowning. "I'll come back to tell you what we've found, if anything."

He did not move from where he stood. Edith regarded him with pain in her bosom. She'd hurt him, and she had no means of undoing it.

A long sigh escaped him and he turned back to her, the crooked smile appearing. One hand came up, and Edith felt his fingers caress her face.

"I can't leave you like this. I won't be properly alert if I'm picturing you in a state of upset."

She summoned her old ally. At least she could set his mind at rest. "Ever the soldier, my lord Hetherington? Then let me send you off to the wars in good heart. You have my blessing."

Warmth was in his eyes. "I'd rather have a kiss."

Edith felt herself flushing. "Certainly not! Content yourself with a promise."

"Promise of what?"

"Why, of a kiss — when you've slain the dragon."

She stepped back out of reach as she spoke, and Niall laughed.

"Then I'd best go and mount my charger, lady."

With which he left her, and Edith's spirits were a little buoyed to think she'd done what she might to lighten his mood. Her own soon drooped as she reflected how much damage Kilshaw had done. Even were he defeated, Edith did not know if a repair was possible.

Chapter Twenty-two

Progress was necessarily slow, Niall choosing to keep an eye open for any likely ale house out of the common way. He had opted to take the road that led past Tazewell Manor, leaving Eddows to ride along the northern path in the direction of Warwick. In Niall's judgement, Kilshaw was more likely to conceal himself on the road leading eventually to London, that being his prospective destination. Where he had it in mind to take Edith, should he succeed in capturing her, was another matter.

The thought caused a burning sensation within him. Why trouble himself with the question? It was never going to happen. Not if he had anything to say to it.

Yet despite his unalterable determination to keep Edith out of Kilshaw's hands at all costs, the question persisted. Habit dictated the need to look at all possibilities. Only then could one be ready to counter them. The fellow had spoken of a house, had he not? The sort of establishment where a rich man might set up his mistress.

Niall struggled against the rage. He must keep a cool head. Easier when he was a soldier and had no vested interest in the fight to come beyond his dedication to the task of frustrating England's enemies. This was personal, had become so all too readily, clouding his ability to think dispassionately. Yet his thoughts persisted even as his gaze swept the buildings he encountered as he rode, discarding those which were obviously private dwellings.

A house in London? He'd hinted as much. But would he take her there, knowing Niall would be on his heels? Would he not more likely find her a lodging in Bath, since his estates were near there? Or had he more than one place at his disposal? A hunting box? A suitable place for a mistress, provided she was willing to play hostess to his male guests. Impossible to picture Edith in such a guise. No, if he meant to hold her, Kilshaw would be obliged to keep her in some isolated spot from where it must be hard for her to run.

Though where would she go? His guts went hard on him. Despoiled, ruined, what was left for her? Who would take her in? Where would she find sanctuary even if she escaped?

Niall had seen women enough left in the wake of a retreating army to imagine the likely fate of one no longer fit for marriage. The lucky ones had accepted the protection of a soldier and followed the drum. The rest? Reduced to beggary and prostitution or an early death. And these were of common stock. A woman of genteel birth, as Edith was, had even fewer choices. The life of a governess or teacher could no longer be open to her. Without references, no respectable matron would receive her into the household.

Which brought him back to the vexed question to which he could not demand an answer. What the devil had happened in Bath? Edith's departure from the Academy had less to do with her illness, Niall was certain, than her dealings with Kilshaw. Which suggested she'd been dismissed. Or had she been driven to an ignominious retreat, leaving her with no better option than to seek refuge with her uncle?

He recalled Edith speaking of looking for another post, and the gloom engendered by these thoughts lightened a trifle. If she was confident of acceptance in the capacity of teacher of some kind, she must have been given a reference. A better proposition than he'd feared.

Not that it made the slightest difference, as far as he was concerned. But he knew Edith to be morbidly sensitive on the subject. Unless and until he was in possession of the facts, he suspected she would continue to resist him. Did she trust him enough to tell him? Did she care enough? Or was her eager welcome due to her need of his protection?

Once or twice he had felt convinced of her regard. But the way she had of distancing him, using her tongue and her wit if not an outright withdrawal, kept him on a tightrope of uncertainty.

When the menace of Kilshaw was out of the way, he would have a chance to woo her in form, if he must. The necessity to eliminate the enemy was paramount.

Yearning curled his stomach. He would kill the fellow without compunction. But he was not on a battlefield now. Hard to remember his civilian status, which made it impossible to get rid of the man in the simplest way. Niall had no doubt he could best him with either sword or pistol. He would swear he was the more in practice with both weapons. He'd known men of Kilshaw's brand of arrogance, so set up in their own conceit they believed themselves invincible.

Well, you are not invincible, my friend. And Niall intended to demonstrate as much.

Catching sight of a small wayside inn, he reined his horse to a walk and approached it with caution, keeping his eyes peeled. A trifle dilapidated, sides browned by dust from the road and the thatch in need of repair, it appeared deserted. A battered sign depicted a crowing cockerel.

Niall swung off his horse and tied the animal to a post. There was no sign of an ostler. Could Kilshaw have chosen to stay at such an unpromising establishment?

Striding to the door, Niall clicked the latch and entered. A fug of smoke and the smell of stale beer hit him in a small hallway with a rickety stair to one side. To the other was an open door, through which emanated a murmur of voices and the clink of tankards. A glimpse of a couple of elderly countrymen lounging on a bench, one puffing at a long pipe, told Niall this was the taproom.

His entrance caused the murmurs to die off, and a battery of eyes to turn in his direction. Niall cast a cursory glance at them and headed for the counter, behind which stood a large fellow in a greasy apron, sporting beefy arms and a beard. He stared at Niall in the way of country people, half belligerent and half in surprise. He laid a pair of big hands on the counter and thrust his head forward.

"What be you wantin', yer honour?"

It was not encouraging. Niall was not intimidated. He'd met far worse receptions. He went directly to the point. "I'm looking for a gentleman who might perhaps be staying here."

A pair of bushy eyebrows climbed the fellow's forehead. "My lord Tazewell, d'ye mean? What'd he want here when he's a whole manor to hisself?"

He looked round as he spoke, clearly expecting his audience to be entertained. He was not disappointed. The elderly fellows cackled and a couple of raw farm boys, enjoying a luncheon of thick meat sandwiches, emitted jeering laughs.

Niall caught the landlord's eye and gave him a gimlet stare. The man began to fidget and the ruddy colour in his cheeks deepened. He sniffed and changed his tone.

"Bain't no gennelman staying here, yer honour."

"You've not seen one either? A tall man, extremely well looking and elegant in his dress, with black hair and dark eyes. Goes by the name of Kilshaw."

The landlord shook his bull-like head. "None like it, yer honour."

A movement in the periphery of Niall's vision made him jerk his head round. A man he'd not before noticed was sitting in a corner of the inglenook, half-concealed by the prevailing smoke. He'd leaned forward suddenly, catching Niall's attention.

There was time only to take in an odd look upon a face that to Niall was vaguely familiar, before the fellow pulled back into the gloom.

"What the devil —?"

Only half aware he'd muttered aloud, Niall peered towards the man, trying to see him better. The face was unclear and he took a step or two in the fellow's direction.

To his astonishment, the man leapt up and, pushing his way past the two elderly fellows on the bench, made for the door. Niall plunged after him, making a grab at the man's shoulder. But his quarry evaded him and was out of the door in a trice.

Without hesitation, Niall followed him into the hall, but the place was empty. Hesitating only an instant as he got his bearings, he went swiftly down the hall and flung open a door at the back. A short corridor and a strong smell of onions led him to an overheated kitchen, where a red-faced woman of ample proportions turned from the fire with a skillet in her hand to stare at him. A slovenly girl, peeling vegetables at the table, ceased her labours and gaped.

Niall cast a glance at the back door. The man could not have come this way. With a brief nod to the women, he returned to the hall by way of the corridor and found the landlord waiting for him, arms akimbo.

"What be yer wanting with that 'un?"

"He left in something of a hurry."

Niall pushed past him to the front door as he spoke. He opened it and went out into the yard. His horse was standing quietly where he'd left it, much to his relief. At least the fellow wasn't a thief. There was no sign of him, and Niall came to the conclusion he was long gone. Unless he'd taken the stairs?

The doorway was blocked by the landlord's bulk.

"Who was that fellow, do you know?"

The man shook his head slowly, moving back into the hall and allowing Niall access. "Never see him afore. Bain't from these parts. He come early and took a plate of ham and eggs for his breakfast. Sat there since. A-waitin' or summat."

Niall pictured the man in his mind's eye and was struck by the fellow's dress. Shag breeches topped with a blue frockcoat with decorative frogs, over a waistcoat adorned with pewter buttons, and sporting a slouch hat and top boots. A groom? Niall was certain he'd seen him before, but he could not think where. Still, there was no reason to suppose he had anything to do with Kilshaw. Except for his rushing out in that fashion, Niall would have thought nothing of it. More likely he was one of his tenants, and did not wish Niall to think he'd been lingering in an alehouse instead of pursuing his labours. Though he was unknown to the landlord here. But then this was Tazewell's land.

He slipped the landlord a shilling, tempted to ask him to send word if the man should call again. But what was the point? He'd do better to keep up the search for a few more miles.

Yet the episode niggled at the back of his mind as he rode on, and was still there when at last he called a halt. He'd passed through several villages and tried each of the inns he encountered, with no result. Either Kilshaw was staying farther afield or he'd holed up somewhere out of the way. One could hardly search every village for miles roundabout. But at least he had established that the fellow was not in the immediate vicinity.

It was late by the time he rode back into Itchington Bishops. He'd taken advantage of one of the better class of inns he visited and downed a glass of ale and eaten a sandwich. But his horse was in need of rest and a feed, and he knew Eddows would be waiting for him at home. Besides, by this time he must be rank with sweat and the stink of horse and the Lord knew what else. He could scarcely present himself before Edith in this condition.

He was obliged to forgo another visit to the vicarage, only pausing to leave a brief message for the vicar with one of his lads. Jonny was on duty near the church, covering the road that led to Long Itchington and Lowrie Court.

"When you exchange, Jonny, pray go to the vicar and tell him I've had no success and will see him tomorrow."

He trusted the message would be conveyed to Edith, and she would take it to herself. He could scarcely address it directly to her, even though he could not doubt his predilection for her society was well-known in the village.

He rode home in a mood of disquiet, the nag of the odd occurrence in that wayside inn never far from his mind.

Chapter Twenty-three

The night had dragged. Edith slept but fitfully, waking several times and fidgeting until she dropped off again. The bedclothes became tangled, and discomfort was added to the dreams that plagued her asleep and the disturbances of her mind awake.

Strangely, the traitorous letter figured less than the cryptic message Niall had sent by Jonny. Try as she would, Edith could not shake off her dismay that he'd not called in to give it in person. She could think of a hundred reasons why he might not, and only one why he might. Because he could not endure to pass the vicarage without coming in to see how she did.

Only he had not come in. And what did that mean? Was he offended by the little contretemps between them earlier in the day? Offended, no. Not Niall. Hurt? Or had the smart of thinking her impure, having raised its ugly head in his mind, settled there to erode his regard?

There. She'd given it voice in her head. This was the truth of it. Her distrust was rooted in the fear Niall would cease to love her. Suspicion, even though she told him all, could so readily poison his mind against her. And here she was, merely because he could not, for whatever reason, attend her as he'd said he would after hunting for where Kilshaw might be staying, convinced he did not come because his heart was hardened against her.

Oh, stop it, Edith Westacott! This was nonsense and she knew it. Yet the notion persisted, jumping into her head the moment she woke, the dream fading from her mind. Which was as well, or she would be seeking meaning in that too. A waste of time. She was bound to have troubled dreams at such a time. She'd been obliged to soothe many a young mind after a bad night. Always it had its origin in some upset of the day.

She was restless again, unable to breathe in the enforced confinement of the vicarage. She felt as if she would never be free of the menace. Her state of mind was as bad as it had been in those early days, when she'd been driven to walk in the woods and collapsed in her debilitated state.

She could not avoid contrasting that day, when she'd first met Niall and had only Kilshaw to worry about, with this one when both men had become tigers in her mind. For different reasons, but tigers just the same, ready to bite and scratch at her life and heart.

No, stop it at once! How could she think of Niall in that way, when he thought only of her interests? It was mean-spirited. Yet, even as she went down to breakfast, greeting her uncle with a semblance of calm, she felt Niall as an ogre in the background of her mind, his own poisoned against her. Almost she dreaded his coming, though she hoped for it. Longed for it.

She ate without tasting the food, mechanically buttering a roll and forking scrambled egg into her mouth. Only the coffee made itself felt, at least providing a modicum of comfort.

"Do you mean to continue copying today, my dear?"

Her uncle's voice startled her into tipping her cup. A little of the coffee spilled onto the edge of her platter and over it, staining the cloth and ruining the remains of egg.

With a muttered expletive, she dabbed at it with her napkin.

"My dear Ede, whatever is the matter?"

She looked round to find the vicar regarding her with a frowning brow.

"I was miles away, Uncle, I'm sorry."

"This is not like you, my dear. Are you still troubled by that letter?"

She seized the excuse. "A little. I can't get it out of my mind." A prevarication, but better than having to speak of her dealings with Niall.

Her uncle tutted, setting down his own cup. "Oh, dear, and I must do my rounds today. I have been sadly neglectful."

Edith's conscience pricked. "Which is my fault. I wish —"

"Now do not be foolish, my dear Ede. There can be nothing of more importance to me than your safety. No one has died and those in need have sought me here, so do not be thinking you have kept me from my duty."

"Yes, but I have, sir. You've just said you've neglected it."

He got up, shaking his head at her. "I meant no reproach to you, Ede. Only to myself. I could very well have left you in Mrs Tuffin's care, so let us have no more of that."

Edith saw it was of no use to pursue the matter. But she might at least be of some use to him. "I'm behind with the copying, I'm afraid. I ruined a sheet yesterday and had to redo it. Have you another piece you wish me to do for you?"

"Only my correspondence, my dear. I wrote a somewhat lengthy letter to the Archbishop yesterday, and he insists I should keep a copy of everything I send, in case it should go astray. But if you are behind —"

"No, give it to me, sir, and I will do that first."

He agreed to it, and Edith felt some degree of relief to have a task which might keep her from brooding. It did not entirely succeed in this, but while she concentrated she was able to put her megrims aside. She had just completed the copy of the letter and was carefully blotting it when the front doorbell rang.

At once her nerves went awry. Was it Niall?

The guardian in the hall had been detailed to answer the door by Mrs Tuffin, who'd told him he might as well make himself useful. Edith recognised his step and her heart sank. Niall had not come.

A knock on the open door of the back family room where she was working brought her head round. Owen was standing there with a note in his hand.

Edith's pulse leapt into high gear. Not another one. Had Kilshaw written again? A thumping started up in her chest, and she wanted more than anything in the world to leap out of the window and run as far away as she could.

She got up, and her feet took her to the door as if they carried an automaton.

"A letter for you, miss."

Yes, that much she'd gathered. Holding out a shaking hand, aware of the lad's regard, she took the folded sheet without looking at it. "Thank you."

With deliberation, she closed the door, forcing the lad to retreat. She waited until his steps had gone back to the hall, and then turned and sank into the nearest chair.

Gathering her courage, she at last looked at the letter and her mind froze. The same black writing. The same plain inscription of her name.

Edith gazed at it for a timeless moment, every instinct urging her to tear it to pieces without reading it. At last, her fingers fumbling with the violence of the tremors that shook them, she broke the seal and spread open the single sheet. One short sentence was set in the middle of the page, its message springing to her eyes.

"*I am coming for you.*"

Her ears were buzzing, her head thick as cotton wool. Spots danced in her vision. The letter slipped from her hand to the floor as blackness claimed her.

Chapter Twenty-four

Edith's head swam. Voices sounded somewhere far above her.

"How long has she been like this?"

"I don't know, my lord. I found her only a moment ago."

"Stand aside."

She felt herself lifted and hung helpless in the arms that held her. Then she was set down on a soft surface, her head coming to rest on a bank of cushions. The whirling sensation started to recede and her stomach, which had threatened a revolt, began to settle.

"Will you fetch a glass of water, Mrs Tuffin, if you please?"

Recognition filtered into her head and Edith opened her eyes, trying to focus.

"Niall?"

"Stay still, Edith. You've been in a swoon."

His face was above her, and she felt her hand taken in a warm clasp. Remembrance crept back and she uttered a faint cry. "The letter!"

Grimness entered his features. "I have it. No need to ask why you fainted."

Edith's breath felt tight, and all the misery of the night came back to haunt her. "I can't stay here."

Niall moved to pull up a chair beside the sofa, and dropped into it. "We'll discuss that when you are recovered. Lie quiet for now, Ede."

Her senses were returning, though she still felt weak and half inclined to burst into tears. Without thinking, she groped for his hand and it closed about hers again. "You didn't come yesterday." She hadn't meant to reproach him, but the words escaped her without will.

"I wished to, but it was late and I was in no fit state to visit, if you want the truth."

Her eyes sought his. "No fit state?"

The lopsided grin appeared. "Sweat-ridden and stinking of my horse. There are penalties to knight errantry, you know."

Amusement briefly lightened the darkness. "I would not have minded."

"But I would."

"Chivalrous as ever."

He lifted her hand to his lips and kissed it, and then released it as Mrs Tuffin's voice was heard.

"I've made tea, my lord. Here's the water. But tea will revive her more."

Edith was bidden to sit up. Her head swam a little again and then steadied. She drank a measure of the water at Niall's peremptory command, and was at last able to swing her legs to the floor. She gave a wavering smile to the hovering housekeeper.

"Tea will be welcome, Mrs Tuffin."

A cup and saucer was placed into her hands, but Niall took it from her, and handed the glass back to the housekeeper. He lifted the cup and held it to her lips. Aware of the knowing expression in Mrs Tuffin's face, Edith brought wavering hands up and took possession of the cup.

"I can manage, sir."

Niall allowed her to take it, nevertheless keeping a slight pressure on the bottom with one finger. A precaution she'd employed herself on occasion. A chuckle escaped her.

"I never thought to rival my pupils in needing a nursemaid merely to drink a cup of tea."

Niall's finger came away, and his mouth slipped sideways with the smile in the way she had come to love. "You need not become accustomed. This coddling is merely temporary, I assure you."

"Oh? Do you mean to ring a peal over me when I am better?"

"By no means." He turned to Mrs Tuffin. "She'll do now."

It was a clear dismissal and Edith glanced at the housekeeper, expecting to see her pokering up. Instead, she found a look of complacence in the older woman's face, and she was at once assailed by an echo of her troubled thoughts of the night. If Mrs Tuffin supposed all was in train for a bridal, she might find herself disappointed.

She took refuge in her tea, which had indeed a revivifying effect upon her senses.

Niall did not speak until the housekeeper had bustled out. "When you are quite recovered, I'm going to take you for a drive."

Startled, Edith looked up. "A drive?"

"You've been cooped up here too long, and I've no doubt it's making this whole affair prey upon your mind."

A flood of gratitude washed through Edith. "Niall! You could not have hit upon anything more like to lift my spirits."

"Drink your tea."

She lifted the cup again, but could not resist a sally. "You are excessively masterful this morning. Am I being treated to the officer in command, or is this the true Niall? If so, I have been grossly deceived."

His brows rose, but his lips twitched. "How so?"

"Well, when you have been a *veray parfit gentil* knight up to now."

His laughter warmed her. "A lesson for you, Miss Schoolmistress."

She smiled her acknowledgement and subsided, addressing herself to the remainder of the sweetened tea, to which Mrs Tuffin had added a dollop of cream. An effective remedy, for she was feeling much more like herself.

The remembrance of why she had fainted crept into her mind, and she set the empty cup down into the saucer Niall was still holding. She watched him lay it aside.

"Niall." He turned with an instant frown, and Edith half regretted the portent that must have sounded in her voice. She hastened to explain. "I don't mean to harp on about it, but do you suppose he means it?"

"Kilshaw's letter? All he means is to keep you on tenterhooks so that you will be off your guard."

"Surely it must have the opposite effect? I can scarce look towards a window without expecting to see him. How should he take me off guard?"

Niall picked up one of the hands resting in her lap and enfolded it within his own.

"You swooned merely at sight of the letter. If he should appear with no one by to assist you, shock is likely to freeze you. Kilshaw could take you before you had a chance to gather your wits."

His tone was matter-of-fact, devoid of feeling, but his hand tightened on hers. She drew a breath and sighed it out. "You are right. I must toughen myself against it. I should not allow it to overwhelm me."

He released her fingers. "It is natural you would react as you have done, but to know your enemy is to be armed against him."

"Another lesson? I am privileged indeed."

Niall's features softened into amusement. "And that is precisely the sort of remark to remind me why I fell in love with you."

Warmth flooded her face and she had to look away. She was grateful when he did not pursue it, instead asking if she felt ready to be driven out.

"Yes, indeed." She got up, finding her knees steady enough. "Only give me a moment to put on a bonnet and a wrap of some kind."

It did not take her long to prepare, though she took the precaution of offloading the liquids she'd imbibed before subjecting her person to the jolting of a carriage. Niall was waiting, his hat on his head. He regarded the spencer she'd donned with approval.

"It is warm enough, but there is a little wind. I've a rug in the phaeton, however, if you should be cold."

So eager was Edith to be out of the house at last, even for a short time, she thought it immaterial if she became a trifle chilled. In the event, the sun was strong enough this early August day to provide a constant source of pleasant heat, despite the slight breeze induced by the passage of the carriage. Edith settled to enjoyment, relishing the different views and the open countryside, drawing fresh air into her lungs. She felt immeasurably more relaxed, the stresses of the past days fading from her immediate thoughts. This was precisely what she needed.

Chapter Twenty-five

Niall kept his horses to a trot and headed along the road leading back to his estates. He was gratified to see Edith's shoulders relax as she sat back, holding her face up to the sun.

"This is heavenly."

"Yes, it's a fine day."

He would have wished to answer in a more intimate manner, but the presence of his groom up behind precluded anything but the most commonplace of conversations. Besides, if he meant to free Edith from the burden of her fear, the less said about Kilshaw the better. Only he was equally unable to say anything to further his suit, which he longed to do.

In a short while, Edith spoke, relieving him of finding an innocuous subject.

"This is your land, is it not?" She gave a casual wave towards the woods on the left. "I was used to roam here as a child, you know."

"Trespassing, eh?"

A light laugh escaped her. "In fact, I had permission from your predecessor's father. At least, he was generally amenable to the village children sallying forth to play at Robin Hood or some such thing. As long as we did not disturb his birds or steal eggs from their nests."

He glanced round at her and found her twinkling at him. Suspicion burdened.

"We? Are you expecting me to believe you were allowed to tag along after the boys?"

"Gracious, no. They would have threatened us with stones from their sling shots if we got too close."

"You and who else?"

"My friend the Dancing Bear."

Niall jerked his head round, startled. "The what?"

She erupted into gurgling laughter, and the carefree sound sent warmth into Niall's chest.

"You are roasting me, are you not?"

"Oh, no, I did have a dancing bear for a friend, only no one else could see him."

A pang smote Niall. She had evidently been a lonely child, for all the vicar's kindness. He knew not what to say that could be said within his groom's hearing. But Edith did not wait for his reply.

"You need not be thinking I had no friends. There were one or two girls in the village, but they had little leisure."

"But you surely did not wander the woods alone?"

"I wasn't alone. I had Dancing Bear." He must have shown his disapproval, for she broke into laughter again. "You are such an easy target, my lord. Of course there was a nursemaid with me. Extremely bored, poor girl, and disinclined to join in our dance."

"So you and Dancing Bear performed solo?"

"Well, I cannot altogether blame her. He had a marked preference for the minuet, and of course my nurse had not been taught the steps."

He had to laugh. "I can see why your pupils found enjoyment in you if you allowed your imagination rein on their behalf too."

"Heavens, don't say you doubt me! Why, Dancing Bear came with me to Bath, you must know, and I introduced him to several of my girls."

"I'll warrant you did."

He was both amused and touched. If he had delighted in her wit, Niall was the more charmed to discover the depth of her sympathetic nature. What a treasure he had chosen for his bride. If, he reminded himself, he succeeded in winning her.

The sound of hoof beats in the rear of the carriage made him draw a little in to one side of the road.

"Someone is in a hurry," Edith remarked, with a glance behind.

"We will allow them to pass. I've no wish to proceed at that pace."

"No, indeed."

"How far behind is it, Sorrell?"

His groom was craning his neck to see. "Out of sight behind the bend, my lord, but sounds like several horses. Might be a coach."

"Travelling at that speed? I hardly think so."

The hoof beats became louder, and Niall caught a flash of a vehicle in the periphery of his vision.

"Curricle and four, my lord," reported the groom.

Niall's own pair were growing restive. He held them in, uttering soft blandishments. "Steady, now! Steady!" He waited for the vehicle to pass but he saw no creeping horses' heads to his right. "What the devil is the fellow doing?"

"He's holding the road, my lord. Don't look as if he means to pass."

Niall threw a glance behind and saw the curricle coming up on the rear of the phaeton. The driver had not abated his shocking pace.

"He's gaining on us, my lord."

"Well, damn it, he'll have to slow down!"

Edith had said no word up to now and he looked round, intending to reassure her that he had his horses well in hand.

She was half turned in her seat, looking back towards the vehicle behind, her face stark white. A whisper left her lips. "It's Kilshaw!"

Niall's expletive rent the air and his sudden urgency communicated to his horses, who sped up without his giving them the office. As well, for the curricle behind had almost come up with the phaeton.

"He's slowing down, my lord."

But the curricle slowed only enough to keep pace with Niall's pair. If he allowed them to drop back, the horses behind would tangle with the back of his own vehicle. Niall cursed. "The man's a lunatic!"

Madman or no, his antics were like to bring the lot of them to grief. Niall took his pair to a fast canter, aware of the danger of the manoeuvre.

"Take care, my lord, you'll have us over!"

Niall ignored his groom's warning. "Keep your eye out for a likely lane."

He was himself sweeping the edges of the woods on either side, his sharpened gaze half on the prospect of his escape and half on the road ahead. Thank the Lord it was free of traffic! They'd seen none but a yokel trudging at the side of the road with a basket on his shoulders and a loaded wagon Niall had passed a mile back.

"He's holding behind, my lord."

Of which Niall was only too well aware. He knew too how the country road was not near as wide as the main arteries that criss-crossed Warwickshire, giving access to the bigger towns. If the phaeton and its pursuing curricle should come upon another vehicle, a spill was almost inevitable.

"Hold hard, Sorrell! I'm going to try something."

"Have a care, my lord, for he's right on your tail!"

Sound advice, but what choice had he? Niall glanced once at Edith, who had not moved from her skewed position, her eyes fixed upon Kilshaw in the vehicle behind.

"Hang on tight, Edith!"

Her gaze spun, meeting his for a brief second, enough for Niall to read the terror within. She said never a word, but tightened her grip on the side and edge of the seat, only nodding once.

"Good girl!"

Bracing, Niall steadied his hands upon the reins and set his pair to the gallop. The vehicle shot forward, drawing away from the curricle. But the speed was as shocking as Kilshaw's had been when he caught them up.

The phaeton rattled and shook, bouncing over the uneven surface. Niall dared not look round, but the sound of the hoofs behind told him Kilshaw was following suit.

"He's keeping up, my lord," the groom confirmed.

Just as Niall had expected. The road ahead was straight and clear. He let the horses have their heads for the space of half a minute. He gave a brief warning. "Wait for it!"

Then he tightened his hands on the reins, guiding his pair to the right. The horses plunged across the road. The vehicle swung violently, the passengers in imminent danger of being thrown out.

The curricle thundered past on the left. Niall instantly hauled on the reins, bringing the pace of his animals under control again.

"It worked, my lord. He was going too fast to change direction."

Exactly as Niall had foreseen. Or at least hoped. He took his eyes off his horses briefly, looking ahead to the curricle which had gone some distance. With four horses to control, Kilshaw's task was a deal trickier than Niall's.

Edith's voice came, tight with tension. "He's slowing down. He does not mean to let us alone."

The curricle's pace was indeed slowing, much to Niall's chagrin. Though what the devil had he expected? The man was off his head!

A ball of tightness in his gut, Niall slowed the pace again, scanning the woods. The set of the trees took on familiarity. He knew this part. He'd ridden here with Eddows. Now where was it they had left the main thoroughfare?

"My lord, I think he's going to block the road!"

Niall glanced back at the curricle. Kilshaw had pulled up his team and was backing them.

"Damn the fellow to hell!"

Perforce, Niall slowed to a walk, keeping to the right side of the road.

The curricle came to a stop again and then began to move forward, matching the phaeton's pace. It swung directly into Niall's path.

"He's not going to let you pass, my lord."

"No sense in passing him. He's got twice my speed and would catch up in a trice."

"What do you mean to do, my lord?"

"Turn off, if I can."

He was angry now, but he thrust it down. He was not a soldier for nothing. He'd learned to keep his head and let his emotions go hang. But Edith was not similarly trained. He looked round to see her sitting rigid in the seat, staring ahead. "Don't lose heart, Edith. We'll get out of this."

She threw him a glance, her features strained. "Don't mind me. Do what you have to do."

Niall nodded and she turned away again. He concentrated on the task in hand and his mind presented him with an image. Was there not a worn path a little further on the left? It led into his own lands, short cutting towards a couple of farms. It was scarcely a road or lane, not even a bridle path, but the farmers were apt to draw small carts along it, Eddows had told him.

He measured the distance between his own vehicle and the curricle. If he took the man by surprise again, it might work.

"Now we'll see," he muttered, and urged his horses to a trot.

Kilshaw, presumably alerted by the groom beside him, who was watching, did the same.

Within a couple of hundred yards, Niall spotted the break in the trees to the left which signalled the position of the lane. He did not have long.

Shifting his horses to the centre of the road, he watched the curricle follow suit. He held the crown of the road, keeping his eyes on the break. With a short distance to go, he suddenly swung to the right again and waited for the curricle to follow. Then he swung left, speeding up as he did so. The horses cantered across the road, heading for the break. Despite himself, Niall's heart was in his mouth as he kept an eye out for what Kilshaw might do.

"Brace yourselves!"

As well he yelled, for the curricle swerved just as Niall was about to take the turn. For a second, a collision seemed inevitable. Abandoning his plan, Niall whipped up his horses and shot past the curricle, narrowly avoiding his vehicle being squashed into the trees on the left.

A cry escaped Edith's lips and his groom swore aloud.

And then hell was let loose as the curricle speeded up behind, forcing Niall to keep his horses at the gallop.

The phaeton bounced alarmingly and he had all to do to keep it from overturning. He'd bungled his chance to escape and was doomed to hold to this shocking pace.

He heard his groom shouting above the thunder of hooves.

"I've got my pistol, my lord! I can fire over his head!"

"No, for God's sake! That will mean the devil to pay. You'll spook the horses."

His own pair was already in a lather of fear and fit to bolt. He could feel them straining. They'd be spent in a matter of minutes if he couldn't bring them down from the gallop. His own muscles were stretched to breaking. He had to do something!

A gap in the trees showed up on the right. In a split second decision, Niall swung right off the road. With a crashing of wood against branches, the phaeton plunged into the trees.

His attention fully engaged, Niall negotiated what he took to be an ancient track, well overgrown. He slowed the horses to a walk, certain the curricle could not follow. Besides, at that pace, Kilshaw would have had an impossible job to swerve a team.

"He's gone past, my lord," confirmed the groom even as the thought occurred. "Couldn't get them in here."

"Keep your eyes on him, Sorrell. Watch what he does. And duck!"

A branch directly ahead cut right across the track. Dipping his own head, Niall felt the leaves brush his head and realised he must have lost his hat in the wild ride. He kept on going, though there was only just room for the phaeton, its wheels flaying twigs and leaves from the trees at either side.

"Road's out of sight, my lord. I can't see him any more."

They must have penetrated a good two or three hundred yards into the forest. Niall caught sight of a small glade off to one side and directed his horses into it, at last bringing the vehicle to a halt.

"Go to their heads, Sorrell!"

The groom jumped down and ran to soothe the horses. Their sides were heaving. Even from here, Niall could see flecks of foam flying from their mouths. Steam rose from the velvet backs.

Niall found himself panting as hard as his cattle as he released the reins at last, and flexed his hands against the pain in the muscles there.

He turned at last to Edith. She was white of face, her body shaken by violent tremors. Without hesitation, Niall gathered her into a close embrace, holding her hard and murmuring words over which he had no control.

"I'm sorry. So sorry. You're safe now, my love. It's all over."

She made no attempt to free herself, and he kept her enfolded in his embrace until the shivers began to abate.

Chapter Twenty-six

With the panic over, the enormity of the danger in which they'd stood loomed large in Edith's mind. She recognised her body's trembling as the after-effect of shock and was grateful for Niall's comforting hold. She lost it soon enough.

Releasing her, he took her by the shoulders, a frown in his eyes. "Are you sufficiently recovered to manage without me for a space?"

She drew a shaky breath. "I will do."

There was no smile, and it struck her he was blazingly angry. His voice remained steady, although Edith detected a hard edge.

"Don't move from here. I'm going to check on Kilshaw."

He fumbled under the seat and Edith's shock revived when he produced a pair of pistols.

"What are you going to do?"

He jumped down from the phaeton, turning with a grim look in his face. "I won't shoot him out of hand, don't worry. Though I'd give much to do just that."

"But two pistols, Niall?"

"I may need to fire a warning shot. If I discharge one, I still won't be disarmed."

The thought flashed through her mind that this was the soldier at work, and she felt a flare of admiration as he turned to his groom.

"You have yours, Sorrell?"

She watched the servant unearth a rough-looking weapon from his own pocket, and Niall nodded approval.

"Keep an eye out! I'm relying on you to take care of Miss Westacott."

And then he was away, creeping through the trees almost without sound in the direction of the road. It was evident he had ample experience of a like situation, for Edith lost sight of him in a moment and she could swear she'd seen him slip from tree to tree for the first fifty yards or so.

Her pulse had begun to settle, but its rhythm speeded up again as Edith's mind presented her with the possibility of Lord Kilshaw seeing Niall first. He would have no compunction in pulling the trigger. A man who could risk so many lives in such a hazardous enterprise as that in which he'd just engaged would think nothing of putting a period to Niall's existence. She'd known he was determined, ruthless even. But the fear he was indeed insane now gripped her.

What else was one to think of a man so obsessed he cared nothing for her feelings or wishes? A man in possession of his senses would not seek to terrorise the female he wanted to win. And he had put her in terror, with his spying and veiled messages, and now this.

Edith could not remember ever having experienced a like depth of fear. Even now, the memory of the clamour of hooves that had frozen thought had the power to revive it in echo. She'd had all to do to keep her seat with the swaying and bouncing of the carriage. How Niall had held his horses together through it all, she'd never know. His skill with the ribbons was masterly, his strength unparalleled.

Her heart glowed, and then fired with renewed fear for his safety. She wanted to run after him, to fly to his defence if she could. Common sense told her she'd be in his way, only adding to his difficulties for he would be obliged to think of her safety as well as his own.

An explosion made her jump with some violence, the breath suspended in her chest.

Edith heard the groom's curse, but the sudden jerk of the phaeton as the horses tried to bolt forced her to seize hold of its side. To her relief, the groom brought them swiftly under control again, uttering soft blandishments and stroking their noses.

Craning over the side of the phaeton, Edith looked wildly through the trees, sweeping her gaze this way and that. "Oh, dear Lord, is he hurt?"

"Devil a bit, miss! The master is behind the gun."

Sorrell's words gave her scant reassurance. Her heart was beating a painful tattoo in her breast, and it was all she could do to stop herself leaping from the phaeton and rushing to find Niall.

An answering shot came, a little distant, yet loud enough to cause the horses to panic. One of them emitted a terrified whinny and reared, trying to rid itself of the encumbrance behind.

"Whoa, there, Rufus, whoa!"

But his fellow's distress upset the second animal, who added his strength to the attempt to flee. The phaeton began to drag through the glade despite the groom's efforts, slowed only by the difficult terrain.

Her heart leaping into high gear, Edith acted on instinct, making a grab for the reins. She'd not driven since her youth, and then only her uncle's gig. But she knew enough to haul on the reins. It took every ounce of strength she had, and she was almost dragged over the front of the vehicle from the force of the pull against her. The phaeton moved a good few feet before the horses came to a halt.

"Well done, miss! Hold 'em hard a moment."

She did as Sorrell asked, keeping the reins taut while he held the two horses at the bridle above the bit and soothed them, murmuring and stroking until they were quiet again. It seemed many minutes she sat thus, her ears alert for another shot, her muscles poised to pull again at need.

At last the groom looked across, speaking in a near-whisper. "You can let go now, miss."

Edith relaxed her grip, but kept the reins under her hands as she flexed them. Her fingers felt strained and her palms were stinging. She pulled off one of the cotton gloves she was wearing and found a red weal across the palm and lower part of the fingers, where the reins had cut into them.

She regarded it with interest, not unmixed with relief. Her injuries could have been so much worse. Indeed, if Niall had not been so skilled, she might have lost her life.

It struck her the woods were quiet. Too quiet? Her heartbeat sped up again as fear for Niall's safety returned. She strained to hear, extending her attention out towards the unseen road. No clop of horses. Had Kilshaw gone?

She distinguished sounds near at hand. A whiffle from one of the horses, the slight jingle of harness as a hoof shifted in the grass, the cheep of a bird, a cracking twig. The last brought her head round. Niall's tall figure appeared between the trees, and Edith almost cried out in relief.

Instinct urged her to climb down from the phaeton and run to his arms, but caution won. She ought not to let the reins fall away again. Besides, she'd not yet won the trust that could permit her to make free with Niall's regard for her.

He addressed the groom as he approached. "Is all well here?"

Sorrell threw up his head in an exasperated gesture. "As well as it could be, my lord, with these two taking exception to them pistol shots. If we'd had 'em with us in India, it'd be different. But they ain't trained for battle, my lord."

"It's scarcely battle, Sorrell, but I'm relieved you held them."

"It were miss there as saved the day, my lord. Seized the reins and hauled on 'em hard."

Niall had reached the phaeton and he looked up with a startled frown, his eyes going to the reins caught under Edith's wrists. She forestalled comment.

"Between us, we managed to hold them." Anxiety surfaced. "Has he gone? I was afraid he might have fired on you and killed you, it was so quiet."

"He tried, but I was a moving target and knew better than to give him a clear shot."

"But has he driven away?"

"For the time being. I can't depend on his having gone for good, however." He looked at the groom. "Did you take note of his groom up beside him, Sorrell?"

"Not particular, my lord. Didn't have no call to be watching him. Why?"

"I'm pretty certain he's the man who ran off from the Cock, back when I was hunting for Kilshaw along the road south."

Edith eyed him. "What man? You said nothing of this before."

"He had the look of a groom and was mighty anxious not to be seen by me. Or so I thought, at the time. If he is Kilshaw's groom, it fits."

"Would you recognise him again?"

"Yes, but I doubt you would, which is more to the point."

The tattoo started up in Edith's bosom again. "You think Lord Kilshaw might employ him for his tricks?"

Niall nodded. "Which is why you'll take no messages from any man you don't know, is that understood?"

She was nettled. "I would not in any event. I'm not a fool, my lord."

A slight smile deprecated her irritation. "No, I know."

Brisk, he addressed the groom. "Go up to the road and keep watch, Sorrell. If he comes back, fire into the air. If we've heard nothing from you within ten minutes or so, I'll drive us out of here."

"Right you are, my lord. Though you'll have the devil's own job, if you'll pardon me, to turn them in this here glade."

Niall agreed to this and jumped up into the phaeton, taking the reins from Edith, who dropped her glove and bent down to retrieve it.

"You'd best help me guide them back onto the track first."

It took several moments to manoeuvre the horses into turning the phaeton in the enclosed space, but when the vehicle was finally set in position to reach the track, Niall halted his pair. The groom went off on his mission and Edith was at last alone with Niall. There was so much to say and so much to ask, she scarcely knew where to begin.

He was silent, his hands lightly holding the reins, staring ahead of him in a kind of brown study. Edith eyed his profile, aware of a stronger male scent than she had before associated with him, due no doubt to his recent exertions. It was not unpleasant to her nostrils. The opposite indeed, arousing an odd sensation within her that made her yearn to close in to him and breathe it in more intensely.

Impelled, Edith broke into his abstraction. "What are you thinking?"

He started slightly, looking round, his brows still drawn close together. "I'm wondering if the vicar would permit me to take you to Lowrie Court."

Startled, Edith stared at him. "Your home?"

"It's possibly the one place Kilshaw could not get into."

Edith shivered involuntarily. "I would not count on it, Niall. He's like a spectre, appearing just when you least expect him. Even at the Academy, with Lord knows how many persons in the place, he got into my —" She stopped, aghast at having been betrayed into saying it.

"Into your —?"

Niall's tone was sharp. She swung her gaze away, biting her lip. She'd forgotten caution. In all the ferment of the hair-raising chase and the subsequent wild ride through the woods, she had lost control of what she said to him.

"Don't leave it there, Edith. Your bedchamber, is that it?"

She drew a gasping breath as the memory of that fell day swept into her mind, blotting out everything else. "I can't…"

"Yes, you can, Edith. Tell me!"

His tone was gentle, yet the command within it had power to loosen her tongue.

"I see him in my dreams, standing before the door. It was like a nightmare at the time… I was still hazy with the remnants of the fever." Remembrance brought the image back. Lord Kilshaw's handsome features, his predatory eyes fixed on her as he approached. "I was so weak … could barely rise from my bed as yet. I could not understand why he was there, where he had no business to be."

She hardly knew she was speaking, haltingly as the memories crowded in from the secret place to which she had banished them.

"I was half asleep … thought it a delirium, a dream of some kind. Later I learned he'd bribed young Lucy. She was dismissed, poor girl." Her chest tightened. She could hear his voice in her head, the silky tones still with power to chill her. "When I asked him what he wanted, he said I knew very well.

He came to the bed … smiling in that unctuous way. He said I wanted it too, but I didn't. I didn't! I knew by then what he was."

Her breath came short and fast, as it had that awful day. She was only half aware of the tears trickling down her cheeks, of the still, tense figure beside her, listening to the words she'd sworn she could never speak.

Too late now. She'd said too much. She had as well say it all. Once it was known, it would not matter. Nothing mattered any longer. The feeling swamped her just as it had then, when ruin stared her in the face even as it now did with Kilshaw's madness at full stretch and ready to take her into oblivion.

"Did he rape you?"

The question, uttered low and with a deep intensity that echoed in her core, brought her head round. She gazed directly into Niall's eyes, slits of steel in the swarthy features. So much the opposite of that other countenance in every way.

Her voice was a whisper on her breath as she answered. "Very nearly. I could not fight him, though I tried. I had no strength to scream, though I tried. I whimpered rather."

She recalled Kilshaw's hot breath on her face, the heavy body holding her down, the rough hands parting her thighs. She shuddered at the memory, closing her thighs tight as she always did when it came again, as if to repel the beast that had come so close to conquest.

"One of the girls saved me. Oh, not directly. I heard the latch of the door as she crept into the room. She'd been charged with bringing the dose prescribed by the doctor. She screamed and ran, calling for Mrs Vinson. She was only seven. She had no notion what that man was doing there."

"But it stopped him?"

Edith could hear the vibrant rage behind the question. Her gaze had shifted as she talked, but now she looked at him again, sobbing in a taut breath.

"You would think so, would you not? But you've seen what kind of man he is. He threw himself off me only briefly, turning to see who it was. Then he said — he said… 'We've not much time' as if he meant to pursue his purpose even then. Indeed, he began to cover me, but the interruption had dragged strength in me from somewhere and I resisted. I think I rolled away. However it was, I fell out of the bed. By the time he could come around to drag me up again, the cacophony outside the door prevented any further assault. Mrs Vinson flung open the door and…" Her voice died and she drew an unsteady breath, waving an impatient hand. "You may imagine the rest."

"I think I may safely do so."

His tone was heavy and Edith turned away, staring into the trees. She felt exhausted, as if she'd run for miles. She spoke without thought. "I thought I had endured enough this day, but it seems I was mistaken."

Niall did not answer this. Instead, he caught the hand she had not known she was flailing. His voice changed. "You've hurt your hand. Had you no gloves?"

Edith held up her other gloved hand. "Cotton ones only."

"No protection at all."

A faint laugh escaped her. "I had not anticipated being obliged to take the reins."

Niall lifted her hand to his lips and kissed her palm. A shiver of a different sort ran through Edith. She met his gaze, finding his expression unfathomable. But she was encouraged by his action, and allowed him to retain her hand in his.

She had not meant to ask, but the words came nevertheless. "Do you believe me, Niall?"

"I should have believed you at the outset. Lord above, I'm as bad as Kilshaw!"

She drew an unsteady breath, her eyes pricking. "You are as unlike him as you could possibly be."

He stroked her cheek with one finger. "This Mrs Vinson of yours sent you away, I presume? Could she not have given you the benefit of the doubt?"

"She was generosity itself, but she had no choice. Too many people had been witness to the event, and you may imagine how gossip spread."

"She believed in your innocence?"

As you did not, Edith wanted to say, but she was too relieved to find he had not turned from her in disgust to pinch at him. "She would have let me remain until I was well again, although of course I could have nothing further to do with the girls."

"But you were too proud to wait," he said, a mix of understanding and disapproval in his voice. "You left before you were returned to strength."

"Too proud and too ashamed. And afraid of what Lord Kilshaw would do, if you want the truth." A riffle of anger swept through her. "Would you believe he had the audacity to write to me by the agency of one of his daughters?"

"I'd believe anything of that fiend." Niall's tone had hardened again. "What did he write?"

"What do you suppose? That he was not done with me. That he cared for me too deeply to let me go. That if I was sent away, I need not fret for he would find me again and succour me from disgrace and love me forever." She could not help the embittered note, knowing now how false had been the words. "Any number of lying sentiments that I was fool enough to take at face value. I did not respond, but it hastened my departure."

Niall's hold tightened on her hand. "And you've been on tenterhooks since you came home, worried he might find you?"

"Yes, exactly so. And of course he did, just as I knew he would." She turned to him, gripping his wrist with her free hand. "He is insane, Niall. I am convinced of it now."

"If obsession may be considered an insanity, I agree." He drew out his pocket watch and consulted the time. "We have given him long enough. There's been no signal from Sorrell, so let us assume Kilshaw has done his worst for today."

"A worst that could readily have proved fatal."

He had no answer to this, and Edith supposed he knew it as well as she.

"My horses are in dire need and must be watered and well rubbed down. And I must get you home."

His earlier proposal leapt into Edith's mind, and she spoke before she could think. "Not your home, Niall. Only think of the scandal. Things are bad enough."

He had released her hand to take better hold of the reins, but at this he caught her face and caressed her cheek. "Not if you will agree to marry me."

She hesitated, meeting his eyes, uncertainty in her heart. He was waiting for her answer and she felt suddenly breathless.

"Niall, I…" She stopped and his brows drew together.

"What is it? You don't care for me, is that it?"

"Oh, I do, Niall! Too much, if truth be told."

His brow cleared. "It could never be too much for me."

She smiled a little, but as he moved closer, she reached up a hand to his chest to hold him off. "Don't, pray!"

His eyes clouded. "You're afraid!"

"A little."

"I won't hurt you, Edith. I only want to kiss you."

She shifted back a little. "But if you do that, there's no going back, Niall."

"And?"

She drew a breath and out it came in a rush. "I want to be free to accept you. I don't want to say I will marry you with this threat still hanging over my head. If he should succeed —"

"He won't succeed. My word on it."

"But it's a word you may not be able to keep, Niall, don't you see?"

For a moment, he looked as if he might overbear her protests and kiss her in any event. And then he sighed and spoke with obvious reluctance.

"I am being selfish, am I not? I want you safe so badly it half kills me to let you out of my sight, and that's the truth."

She released her hold on his chest and instead touched her hand to his cheek, stroking along the scar, a rush of tenderness in her breast. "Indulge me in this, if you please, Niall. Let me come to you with a full heart, not one burdened by fear of another man."

He eyed her for a moment in silence. Then a smile crept into his eyes and he leaned toward her, dropping a light kiss on her forehead. "Your word is my command, my lady."

Edith's vision blurred. "My perfect gentle knight."

He laughed and looped the reins through his fingers, clicking his tongue at the horses, who had been standing quietly throughout.

"Did your reverend uncle teach you to drive?"

His tone was conversational and Edith responded in kind, yet feeling perfectly battered as they began the short journey back to the vicarage.

Chapter Twenty-seven

The last thing Edith needed was to be obliged to entertain the ladies from the Manor. She had barely recovered from the appalling adventure in the phaeton, with its hideous culmination of confession, when young Lady Tazewell and her friend made a wholly unexpected appearance at the vicarage, agog with excitement.

"My dear Miss Westacott, what in the world is this I'm hearing? Such stirring doings in Itchington and we've missed it all!"

Feeling a flush rise into her cheeks, Edith hardly knew whether to scream or burst into tears. Distress, rage and frustration rose, rapidly succeeding one another in her breast and she uttered ill-considered words, bitter in tone. "You might have had my place for the asking. And if you suppose I've had the least bit of enjoyment in being hunted like a hare, you must have windmills in your head!" Dismay overspread the charming countenance, and Edith was instantly smitten with guilt. She put out a shaking hand. "Forgive me. You could not know. I have been overset for some days and have little control over my temper."

Lady Tazewell gazed at her mumchance, but Delia Burloyne, whose face had mirrored her friend's at the outset but now sported a deep frown, stepped into the breach.

"No, you must forgive us, Miss Westacott — or rather, Edith. We didn't think." A deprecating smile creased her mouth. "We never do, you know."

Edith gave her an answering smile, though she felt little amusement. Young Lady Tazewell pushed in again, her eyes suspiciously bright.

"How Tom would scold me if he knew! He forbade me to speak of it to you, and see what has come of my disobedience. I am so very sorry, Miss Westacott."

Edith could not but be mollified. She invited them to sit down and went to the bell pull. Even as she put her hand on it, the housekeeper appeared in the doorway with a loaded tray.

"Ah, you've anticipated our need. Thank you, Mrs Tuffin."

The necessity to pour gave Edith time to compose herself. The housekeeper had chosen to break into her precious supply of tea rather than the customary coffee. No doubt in honour of the status of the guests. By the time she had offered the ratafia cakes, Edith was able to speak with a semblance of her usual calm.

"I thought you did not mean to return so soon, Lady Tazewell. We were not expecting you to arrive in time for the Fair."

The youthful woman brightened. "But that is precisely what brought us home, Miss Westacott. Tom would have remained with his parents longer, but I pleaded with him to come back in time. I was not here for it last year, of course, and I do so love a fair."

"She's dying to see the battle of the villagers," cut in her friend with an amused look.

"I am not! How can you say so, Delia?"

"Don't sit there and pretend you are not eager to watch young men having at each other with their fists, Jocasta, because I know very well you are."

"Oh, I shall throw my tea all over you in a minute, you wretch," cried Lady Tazewell, breaking into laughter. She turned her once more sparkling eyes upon Edith. "It is true, alas. You will think it shocking in me, I dare say, and my mama would shriek, though Justin would only laugh. He is my brother and the most delightful creature."

"You would get short shrift from Marianne too," observed her friend.

"Oh, she would not mind. Marianne is my sister-in-law, Miss Westacott, and no one could better understand the horrid restrictions of being female. One is not permitted to do anything remotely exciting. Do not you find it a great bore too?"

Edith was finding the nonsensical chatter oddly soothing, as if the possibility of an ordinary life had not been turned upside down. She felt as if she dwelled in a twilight world somewhere between normality and the nightmare that still threatened. She answered in a voice that did not seem to belong to her.

"There are disadvantages certainly."

Lady Tazewell eyed her in a way that made Edith feel acutely assailable. Was she wondering whether to ask again about what had been happening here? A quick glance at Delia was enough to show Edith both girls were big with curiosity, though neither had the temerity to bring up the subject again.

She took a sip of her tea and set the cup down in a decided fashion, looking from one to the other. "Well? How much do you already know?"

The tart tone had the effect of bringing colour into Lady Tazewell's cheek, and Delia's gaze dropped to her cup. Edith sighed. "Let me give you a round tale, for I feel sure the gossip has given you a false impression."

Lady Tazewell gave a relieved little sigh. "Oh, I wish you would. It is dreadful to be gossiping with the servants, I know, and Tom became quite cross with me and he never does so as a rule."

Delia threw her a quelling glance. "All we know, Edith, is that several sturdy young men have been patrolling the village under Lord Hetherington's direction. There's talk of a break-in and attempted murder."

"Murder! Heavens above, is that what they think?"

Lady Tazewell's eyes were round. "Yes, Edith, and — oh, I beg your pardon!"

"You need not. Pray use my name if you wish."

"Oh, I will then. And you must call me Jocasta. But is it true you are betrothed to Lord Hetherington?"

"No!" Warmth flooded Edith's face. "At least, not yet."

Delia's eyes widened. "Not yet?"

Edith put a hand to her head, beginning to feel perfectly disoriented. It was two days since the fateful race, and she had seen Niall but once when he was fully taken up with allaying her uncle's alarms.

The vicar's distress on hearing of Kilshaw's latest antics had been unbounded, and he was ready to leave his duties and take Edith away somewhere, if that would secure her safety. It had taken both patience and argument to persuade him that it were better to face the threat while it was in full sight and ensure it was routed, rather than to take flight and never know when it might return. Uncle Lionel had agreed in the end, but he could hardly bear to let Edith out of his sight.

A circumstance which had effectively barred her from allowing her thoughts to become preoccupied with recollection of Niall's reaction to her revelation in the phaeton that day. Was she churlish to have insisted upon waiting? And here were the Manor ladies ready to marry her off regardless.

"There is a man," she said aloud, "who won't take no for an answer. He … he is desirous of…" She faded out, unable to put the threat into words that might be acceptable to be spoken in front of these two. The matter was taken out of her hands.

"A suitor?" Jocasta looked bewildered. "But if you are attached to Lord Hetherington, surely he can't expect you to marry him?"

"He is already married."

It came out flat and hard, and the effect on her auditors might, in other circumstances, have made her laugh. Jocasta's jaw dropped, her eyes popping, and Delia threw her hands to her mouth, looking over them at Edith in evident alarm.

"Shocking, is it not?"

Delia found her tongue first. "It is worse than shocking, Edith. How perfectly dreadful for you."

"Yes, indeed," broke from Jocasta in a trembling tone. "I can hardly believe it. Is it your position in that school? Does he suppose you are not genteel?"

"He knows just what I am and he does not care. But I pray you say nothing of this. Let the villagers retain their lurid imaginings. The truth is so much more disrespectful, to say the least."

"Disrespectful? It is disgraceful, Edith!" Sparks of anger shone in Jocasta's eyes. "How dare he? Who is he?"

Delia leaned forward. "Never mind that. How may we help you?"

"Yes, pray tell us. We will do anything we can, I assure you."

Touched, Edith gave the first genuine smile since the girls had arrived. "I doubt there is anything you can do." Then a thought occurred. "Stay! Yes, there is. Could you remain close to me at the Fair? Niall — I mean, Lord Hetherington — is fretting that he must be otherwise engaged and cannot stay by my side throughout."

Both ladies instantly proclaimed their willingness to stand guard with her, and Edith was able to contemplate the coming event with a little less apprehension.

"From what your uncle has told me, it is precisely the sort of occasion to provide Kilshaw with a chance at you," Niall had said. "What with the place teeming with people, any stranger must pass unnoticed."

When Saturday dawned, however, Edith found he had detailed her guardians to take turns in remaining near. Edith was a little on the fidgets, for nothing had been seen or heard of Lord Kilshaw for several days and she could not but anticipate some movement from him at such a promising venue. She was by no means lulled into a false sense of security, and would certainly be on her guard, but she could not help a twinge of guilt on behalf of the youths who must trail around after her.

"It is hard if the lads are excluded from enjoying the day, Niall. They get scant opportunity for holidays as it is."

"Precisely why I've ordered them to take an hour at a time."

When she told him the two Manor ladies had the intention of remaining at her side, Niall was sceptical. "I cannot think it a sufficient deterrent. And if Kilshaw were to make a touch at you, neither of them could prevent him. No, you will have a man with you at all times."

She was glad to submit, and he left her to her breakfast, which he had interrupted, and went off with her uncle to confer with the Parish Clerk and the Churchwardens who were the organisers of the day. She began to appreciate his reasoning as the green filled with makeshift booths and trestles put up by travelling traders to display their wares. Its situation on the edge of the green opened the vicarage to the sound of rumbling wheels, shouts and hammerings, all the noise of preparation for a fair, albeit a small one.

Through the window in the dining parlour, Edith could already see enough strange persons to provide cover for twenty Kilshaws.

Niall was right. He was likely to be occupied all day, and it was doubtful she would catch more than a glimpse of him. Her uncle likewise had his hands full, and Mrs Tuffin would soon be off to man her stall of muffins and scones she'd been baking from the early hours.

The ladies from the Manor duly arrived, both prettily attired in figured muslins, Delia with a tippet, her friend sporting a purple handkerchief crossed about her bosom, and both with straw bonnets and parasols to protect their complexions from the sun. Lady Tazewell was in a high state of excitement, bubbling with eager anticipation.

"I declare, I have not been this much delighted since my dearest Tom proposed! It is the drollest thing. Have you been out yet, Miss Westacott? Oh, I am being formal again. Edith! But have you seen what diversions we have in store?"

Delia Burloyne shook her head at her friend. "Edith won't have gone out, henwit! She was waiting for our escort."

"Oh, yes, I forgot. And you need not fret, Edith, for Tom insisted upon our having Monkton at our heels. He said he must do what he may to guide Lord Hetherington, for you must know he has presided over these affairs for years and years."

Edith stemmed the flow. "I have no doubt Lord Hetherington will be glad of his guidance. And we shall be glad of your footman, for Niall insisted upon one of my stout guardians remaining with me too, so we should all of us be safe."

She spoke in an easy tone, but she did in fact feel a weight lift. It must pose a severe problem to any plans Lord Kilshaw might cherish. Even he could scarcely imagine he might snatch her if she was surrounded by a coterie of persons. In broad daylight too. She began to entertain some hope of being able to enjoy the amusements of the day.

Jocasta being impatient to set off, Edith made haste to don a bonnet and lay a light shawl across her elbows, though the day proved warm. They left by the back door, and Edith popped the key into a receptacle attached to the chain she had chosen to wear about her neck, feeling it to be safer than a reticule which might readily be snatched by one of the thieves inevitably to be found at such a gathering.

Urging her companions to hurry, Jocasta set a smart pace, which sent her footman scurrying after her. Edith could not but be amused at Delia's look of exasperation. It became evident, as the younger girl exclaimed at a stall of colourful scarves and darted to another with a selection of cheap shiny brooches on display, that Delia Burloyne had taken Edith's advice to heart. She no longer emulated Jocasta's bubbling enthusiasm, although she stopped to rummage in a collection of embroidery silks, setting aside several hanks for purchase. Her appreciation was couched in a much less bubbling fashion than that of her friend, and Edith suspected this was the real Delia, rather than the puppet she had first encountered. And a deal more attractive she was too, acting like a sensible woman instead of a giddy girl.

Although Edith derived a good deal of entertainment from Jocasta's antics. She was like a child, flitting from one toy to another, unable to decide with which to play. She soon dissipated her supply of funds, loading up the fellow Monkton with small packages as she went.

"Oh, I have run out of coin! We must find Tom at once."

Fortunately, since the prospect of winding through the press of humanity to locate Lord Tazewell looked to Edith to be singularly unmanageable, her husband himself appeared, cutting a path through the throng.

"Here he is!" Jocasta hurried up to him. "Oh, Tom, I am so glad to see you for I was just coming to find you. I hope you have some money on you, for I have spent all mine."

He received her outstretched hands in his, smiling in an indulgent fashion. "Run out already, my love? I thought you would." Disengaging one hand, he dove into a pocket and produced a handful of silver. "Here you are."

"Oh, you are the best of husbands, Tom," declared his lady as he allowed the coins to fall from his fingers to fill the empty purse she was holding open. "I have bought all manner of useless fairings, I'm afraid, but pray don't scold."

He grinned, chucking her under the chin. "Are you enjoying yourself?"

Edith watched Jocasta's pretty features break into mischief. "Oh, enormously! I was never so diverted. I am so happy you brought me back. Thank you a thousand times!"

"I'm glad it's giving you pleasure," said her spouse, regarding her with doting fondness.

Edith felt a pang of jealousy. Would fate permit her a like happiness? She had no opportunity to pursue this thought, Lord Tazewell turning to extend a greeting to her, asking in his punctilious fashion if she found herself recovered now from her recent illness.

"The effects scarcely trouble me, sir, I thank you."

He returned a bland answer, neither by word nor look showing his awareness of what had transpired in his absence. Edith was relieved, for Jocasta's artless outpourings had told her he was au fait with the rumours at least.

"Don't tire yourself out, Jocasta!"

"Oh no, Tom, I am perfectly well, I assure you. I promise I will rest if I grow tired."

This assurance appeared to content Lord Tazewell, who left them to themselves, saying he had given his word to Lord Hetherington to aid him in judging the sheep and pigs presented in competition. The moment he was out of earshot, Jocasta closed with Edith, addressing her in an excited whisper.

"Tom is a little anxious, for we think I may be enceinte, only the doctor says we must wait a few weeks to be sure."

This piece of news naturally invited congratulation and Edith did her duty, resolving to insist upon the ladies taking a break at the vicarage in due time. For which she had a ready excuse.

"Mrs Tuffin has left a cold collation in the dining parlour, and she will be offended if we do not partake of it."

As it chanced, even Jocasta became decidedly weary after several hours wandering along the booths and she made no objection, declaring she was hungry despite having eaten a bun and a toffee apple purchased along the way. Since it was after two in the afternoon, Edith found this unsurprising.

Accordingly, she led her charges — as she had begun to feel them rather than the other way about — towards the break in the wall that ran alongside the lane. They were obliged to negotiate a line of carts in which traders had brought their wares, one of which had been left standing right by the vicarage wall. A fellow in rough clothes and a slouch hat was engaged in shifting a load of some kind within the cart, while a village lad, likely earning himself a penny or two, held the horse's head.

Owen, who was on duty behind her, slipped forward and went up to the cart.

"Move un forward, if yer can. I've to get the leddies through gate and this here cart be blockin' us."

The man looked up, casting a glance at Edith, as she thought. Her pulses kicked and she drew back a step, putting out a hand to stop Jocasta beside her. Was she being needlessly nervous? His manner was not threatening, though he looked a trifle surly at being asked to move his cart. Emitting a grunt, which might have been of assent, he jumped down and went round to take his horse's rein. The cart rumbled forward for several yards and stopped again.

Its owner threw a look at Owen. "Far enough for yer?"

Edith did not wait for Owen's response, but hurried across the road and through the gate, extracting the back door key from the receptacle on her chain with fingers that fumbled a little. Even with the cart out of sight, she could not settle the apprehension that had risen in her breast.

It was a relief to be back inside the relative safety of the house. Not that she'd felt exposed in the Fair. Indeed, she had not been as relaxed for some time. But whether it was the situation of the cart or its unfriendly owner, the little episode had brought the menace back into her mind. In all probability, the fellow's presence was completely innocent, but the suspicion, however unfounded, would not be suppressed.

It sunk a little under the soothing chatter of the Manor ladies as they partook of the viands, pasties and tarts presented for their delectation under the covered dishes in the dining parlour. Delia seemed bent upon deprecating most of Jocasta's purchases, which the latter defended with a vigour that belied her condition, if she was indeed pregnant. She certainly cherished no notion of abandoning the Fair, as was made clear when Delia suggested they had seen all there was to be seen.

"Oh, no, how can you say such a thing? Why, there are the races and the man who juggles with fire. And I am determined to visit the gypsy too."

"What, and have some ridiculous future outlined for you? I can't think what you could be wishing for in any event. You have already found your fortune in marrying Lord Tazewell."

"The very thing!" Jocasta pointed her knife at her friend. "You should visit the gypsy. She might see your future husband in a crystal ball."

Delia snorted. "I thank you, but I prefer to remain ignorant of what is likely at best to be a middle-aged widower in need of a stepmother for his children."

A laugh escaped Edith, despite her inward alarms. "I should highly doubt that to be a likely fate for you, Delia."

"No," agreed Jocasta, "and only think if the gypsy should prophesy an exciting adventure."

"I should not believe a word of it if she did."

"I declare, you have become decidedly unambitious all of a sudden. Don't you wish to find a husband any more?"

Edith caught a wry glance from Delia and felt compelled to intervene. "Do you know, Jocasta, I feel sure she is much more likely to find him if she stops looking. It never does to appear too anxious. It only makes gentlemen wary."

Jocasta looked struck. "I never thought of that. But it could do no harm to hear what the gypsy says, surely?"

"I dare say Delia does not wish to have expectations raised that might not be fulfilled, and so be disappointed."

"Oh." Jocasta eyed her friend as one observing a stranger. "Oh, dear, Delia, is it so?"

A little sigh came from the other girl. "Truly, I don't want to have my fortune read, Jocasta. You may do so, if you wish, but I still can't think why."

"So that I may know if I am carrying Tazewell's heir, of course."

"Well, she's not going to be able to tell that, silly."

Which set them off arguing again. Edith retired from the discussion, feeling unequal to participation. It was too reminiscent of the Academy, and all such memories had been ruined by Lord Kilshaw.

She could hear Owen and Jocasta's footman talking in a desultory fashion in the kitchen, consuming the sandwiches the housekeeper had provided. Edith felt sorry for them both, obliged to dawdle here when they might be enjoying the diversions on the green. She made no objection therefore, once the ladies had eaten their fill, washed down with lemonade, and been directed to her bedchamber to freshen up, to returning to the Fair without delay.

She looked instantly down the lane as they exited through the gate, but the cart had gone. For no observable reason, Edith found this disquieting. Had the man moved it elsewhere? He surely would not leave the Fair while so many people still wandered the booths, ready to squander their hard-earned pennies. She looked about as she crossed the lane with the ladies and the guardian males in tow, but there was no sign of the unpleasant owner.

She caught herself on the thought, following as Jocasta began threading her way to the gypsy's gaily striped little tent. Unpleasant? Or merely chafed? The traders were at work, after all. They had come from far and wide, she knew from previous years, a motley collection who took their wares from fair to fair through the summer months, scratching a living that must keep them through the winter.

The races had begun in the enclosure created with a set of flagpoles and bunting. Since the gypsy's tent was situated nearby, Edith and Delia were able to watch a gaggle of young women being carried piggyback by stout young lads, along with much shrieking and mirth from the audience as an overfed little fellow came to grief along with his fair jockey.

Edith caught sight of Niall, flanked by Lord Tazewell, on the other side of the enclosure and waved. His attention was elsewhere and he did not see her, to her disappointment. She found herself wishing he was not too busy to attend her, if only for a moment, knowing his presence served to allay her nervousness.

Jocasta presently emerged from the gypsy's tent, airily saying it had not been worth the outlay, but looking a trifle disheartened.

"What did she say?" asked Delia, over the squealing set up by the piglets now being urged down the field by a set of determined little boys, striving for their entry to win.

"Nothing to the purpose." Jocasta pouted a little. "She would keep harping on saying the day will end darkly, as if we didn't know the sun must go down in the end."

A chill sneaked through Edith's veins. Jocasta had entirely failed to interpret this warning in the way it was clearly meant. But it was Jocasta's fortune, not her own. She must not be beguiled into taking account of nonsense.

"I told you it was a waste of time."

"True, but I had hoped... Oh, do but look! They are preparing for the tug of war."

Edith did not share Jocasta's eagerness. She knew what this portended. "If that is so, then we need to remove from the area, ladies."

"No! It's what I came for!"

"Oh, Jocasta, don't be silly!"

Edith cut in at once. "You can still watch, but we should be farther back. The tug of war invariably ends in fisticuffs and Lord Tazewell, I am persuaded, would not wish you to remain in a position of danger."

"Pooh! How could I be in danger, pray? No one is going to throw a punch at me."

A sigh escaped Edith. "You don't understand, my dear. The fight will not be confined to the warriors on the rope. It's what the villagers look forward to. See! The traders are packing up. They know enough to get themselves and their goods out of the way as fast as they can."

Between her urgings and Delia's scolding, Jocasta was persuaded to retire some distance from the enclosure. As well, since the area around it was rapidly filling with eager spectators, creating a sad crush.

Yet young Lady Tazewell became reconciled only when her footman engaged with one of the locals who had, like Mrs Tuffin, set up his own trestle table for a stall, to allow her ladyship to step up and stand upon its now empty surface.

"Will it hold her in safety?"

"Of course it will. Pray don't spoil sport, Edith. It is the very thing."

The villager thumped the table a time or two with his closed fist to demonstrate its solidity. "It'll do her leddyship fine, miss, and welcome."

Upon her command, Monkton lifted Jocasta onto the table, standing in a suitable position to catch her if she fell. Gleeful, she declared her view to be the best on the green and invited her friend to join her.

"No, I thank you. I prefer to remain on terra firma. Besides, there is no charm for me in fisticuffs."

Edith could not help laughing. "You might enjoy the tug of war, however. We are expected to root for our village, you must know."

"Well, as I don't live here, I have no such duty."

But even Delia became excited once the two teams were in place — which appeared to take a deal of argumentative organisation — and Niall was seen to be standing in the centre ready to give the signal with pocket handkerchief held high in one hand.

"He's dropped it!"

Jocasta's exclamation made her friend crane her neck to see as a terrific grunting and roaring issued from the competitors, accompanied by encouraging shouts and catcalls from the crowd. Edith caught glimpses through slight gaps in the press of people as the line dragged one way and then the other, the heaving men with muscles straining at full stretch leaning back as they tried to hold purchase with their feet in the worn turf, by this time churned half into mud by the various races. She could in no way tell which side was which, with supporters from both villages mixed together.

At last one side succeeded in tugging their opponents across the line. The roar from the crowd was deafening. Within seconds, a few feet away, a fellow in homespuns turned to his neighbour and threw a punch that knocked him into another behind.

Edith heard Jocasta's shriek as the innocent bystander retaliated. In a moment, the air was full of curses and wildly swinging fists. The crowd turned rapidly into a struggling mêlée.

"Quickly, ladies! Let us get back to the vicarage."

She turned to her designated escort, but he was not there. Instead, a strange man loomed up. Before she could react, a strong arm came about her and a handkerchief was thrust against her nose and mouth.

She had no chance to struggle more than to strive against the iron hold, for a pungent aroma stung in her nostrils, rendering her dizzy. On instinct she opened her mouth to breathe, but was overcome by a heady sensation.

In the instant before she lost consciousness, she recalled the face she'd seen as that of the surly trader who had been obliged to move his cart.

Chapter Twenty-eight

On Tazewell's strongly worded advice, Niall had retired circumspectly once he'd dropped the handkerchief. He'd viewed the tug of war from just within the enclosure with a good deal of amusement and some interest, since several of the stout fellows on the rope were his tenants. As they were divided among both sides, he would have remained impartial even had it not been his duty as the designated judge.

He was obliged to keep his eye on the line that had been drawn across the turf by means of a thinner rope than the one in use, hammered into the ground at either end. The moment the feet of the leader of the visiting team crossed the line, he ran forward to declare the home team the winners.

Congratulations and handshaking took some time, and he felt constrained to have consolatory words with the disgruntled losing team from the neighbouring village. The home supporters were jubilant, much to the fury of the visitors, and by the time Niall was ready to leave the arena, battle had been fairly joined.

He contemplated the scene with misgiving, having little hope that the neighbouring competitors would not feel compelled to seek vengeance in a similar fashion. He doubted there was one of them who had not refreshed himself at some point in the Bear, doing a roaring trade today, and was inevitably reminded of the soldiers under his command released on furlough who had conducted themselves in just such a fashion.

Tazewell, who had remained close by in case he might be needed, had gone off before the fight was well underway to make sure his wife had gone to ground at the vicarage, though how he proposed to get through as the crowd closed in, Niall could not imagine. Though he'd had little leisure, a part of his mind had remained on Edith and he trusted she had been escorted home, according to his orders, in time to avoid being caught up in the mayhem.

The vicar, to whose kind offices, along with those of Tazewell, he owed the smoothness of his participation in the events of the day, had ambled away some time ago. He had declared his intention of securing the church in case some wanderer, the worse for wear, took it into his head to nestle there for the duration, which had not been unknown in the past.

Niall was therefore, thank the Lord, only concerned with avoiding personal involvement in the surrounding battle and finding his best way out of it without taking a stray hit. By dint of dodging two young lads throwing wild punches, another pair shoving up against each other, three stout men engaged in a whirling altercation and sundry fallen bodies groaning on the grass as well as carts creeping through to leave, Niall managed to weave across the green and came out at length into the lane alongside the vicarage.

His intention was to head for the gate to the back way in, but he was brought up short by the sight of Tazewell, supporting one of the lads detailed to guard Edith, who had a hand to his head and looked decidedly under the weather.

To one side stood Miss Burloyne, trying in vain to comfort a tearful Lady Tazewell. Adding to the cacophony, the vicar himself, accompanied by his clucking housekeeper, was engaged in firing questions at the lad in an unaccustomed peremptory tone.

Taking in the scene in one comprehensive glance, Niall felt his guts clench. No need to ask what had happened. Edith's absence told its own tale.

He strode forward at the same moment that the Reverend Westacott turned and saw him. The little man threw up his hands, crying out as he came towards Niall in a rush.

"She's been taken, my lord! For pity's sake, what are we to do?"

The clutch on his arm forced Niall to concentrate, despite a blinding rage that rose up, threatening to deprive him of all ability to think.

"Steady, Reverend! Let us get at the facts first."

The vicar released him only to throw agitated hands in the air. "Facts, my lord? Try if you can get any sense out of this fellow, for he's either drunk or mad."

Niall threw a keen glance at Jonny's sickly countenance. He looked as if he might cast up his innards at any moment. "Not drunk, sir. Knocked silly, belike."

"You're in the right of it, Hetherington. He's taken a blow to the back of the head." Tazewell was in the process of assisting the fellow to perch on the vicarage wall, where he sat, groaning with a hand to his head.

"He was found lying near the table where my wife was standing."

Niall's soldiering instincts came alert and his gaze turned to the ladies. "Is that where you lost Miss Westacott?"

A fresh wail issued from Lady Tazewell and she flung herself into her husband's arms. "Oh, Tom, Tom, it's my fault! I should never have insisted upon remaining for the tug of war. Edith said it was dangerous, but I never thought — never suspected — and we were supposed to be keeping her safe!"

"This does not help us, sir," hissed the Reverend Westacott in an urgent under-voice. "We must begin a search at once!"

"My dear Reverend, we can do nothing without knowing the probable direction in which she has been taken. Let us glean as much information as we can first."

Miss Burloyne's head turned from watching her friend sobbing into Tazewell's chest. She was white of face, but she looked resolute. "You will wish to know just what occurred, my lord."

A fleeting surprise struck Niall at finding her as calm as this. He'd written her off as just such another featherhead as Lady Tazewell.

"I would, ma'am. Pray tell me as precisely as you can."

She nodded, moving a little away to be heard above her friend's lamentations.

"All was well, I thought, until the fighting started. Jocasta was watching from her vantage point on the table."

"What, she was standing on it?"

"Yes, and Monkton was by to be at hand in case of accident."

"Which put him off guard as far as Edith was concerned."

Miss Burloyne's eyes showed guilt. "I'm afraid we were all off guard, my lord. I blush to confess it, but I became riveted by the tug of war despite having professed disinterest. But then a fight broke out almost in front of us, and I saw at once that retreat was in order."

Niall curbed his impatience. "Did you see Edith?"

"I remember hearing her saying we should go, and I turned immediately to persuade Jocasta. I'm afraid I fell into argument with her because she was making a fuss about getting down from the table. By the time she had been successfully set upon her feet, we could not see Edith anywhere."

Niall gritted his teeth against the furious words that rose to his tongue. Among God knows how many well-wishers, Kilshaw had still managed to snatch her. He could say nothing, for his bitterest anger was directed at himself. He had presumed too much. He ought to have done the business himself, instead of succumbing to the lure of a duty he could well have insisted upon leaving to Tazewell.

"When did you find my lad Jonny there?"

Miss Burloyne glanced across at the boy, who still looked to Niall to be as sick as a horse.

"Not quite immediately. We cast about and called Edith's name, but to no avail. We thought at first her guardian might have taken her away quickly, and several moments must have passed before we found him. There were already men sitting or lying on the ground, nursing injuries, for the fight was going on all about us."

An exasperated exclamation came from Tazewell, who had managed to quiet his wife. "My man should have had you out of there in a trice."

"He would have done, Tom," cried his wife in a still tearful tone, "but I would not let him take us, for we had to find Edith."

"And then Monkton discovered this poor fellow lying at a slight distance from the table," said Miss Burloyne, taking up the tale again. "He was coming to his senses by then, though he could hardly speak."

Damnation! Useless then to question the boy. "We'll let his fellows take care of him, when I can find them."

Mrs Tuffin spoke for the first time. "Mr Eddows has gone in search of them, my lord. He was here with the Reverend, taking a drop of wine. And that young good-for-nothing son of his ought to be here at any moment for his night duty. Though

I've no doubt he snores his head off up in the spare bedchamber."

Ignoring this aside, which was spoken in the cantankerous tone of one too troubled to be thinking of what she said, Niall thanked her. "You've removed one worry, at least. I need not concern myself with locating my men in this motley assembly."

The housekeeper looked gratified, but gazed up at him with anxious eyes. "Can you find her, my lord?"

"I'll find her, you may be sure, if it takes every ounce of effort of which I am capable." He did not pause to see the effect of his promise, but turned at once to the vicar. "You were questioning the lad when I got here, sir. Did you manage to ascertain whether or not he saw anything before he was struck down?"

"I could get no sense out of him at all, I told you, my lord. It is useless to ask him."

Miss Burloyne intervened, with a pitying glance cast at the victim. "The poor fellow does not know what happened to him, for you may be sure we asked as soon as we found him. At one moment he was behind Edith, and the next he woke up in this state."

"Taken unawares, no doubt, leaving my poor Ede exposed and prey to that villain." The Reverend Westacott again seized Niall's arm. "My lord, I cannot think Kilshaw can have done the thing himself. Unless he chose to assume a disguise of some sort?"

"No, I imagine he employed a tool in the business, one who might pass unnoticed." Niall turned again to Miss Burloyne, as the person most likely to give him a useful answer. "Was there any sign of anyone behaving in an odd fashion? Any stranger perhaps regarding you all with more than casual interest?"

She seemed to ponder, slowly shaking her head. "I cannot say I noticed. To say truth, we were all so much occupied with the diversions, I dare say we paid no attention if there was some such person."

Lady Tazewell suddenly struck her hands together, uttering a shriek. "The cart! Delia, don't you recall? That horrid man who had his cart too close to the gate there, and was perfectly objectionable when he was asked to move it."

Niall's senses pricked. A cart? This was more like.

"His manner was not pleasant, it is true," said Miss Burloyne, "but we have no reason to suppose he was here for any other purpose than to sell his wares."

"But why should he set his cart by our wall?" demanded the vicar on a frantic note, snatching off his spectacles and waving them for emphasis. "There was plenty of room on the edges of the green, and any one of our people would have told him where to go if he was a stranger."

"He must have been, for Edith's guardian at that time did not know him." Miss Burloyne looked at Niall. "Jocasta's footman will know. They were speaking together while we partook of our repast."

Niall had already formed the intention of questioning his lads the moment Eddows succeeded in rounding them up. But this information about the cart and its disgruntled owner could not but set his mind racing. Nothing was more likely than that a cart would be needed to convey Edith wherever she was taken. With so many such conveyances parked around the green, it would pass unnoticed. And the fact of the man's setting it in the lane, apart from where it should have been, suggested it might have stood in readiness for a quick getaway.

He once again looked to the ladies. "Was the cart taken elsewhere?"

"Well, it had gone when we came out again," said Miss Burloyne.

Niall looked at Mrs Tuffin, whose sharp eyes went from one to the other as the story unfolded. "The Reverend told me you would not stay for the tug of war, Mrs Tuffin. Did you happen to notice a cart standing in the lane when you came back?"

She shook her head. "I did not, my lord. It might have been. There were a number of them about, as there always are. I paid no heed, for I had stayed past my time and was in a hurry to get back to my kitchen, for I'd the vicar's dinner to prepare."

Niall thought fast. If the cart in question had indeed been meant for Edith, it ought to have been ready at that time. Although how should the housekeeper have noticed one among so many who must have been loading up preparatory to departure? Yet he'd had occasion to observe that people noticed more than they supposed at the time.

"Think, Mrs Tuffin! Try if you can to regain a picture of the place as it looked when you came back here."

She frowned in an effort of concentration, staring at the ground, plainly willing to do anything that might help to recover Edith. No one spoke, and Niall saw every eye trained upon the woman.

In a moment, her head came up, a new brightness in her eyes. "Yes, my lord, there was one, now you put me in mind of it! Standing against the wall." She pointed along the lane leading to Tazewell Manor. "A little way down, it was. I caught a sight of it as I came across. Thought nothing of it at the time."

"No, of course you did not. Which way was it facing?"

"Towards the woods, my lord."

Niall was seized with a thread of hope. "Miss Burloyne, can you describe the bad-tempered fellow in the cart?"

"I can," chimed in Lady Tazewell, eager now. "He was stocky and wearing a brown coat and corduroy breeches. He had one of those round hats with a floppy brim, and wore his hair tied at the back."

"Excellent, ma'am. And his face?"

"Ruddy in the cheek and a square jaw," supplied her friend.

"With a big nose — and that was red too."

"He sounds a very ruffian," said the vicar in a tone of deep distress. "If my Ede is in the hands of such an one, God help her!"

"If not God, sir, then we must do our part." Niall became brisk. "I fancy I know where to begin my search. Now, where the devil is Eddows?"

Chapter Twenty-nine

A rocking sensation dragged Edith out of the mists that clouded her mind. She became aware of darkness, an unpleasant odour and discomfort at her wrists and hip. The regular clip-clop of hooves penetrated the muffling blanket that covered her. Whatever it was must have been used for the horse, for it stank of that unmistakable animal aroma.

As her head cleared, Edith found she was lying on her side on a hard surface that dug into her hip and shoulder. She tried to adjust her position, pulling her arms towards her, and found she could not move her hands. The villain had tied her wrists!

The realisation she'd been taken struck hard. Despite all Niall's precautions, Kilshaw had succeeded. As she'd known he must. Oh, she'd known it. A wash of grief swept through her. She'd had a chance at happiness and he'd snatched it away. She would never feel Niall's kiss, or his ring sliding onto her finger. Instead, she must endure Lord Kilshaw's hideous caresses and live in degradation for the remainder of her days. From out of engulfing despair, rage rose up. She would die first. Or kill him and end up on the rope. Better that than sink to the depths where the villain sought to drag her.

Instinct set her straining against the bonds, but they were tied too well and it only increased her discomfort. Desisting, she lay quiet, trying to compose her mind to think clearly. And sanely. Useless to rail. Better to plan how she might escape. Small hope, she must suppose, of rescue.

Niall! How could she be such a ninny? He would come after her, of course he would. If he could find in which direction to strike out. How long had it been? How far had the cart travelled? Her mind jumped. Cart! She must be in the back of a cart. The memory leapt into her head. That very cart? Then, by heaven, her instinct had not been at fault! Was that surly fellow even now on the bench above her, guiding the horse?

Impossible to judge how long she'd been in the vehicle, for he'd covered her so thoroughly — for concealment as he left the green of course — with what she suspected was a horse blanket that Edith could not tell if darkness had yet descended. In full summer, it seemed unlikely.

She did not know what he'd used to overpower her. She recalled a sweet and pungent smell. It must have been strong to have sent her into a swoon. Yet it can surely not have been strong enough to have kept her out of her senses for long. She began to entertain a hope of Niall overtaking the cart before ever it reached where Kilshaw was no doubt waiting. But even as the hope flared up, the pace of the vehicle slowed, the rumbling wheels soon coming to a halt.

Edith braced as she heard the sound of movement and then feet thumping to the ground. They came around to the back of the cart and her heartbeat pattered into life, pulsing in her own ears. Better to play dead. She closed her eyes and tried to relax her muscles, letting her tied hands fall away to one side. A grunt sounded and a rude mutter. Edith could not make out the words.

The covering that lay heavily over her was suddenly lifted, and light played across her eyelids. Sun? The day had been warm, the sun playing peek-a-boo throughout. Hope lifted, despite the thump at her breast. It could not be far into the evening yet. Niall had time enough to trace her whereabouts before the daylight faded.

There was time for no more speculation, for rough hands grasped her ankles and pulled, dragging her bodily towards the back of the cart. Only with difficulty did Edith refrain from resisting at this rough treatment. She could feel her petticoats in disarray, likely exposing a good deal of stockinged leg. It made no odds, for all her attention was immediately taken up with the effort to remain limp as she was heaved from the cart and slung over her captor's shoulder, like a sack of potatoes.

The discomfort was acute; Edith's breath near stopped by the combination of hanging upside-down and the restriction her arms made against her breast, tied as she was. She made no sound, trusting the man would suppose her to be still unconscious. In this undignified position, she might dare at least to open her eyes.

It availed her little. But she knew her captor crossed a threshold. She could see a stone floor, dirty with footmarks, and the bottom of a stairway as her bearer turned to one side. A door opened, and she saw bare flags and smelled a combination of stale liquor and tobacco. She'd been taken to an inn of some kind. That augured better. A private house would have been more difficult for Niall to find.

Her thoughts ceased as she was unceremoniously dumped onto a settle, where she landed in disorder, unable any longer to pretend unconsciousness. Without thinking, she strove to gain a purchase on the hard surface, righting herself as best she could without the use of her hands.

"You will forgive the harsh treatment, I trust."

A jolt shot through Edith. That hated voice! Despite foreknowledge — for it must have been Kilshaw who'd had her captured in this rough and ready fashion — the unctuous tone grated on her nerves. Edith looked up and found him standing not two feet from her, the oily smile plastered across his handsome face.

"Dastard! You could not even do your dirty work yourself!" Edith flung the words at him, fury swamping her fear.

The smile did not waver. Rather it broadened, triumph creeping into his eyes.

"What would you, my dearest love, when your importunate cavalier insisted upon putting spokes in my wheel? I could scarcely appear in the matter in person, upon an occasion such as that on the green today."

"But it did not stop you taking advantage of it. Niall knew you would try."

He spread his hands. "As indeed I did. But we ought to say succeeded, do you not think?"

"Don't be too pot-sure. Niall will come after me."

"Oh, I don't doubt it. Which is why, my sweet one, we will proceed upon our journey at once."

Less afraid than she might have been, secure in her conviction Niall would move heaven and earth to retrieve her, Edith managed to produce a sneer. "Do you propose to outrun him in a cart?"

A gentle laugh escaped him. "Pray use the wits I know you to possess, my dear. Am I a fool?"

"Yes, if you suppose Niall will not outwit you."

"No doubt he will pit his best against me, but I think I have the edge. My curricle is being readied at this moment. We will be many miles distant before your precious Niall has scratched about to find which way we are headed."

Doubt smote Edith, but she would not let him see it. She summoned her coolest tone. "Indeed? And where are we headed, sir?"

"Why, to London, of course. And thence to Brighton. Would you not wish to meet the Prince? I feel sure he would be pleased with you."

Fury spat within her. He would dare to present her to his royal crony as his mistress? Fie on him! She lifted her tied hands. "Will you drag me before him like a slave? You had better chain my ankle while you are about it."

He emitted a low laugh. "By God, I like your spirit, Edith! It's why you inflame me, I think. So piquant a conquest when the challenge is high."

Edith drew an unsteady breath, keeping her hands uplifted. "Do you mean to untie me? Am I to make the journey in this state?"

The smile she loathed appeared and he dug a hand into an inner pocket, bringing out a folded knife. He came to her and took hold of her hands, bending them back at the wrist to expose the rope that bound them.

Edith's skin crawled at even this mild touch, but she forced herself to remain quiescent while he cut through her bonds. Released, she felt instant relief, succeeded at once by an ache at her wrists as she instinctively caught at one and then the other to soothe them. Red weals decorated each one, where the rope had cut into her skin.

"Come, my lovely Edith. Unless you require the call of nature, we must be off."

Edith at once claimed she did indeed need such, hoping for a delay at least, and even an opportunity to evade him. But when Lord Kilshaw produced a chamber pot and set it down before her on the floor, with every apparent intention of remaining where he was, she glared at him.

"Do you not mean to retire?"

"There need be no modesty between us, my dear Edith. And I have no mind to offer you a chance to escape. Not that you'd get far, but time is pressing."

Edith rose. "In that case, let us go at once."

She had no intention of performing such an intimate act within his orbit. She must find another way to procure her freedom. A weapon of some kind would come to her hand. If she went down, she would go down fighting.

Chapter Thirty

The temptation to ride like the devil was hard to withstand. Niall kept his horse at a canter, knowing it would only make matters worse if the animal foundered. He'd held in the churning rage and chagrin which overlaid his deep anxiety while occupied with questions and plans. Once on his way, with young Peter Eddows at his back, armed and eager to prove himself, Niall had been buoyed at first with taking action. But as the miles crept by, his imagination fed him such images as threatened to drive him into paroxysms of fear.

He thrust them away, concentrating his mind on the strategy he'd put in place. Kilshaw could not win. If Eddows played his part, a veritable army would be following hard on his heels. Speed was of the essence. Kilshaw must not be permitted to gain too much of a lead.

He had not dared waste time sending to the Court for his cousin's curricle, which he'd not yet used more than a time or two. But he knew Kilshaw to have the benefit of four horses, and his phaeton would be useless if it came to a chase. By this time, his groom should have been driven back to Lowrie Court with Eddows to collect both curricle and phaeton. Tazewell had offered to perform this office, leaving his ladies at the vicarage. Niall had declined his further offer to join the fray, instead detailing Eddows to bring his three uninjured lads, hired to guard Edith, who would travel in the vehicles.

It would take time to fig out the vehicles, but the precaution was necessary. Who knew how far Kilshaw might travel before Niall caught up? Unless his hunch was proved. In any event, he must have a carriage to bring Edith home again. No doubt of his ability to do so troubled him. He had said as much to the Reverend Westacott, in a bid to dissuade him from joining in the chase in his gig.

He doubted Kilshaw had more than the one ruffian who had effected the kidnap in his pay, along with the groom whose odd behaviour that day had given the clue to Edith's possible whereabouts. With himself and six men, there could be no difficulty in overcoming any opposition.

No, he was not troubled by any thought of failure. What he could not shake from his mind was the hideous possibility that he might not catch up before Kilshaw had a chance to force Edith to his will. Which fear had the power to destroy Niall's confidence, for all his experience of conflict. He refused to allow himself to dwell on it. Yet stray thoughts crept across his mind without will.

Kilshaw had tried once to rape Edith. Without compunction or consideration for her state of health. Logic dictated that if he wished to keep Edith from Niall — and had gumption enough to know he would be in pursuit — no better way offered than to bring her to ruin before he was overtaken. He might accomplish the deed in a matter of moments. Edith had not strength enough to withstand a determined assault, though she would fight him with her last breath, that much Niall believed.

Setting aside the consequences, the thought of the woman who had his heart being subjected to that particular brutality caused Niall such agony as he had never thought to endure. With his own eyes he'd seen women ravished by marauding soldiers. He'd executed one of his own for that very crime. It was violent, rude and ruthless. And if Edith…

He wrenched his mind away from the vision that threatened to fill it and found, with a surge of that battle rush he'd once tried to describe to Edith, that they had reached the inn for which he'd been headed.

He put out a hand to young Eddows as he slowed his own mount to a walk. "Steady now, lad. We'll approach with caution."

Bringing the horse to a halt, Niall took a careful sweep of the area in front of the Cock. It was as quiet as it had been the day he saw Kilshaw's groom, who so foolishly drew attention to himself by running off. He had thereby rendered the place suspect, and Niall hoped his instinct had not led him astray.

"Keep watch here, Peter, while I reconnoitre."

Young Eddows obediently sat his horse, setting one hand on the butt of the pistol in his pocket.

"Don't fire at shadows," warned Niall, and rode across to the other side of the inn. There was nothing to be seen but a pile of debris and several empty buckets. But when he walked the horse quietly down the side until he could see behind, he was rewarded by the sight of a cart, empty and tipped up with its shafts in the air.

A door was open at the back, and steam was seen to be drifting from within. Niall recalled the kitchen he'd entered the last time. It was disheartening to find no sign of Kilshaw's curricle. On the other hand, if he'd chosen to press on, there was hope Edith had not been violated. As yet.

The grim reminder of her danger sent him trotting the horse back around to the front, where he signalled young Eddows to join him and dismounted. He tethered the horse as he had done before and, with pistol at the ready, waited for the lad to do the same before lifting the latch and stalking into the noisome hallway. The door to the tap was open, and Niall noted the same stale fug of ale and the smoke and smell of tobacco.

"You can't suppose she's here, my lord!"

Peter's shocked tone brought a grim smile to Niall's mouth. "I doubt it. Not now, anyway. But I intend to find out if she was here, which I strongly suspect. There's a cart out the back."

The lad looked startled. "I'd best cock this then, shall I, my lord?" He indicated his pistol.

"The sight of it will be sufficient, I imagine."

Niall marched into the taproom and looked around for its slovenly landlord. He spotted the man at once, busy gathering empty tankards. The fellow looked round. A flash of recognition in his eyes was swiftly followed by shock at sight of the pistols, at which he stared, frozen.

The taproom went silent. There were only a few patrons, of much the same calibre as Niall recalled from the last occasion. Elderly men, who likely spent their days here and had no interest in attending the Lammas Fair.

He addressed the landlord, his tone peremptory enough to shake the fellow out of his stupor. "I want information, my good man."

The man's head came up, and it was at once evident Niall had guessed aright. Guilt overlaid the fear in his face. Nevertheless, he took to blustering. "I don't know nowt, yer honour."

"Oh, I think you do. You've lately had a visitor here, have you not? The same gentlemen I described to you when we last met, if I'm not much mistaken."

The man's fear deepened. "He bain't here."

"No longer, but he was, was he not? Exactly when did he leave?"

"How would I know? I never said he be here, did I?"

The tone held a trifle of the old belligerence and Niall took a step forward, raising his pistol hand. "Don't play games with me! You had Kilshaw here, in some other room, I surmise. Upstairs?"

"He be over t'other side. 'Tis by way of a coffee room."

"Show me."

The landlord shuffled towards the door, keeping a wary eye on the pistols. Young Peter had followed Niall's moves and now stepped back into the hall, waving his pistol to indicate the man should follow.

"No tricks, you!"

A grim smile curved Niall's mouth as the landlord made haste to get himself across the hall and fling open a door on the other side. Peter pushed him in ahead and Niall followed behind.

The room was small, containing a large table, a couple of wooden settles and little else besides. Light came through a leaded casement but it was gloomy, despite a couple of tallow candles, burning low and smoking. An empty glass and a bottle stood on the table.

Niall crossed and picked up the bottle, sniffing at its open top. Wine? He held up the bottle to one of the candles and found only dregs. Setting it down again, he turned to the landlord. "You had Lord Kilshaw here, waiting for the cart which is now outside the back of your inn. Is it yours? Did he hire it from you?"

Peter's pistol jabbed into the man's belly as he hesitated. "Answer!"

The lad's bark had less effect than the weapon, Niall guessed. But the landlord capitulated. "I didn't know as he meant to bring leddy here, I swear it, yer honour! I'll stake me oath he never said as that were why he wanted cart. I don't hold wi' violence, yer honour, nor I don't hold wi' tying leddies up neither."

The wheedling tone was nauseating, but Niall was far more concerned with the intelligence of the rude handling to which Edith had been subjected. If Kilshaw was capable of that —! His anxiety deepened, his voice sharpening.

"How long was the lady here? When did his lordship leave?"

The landlord shook his head, trying to edge away from Peter's pistol, its barrel still directly pointed towards his oversized belly. "He weren't here more'n a half hour after leddy come. Mebbe less. Fifteen, twenty minutes at outside, I'd say, yer honour."

Time enough. Niall's guts clenched. He must not dwell on the possibility. He jerked his head to Peter to withdraw his pistol.

"How long since he left?"

Still holding his gaze on the gun, despite its being removed, the fellow scratched his chin. "Mebbe an hour? Mebbe not as much?"

"Was he driving a curricle?"

"Aye, that he be, yer honour. Bang-up set-out it be. Only he didn't mean to travel all the way to Lunnon in it."

"How do you know?"

A sour smile creased the landlord's mouth. "For as that there groom of his arst me where his master might hire a coach, didn't he?"

"And what did you tell him?"

"Said as how he'd have to go nor Kington before he'd find one for hire. Bain't no livery stable nearer."

Then it was safe to assume Kilshaw planned to make the change at a suitable inn within reasonable distance of Kington.

"Which is the main coaching house at Kington, do you know?" Another scratch at the fellow's chin and a ruminative look. Niall threw up his eyes. "You'll get nothing out of me, fellow, if you expect to be rewarded for your information. I'm more likely to inform the nearest magistrate that you've aided and abetted in a kidnapping." Which threat was enough to loosen the man's tongue, though he turned surly.

"Well, it be Coach and Horses. Not as you'll catch 'im, not on horseback."

Niall curled his lip. "Saw us arrive, did you? It's my belief you know more about this business than you're saying. Was it you found the ruffian who snatched Miss Westacott? One of your customers, was he?"

The landlord closed his lips firmly together, only his eyes betraying the truth of this accusation.

Niall had no more time to waste on the man. Bidding him to watch out for the constable, he left the place with young Eddows close behind.

The young man spoke as they mounted up. "Do we go on, my lord, or wait for my father?"

"We go on. It's to be hoped they are not long behind us. If that villain of a landlord is to be believed, Kilshaw has nearly an hour's start."

The two horses trotted back onto the road and Niall urged his mount to a canter. Peter followed suit, keeping pace beside him.

"Our quarry must stop to bait at some point, my lord, don't you think?"

"That is my hope."

And his fear, if truth be told. A halt for refreshment must give Kilshaw just the opportunity to make sure of Edith. With an inward shudder, Niall shifted his attention to Sorrell, by now on the road with the curricle, and mentally urged him to hurry.

Chapter Thirty-one

The light was fading when Kilshaw at last slowed the curricle's rattling pace. He had as little regard for the comfort of his cattle as he did for hers, Edith reflected. His team was all but blown, steam beginning to rise from the horses' flanks as they dropped to a trot and were guided through the streets of a small town. Lord Kilshaw slowed them to a walk, and began a turn towards an arched entrance leading to the back of an inn. A sign above the doorway informed Edith that it was the Peacock.

The yard was clear of any other vehicle than a single coach. Edith regarded it with misgiving. She had been wondering if her captor proposed to travel all the way to London in his curricle, exposing her to the general view. Perhaps he did not so intend.

She was tempted to break the silence she had maintained for miles, refusing all Lord Kilshaw's attempts to engage her in conversation until he had laughed.

"I will wait for you to come out of the sulks, my love."

Just as if she was the aggressor. Edith had returned no answer, biting her tongue on the sarcastic comments that itched in her head. If a hostile attitude inflamed him, as he had said, she had no intention of offering him that particular provocation. Above anything else, she must keep him at arm's length.

By this time, however, she was chilled, weary, hungry and heart-sore. Her wounds still hurt and her muscles ached. If this was a respite, she welcomed it. Besides, any delay at all must give Niall more time to catch up.

Lord Kilshaw forestalled her question, turning his head to glance at her. "You will have an opportunity to refresh yourself here, my dear."

And eat too, she hoped. Without sustenance, she would not have strength to resist him, either with words or physically, if it came to that.

She allowed him to assist her down from the curricle, pulling her hand from his the moment she was on the ground. A glance at his face showed his annoyance at this treatment, but the instant he met her eyes, the curling smile appeared.

"Come, my love. A chamber is ready for you here."

Edith's pulses came alive again, jumping in her veins. A chamber? God help her! She could not now remain silent. "I do not require a chamber, sir. I merely want food."

"You will have that too, my dear. A meal has been bespoken."

He took her arm in a strong hold and drew her towards the entrance.

The inn was quiet and Edith's heart sank. Small hope of raising a commotion by screaming or falling into strong hysterics, which she felt as if she might do at any moment.

A bustling landlord appeared as his lordship guided her into a wide hallway.

"Ah, my lord, here you are. All is in readiness. My lady wife has seen to the sheets and your dinner will be served in the parlour, snug as you please."

Relief surged through Edith's bosom. Thank heaven! She'd been afraid she would be forced to eat with the threat of a bed in plain sight. Did the landlord suppose Kilshaw meant to spend the night? Had he made pretence of it? Edith had not the slightest belief that he would. Surely he would press on to put as much distance as he could between himself and Niall?

"Come up, my lord, come up. And my lady too."

This form of address sent a flitter of unease through Edith. Had Lord Kilshaw told this man she was his wife? A hideous possibility raised its head as she perforce began to ascend the stairs in the landlord's wake. Did Lord Kilshaw mean to await Niall's advent? If so, his intention was clear. He would not have hired a bedchamber otherwise.

A tattoo rose in her breast. Useless to wait for rescue. By the time it came, she would be ruined. Fit for nothing more than the life her Nemesis planned for her. Niall would have no choice but to let her go, for Lord Kilshaw intended to display her to him as his harlot.

Through the rise of fear determination built. She would not succumb. She would die rather. Somehow, she would find a way to withstand him.

The landlord opened a door to one side of the upper hall. "This is your bedchamber, my lord."

Edith could barely repress a shudder. But his lordship did not even glance at her and she breathed more easily as he spoke.

"I feel sure it will serve. Where is your parlour?"

Bowing, the landlord closed the bedchamber door and led the way to the front of the house. Ushered into a cosy apartment, Edith went directly to the window and looked out. She listened with only half an ear to the landlord as he outlined the details of the repast which was about to be presented. Darkness was closing in and she could see little beyond a swirl of dust and an urchin hurrying along the road. It must be well after eight if it was already dark. How many hours had passed since her capture? It felt like forever, but it could not have been much above three.

The window let directly onto the street. There could be no escape by this route. But at least she might hope to hear the approach of any vehicle.

"Come and sit down, my dear Edith. Or do you wish to refresh yourself before we dine?"

Lord Kilshaw sounded perfectly composed, just as if her participation in his villainous scheme was in accord with normality. Edith turned to face him, summoning a like manner. "I should much like to freshen up, if I might be permitted a few moments alone."

His lip curled and a gleam came into his eye. "Oh, I think so. You will not object to my remaining outside the door? Not that you could get far if you chose to try and escape me."

"I am hardly likely to do anything so foolish, my lord. I can conceive of nothing more guaranteed to bring me to grief than to be running about the streets at this hour."

"I should have known I might rely on your good sense. Come!"

The peremptory note was not lost on Edith, and a little trepidation assailed her as he held open the door. Did he mean to carry out an assault now? Had she miscalculated? She passed him with her eyes downcast, and walked with swift steps to the door of the bedchamber the landlord had shown them. He spoke as her fingers grasped the handle.

"Don't be long!"

Edith whisked through the door and shut it behind her, leaning against it as a tide of relief washed through her. She cast a comprehensive glance about, looking for a weapon.

A four-poster menaced in the centre of the room, its covers turned down in readiness for occupation. To one side was a narrow chest of drawers with a lighted candelabrum on its surface that threw flickering shadows across the bed. Edith's eye caught on a washstand at its other side and she headed towards it. The jug held warm water, and she poured a little into the basin. With her face and hands washed, she felt a degree more capable of coping with the situation.

She found a chamber pot under the bed and made use of it. As she dried her hands again on the towel that hung off the stand, she took due note of a heavy bible set upon the bedside table. At a pinch, she might manage to wield it against her captor. Or the jug perhaps? Either would slow him, but Edith doubted she could do sufficient damage to hold him, even could she hit him without retaliation. She would have to be fast, and the likelihood was he would catch her before she could grab either weapon.

No, she must find something else. In the parlour. If she waited until he had her in this room, she would be lost. All the advantage lay on his side.

A knock at the door was followed by Lord Kilshaw's immediate entrance.

"Are you not done? The covers have been taken through and I am devilish hungry, if you are not."

Impatience sounded in his voice, and Edith set down the towel she was still holding. "I am quite ready."

He held the door for her, a trifle of suspicion in his eyes. But he said nothing more, merely indicating she should go before him. "Go into the parlour, Edith. I will join you presently."

He vanished back into the bedchamber and Edith hesitated. Dared she run downstairs now? What if she told the landlord she was being held against her will? Would he believe her? Or had Lord Kilshaw primed him?

No, she would do better to pretend to acquiescence. Lull him if she could. She stood more of a chance of besting him if he was off his guard.

She withdrew to the parlour, casting her eyes over the various covered dishes a waiter was setting out, her mind instantly presenting her with images of ways she might incapacitate Lord Kilshaw. One of the silver covers would make a much better weapon than the bible or the jug. And there were two candlesticks on the table, lighted candles adding to the illumination provided by wall sconces and a candelabrum on the dresser to one side.

Feeling more confident every moment, Edith took a seat at the table and allowed her attention to wander to what might be concealed beneath the covers. The aromas were enticing and her mouth watered, reminding her of her empty stomach.

Lord Kilshaw reappeared just as the waiter laid aside his tray and made to lift one of the covers.

"You need not wait. We will serve ourselves. I don't wish to be disturbed."

Edith's confidence faltered as he shut the door behind the waiter and grasped the key in the lock. She heard the click as it shot home and her heart sank. Her captor turned with the key in his fingers and held it up, the mocking curve creasing his fine lips.

"There now, my lovely Edith. We will be perfectly private." With which, he slipped the key into his pocket, still smiling, and came to take his seat at the table, directly opposite. His hand hovered over one of the silver covers. "Now, what have we to tempt you? Ah, a fricassee of some kind. Or would you prefer some of this beef? A little of both perhaps?"

Feeling hollow inside, Edith opted for the fricassee. Her appetite had deserted her, but she knew she must take enough to sustain her for the coming battle.

Lord Kilshaw offered her wine, which Edith refused, instead choosing to drink water. She needed her wits about her. To her dismay, he partook liberally of the claret himself, sinking quite half the bottle before he had consumed the plateful of sliced beef before him.

Edith managed to swallow only a few forkfuls of her portion of fricassee, forcing them down through an increasingly tight throat. She ate slowly, her senses alert to the growing glitter in his lordship's eyes and her ears straining for any sound of hoof beats from the street outside.

Time dragged, but no hint of Niall's catching up with them came to relieve Edith's rising apprehension. She felt in urgent need of some stimulant that would not impair her capability of defending herself. *Coffee!*

On the thought, she set down her fork and looked across at her Nemesis. "Would it be too much to ask if you will send for a pot of coffee?"

He met her eyes, his own unsmiling. A sneer twisted his mouth. "So you may throw hot liquid in my face? I think not, my dear Edith. Do not imagine I am fooled by this show of docility on your part. I am perfectly aware you are plotting how you may best me. You won't, of course, but who am I to protest if it amuses you?"

"Amuses me?" Incensed, Edith gave him a sneer as mocking as his own. "To be sure, it is vastly entertaining for me to be rendered unconscious, tied up so tight I am bruised to pieces —" holding up her closed fists to show her damaged wrists "—thrown into the back of a filthy cart and handed over to a man who intends my ruin. I had not looked for such adventure, I declare."

Lord Kilshaw's lips creased into genuine amusement and he laughed. "Faith, I believe I could keep you indefinitely, Edith. I had thought to hand you over to one of my cronies when I tired of you, but —"

"What, am I a parcel, my lord? All this, so you may have your fill of what you covet only to wrap me up and pass me along to the next man? I wonder you are taking so much trouble, if you mean to discard your prize so readily."

"And lose the pleasure of your wit? No, indeed, my love. The more you spar with me, the likelier I am to keep you."

"I am flattered, my lord. It did not occur to me that your desire was rooted in my head rather than elsewhere."

He went off into a virtual paroxysm of mirth, slapping the table with his hand and making the glasses jump.

Seething, Edith waited for his laughter to abate. It sounded hollow in her ears and the glitter at his eyes warned her he was becoming enraged under the pretended mockery. Well, so was she enraged. And her apparent calm had not fooled him in the least.

His laughter died and he upended her wine glass and poured from the bottle, half filling it with ruby liquid. "I regret you cannot have coffee, my dear. Content you with claret."

Feeling even more in need, Edith snatched up the glass and took a couple of swallows of the wine. Warmth slid down her throat and into her chest. She toyed with the notion of flinging the remainder into that hated face, but caution won. There was no saying how he might react, especially since he had refilled his own glass and was in the act of tipping it down his throat.

Edith watched him empty the bottle into his glass. Merely dregs were left. Lord Kilshaw rose and reached for a second bottle set on the dresser to one side. He ripped out the cork with his teeth and spat it on the floor.

In quick succession, he downed two full glasses and then set down the vessel and the bottle, smacking his lips and gazing across at Edith with an unmistakeable leer.

"I'm ready for you now, my dear. Shall we repair to the bedchamber?"

So bold? Edith's pulse began a slow pumping. She wanted to scream or curse, but her tongue felt thick in her mouth. Her famous wit had deserted her. She could think of nothing to say to hold him. At any moment he might make a move. How to withstand him?

She looked wildly around the room, and her eyes came to rest on the bottle on the table. He picked it up by the neck, turned it upside down so that liquid trickled out. He waved it in a gesture as mocking as it was triumphant.

"I can read your mind, Edith. Face it, my dear, there is no escape. You may as well come to me with a good grace."

He set the bottle aside and reached out a hand to her as he spoke.

"Never!" Without thought, Edith snatched up her discarded fork, rising as she did so. With the full might of her arm, she jabbed the prongs into his hand, bearing it down to the table.

Lord Kilshaw roared and leapt up and forward as the prongs penetrated deep into his flesh and quivered there, blood beginning to spurt.

Edith seized her side of the table and heaved. It tipped, knocking into Kilshaw, who was half standing. He was thrown backwards. His chair went over, crashing to the floor. Dishes, bottles and cutlery slid across the table, crashing down around him.

Her heart was pounding but Edith wasted no time, racing for the door. She turned the handle to no avail, and remembered he had locked it and the key was in his pocket.

He was grunting and cursing on the floor, batting away the debris that had fallen on him, the fork still protruding from his hand.

Edith looked around for another weapon. If she could batter him into unconsciousness, she could get the key. One of the bottles had rolled a little way from Lord Kilshaw and remained intact. Edith darted towards it. As she neared, a hand reached out and seized her ankle.

"Not so fast, you witch! Come here!"

He gave a vicious tug and Edith toppled, grabbed for the table and missed. She came down in a tangle of petticoats, knocking her head on the edge of the table as she did so.

Momentarily stunned, she was unable to move fast enough to evade Lord Kilshaw, who swung himself over her, still bleeding from his hand. Edith saw he'd succeeded in removing the fork and groaned, putting up her hands to try to hold him off.

He was snarling, his fingers digging hard into her shoulders.

"You don't escape me so readily, you fiend! I would have been merciful, but now you deserve what's coming to you!"

Panic gripped Edith as he raised himself enough to permit him to reach down to drag at her petticoats. Panting for breath, she shoved at his chest, but the effort was unavailing. Her legs were imprisoned beneath his, her body crushed by his weight.

From somewhere half outside her consciousness, Edith heard sounds betokening activity without. Voices and footsteps? Had the thumping and clatter within the parlour drawn attention?

No immediate hope of rescue. The room was locked! And Lord Kilshaw had her at his mercy.

Under the impetus of desperation, she turned her head away from his hot regard, vicious now with rising desire. God help her, but he truly was inflamed! Her defiance had served to spur him.

Edith's gaze hunted the debris and lighted upon the bloody fork he had cast away from him. The air washed her bare limbs and she felt his fumble at the fall of his breeches. His breath was hot and heavy on her face, stinking of liquor. No time to lose!

His busy fingers left her hand free. Edith threw it out, groping for the fork, her eyes now on his to keep his attention off the movement of her hand. She felt the prick of the prongs and slid her fingers down to close about the handle.

As he thrust his hand between her thighs, grabbing and shoving hard, Edith brought her weapon up in a violent sweep, and struck below Lord Kilshaw's raised chin.

He froze, his mouth flying open, but no sound came out. He seemed to fight for breath, his grip tightening so hard on her thigh and shoulder that she winced.

The pose held for a timeless moment, blood dripping onto Edith's chest from the wound she had inflicted.

Forever passed in Edith's frozen mind. Then Lord Kilshaw drew a sobbing breath. His grip relaxed suddenly and he collapsed, still half covering Edith's body.

Uttering a cry, she shoved with all her might, dragging herself out from underneath. Her legs were caught, and she had to physically lift his off before she could extricate herself. There was a sob in her throat as her breath came short and fast. She pushed herself to a kneeling position and stared at the wreck of her Nemesis.

He was lying on his side, the fork protruding from his neck. His aspect was deathly, his face drained of colour. Was he breathing?

The fear she'd killed him spurred Edith into action. Reaching towards his hips, she dug her fingers into his visible pocket. They groped in vain. No feel of cold steel rewarded her efforts.

She regarded the heavy body with misgiving. Could she turn him? If the key was in his other pocket, then she must.

The sounds from without had grown louder. She could hear footsteps pounding along the hallway outside. The thought that she was no longer alone with Kilshaw's body spurred Edith.

She staggered to her feet, aware her legs were trembling. She shook out her petticoats and held them up as she stepped gingerly over his still carcase and crossed to the door. Without hesitation, she lifted her fists and hammered on it, yelling out. "Help! Help me, whoever you are! I can't get out!"

The most welcome voice in the world answered her.

"Edith! It is I, Hetherington! Stand away from the door!"

"Niall! Oh, thank God!"

Hardly aware of her own sobbing relief, she flung herself away from the door, landing flat against the wall.

A deafening report made her jump, throwing her hands to her ears. The door cracked open and was thrust back by a kick from a booted foot.

Niall charged into the room, his gaze falling first on Kilshaw on the floor and then sweeping up to find Edith. "Are you hurt? What has happened here?"

Edith staggered forward and fell upon him, feeling his arms close about her in a comforting embrace, his hand holding her head to his shoulder.

"Hush, now, hush, my dear one. It's over now."

She drew a sobbing breath and pulled back, looking up into his face. "Niall, I think I've killed him!"

His brows drew together. "The devil you have!" He glanced down at the body on the floor and then his eyes came back to Edith, reassurance in them as he grasped her shoulders. "Go with Peter, Edith. I'll make all right here."

She allowed herself to be handed over to young Eddows, who took her arm and ushered her out through the door. Edith could not resist a glance back into the shambles behind her. Niall was on one knee beside Lord Kilshaw's still body, checking his pulse.

"Come away, Miss Westacott," urged her escort.

She shuddered, the full horror of what had happened only now coming in upon her. God help her, but she might yet end upon the rope for this night's work!

Chapter Thirty-one

As he hunted for a pulse, Niall searched Kilshaw's pale features. He'd seen enough wounded men on the battlefield to be able to see at once that the villain did not have the waxen look of death upon him. A pity. Niall was tempted to finish the job and send the fiend straight to hell, if the consequences to Edith were not in question.

One glance at the half ripped open fall at the waist of the man's breeches, taken with Edith's dishevelled state, was enough to give Niall a fair notion of what had prompted her to take such drastic measures to protect herself.

Under his fingers, still clasped about Kilshaw's wrist, a slight pumping confirmed the man was still alive. A groan and a flicker of his eyelids betokened returning consciousness. One wavering hand came up, groping at his neck where the fork was embedded, having entered just above the cravat, which was spotted with blood.

Niall grabbed the hand and held it off. "Wait! Don't touch it!"

Kilshaw's eyes flickered open and he gazed up at Niall, blinking blearily. "You!" His voice was hoarse.

"Hold still! I'm going to extract the fork."

"Fork?" The dark eyes rolled a little. "Again? Damn the little vixen to hell!"

Niall did not trouble to answer. It was evident Kilshaw recalled the events prior to his collapse, but this was not the moment to demand details. Though a welter of admiration went through him, tinged with grim humour, at the method Edith had used to save herself.

"I'm going to have to remove your neckcloth first. Just keep still."

The man was evidently in no condition to argue. He let his hand fall and his head sank back. His cravat had come half undone in the late contretemps, and Niall had no difficulty in ripping its folds open, though he had to use care while unwinding it to expose the man's neck and avoid shifting the protruding fork. But it would serve as a bandage after. He caught sight of a discarded napkin amongst the debris in which Kilshaw was lying and snatched it up, bundling it into a thick pad.

"Brace yourself," he told the man and grasped the fork. "It's deep and will likely bleed a good deal."

His victim hissed in a breath as, with some effort, Niall pulled the prongs free from his neck. Blood gushed behind them, and Niall held his makeshift pad to the wound to staunch it. The white cloth reddened with rapidity and Niall took up Kilshaw's hand and put it to the pad.

"Hold this as tight as you can."

The hand wavered a little, but then the man's fingers pressed harder and Niall was able to let go. Folding the long length of the stained cravat in two, he re-tied it around Kilshaw's neck with deft fingers, knotting the ends to keep it in place.

"That should hold it until you can summon a surgeon."

"Obliged to you," grunted Kilshaw. He tried to rise and failed. "Help me up, damn you!"

Niall got up and righted the man's chair. Then he heaved him from the floor and dumped him into it. Kilshaw landed heavily and sat there for a moment, panting, his eyes closed.

Niall surveyed the wreck. Instinct urged him to improve upon Edith's handiwork and slam his fist into that handsome face. Not that the villain was looking his best at this moment. But an innate sense of chivalry prevailed. One did not strike a man when he was down, no matter the provocation.

Kilshaw's eyes opened again and he searched frowningly about the mess below him. "I daresay my bottle did not survive. Damnation! I could do with a dose of liquor."

Niall extracted the slim silver flask he carried from one of his pockets and opened it, holding it out. "You may take this. Though it goes against the grain."

An echo of the villain's customary sneer appeared in his face as he took the flask. "I daresay you'd prefer to fling it in my face." He drank deeply from the flask and handed it back. "That's better."

Niall wiped the opening of the bottle with fastidious fingers and replaced the lid, slipping the flask into his pocket. "Attend to me, Kilshaw!"

The man's brows rose. "A trifle peremptory, sir, towards a wounded man."

"You may thank your stars for that wound, my friend. The one I should have inflicted would have incapacitated you to a greater degree."

Kilshaw's eyes glinted up at him, but his voice was still rough from the rude treatment at his throat. "Is it so, indeed? Well, let us try a fall, my dear Hetherington, when this is mended." He touched one long finger gingerly to the improvised bandage.

Niall snorted. "By no means. You are done, sir. Make up your mind to that."

"Oh? Upon whose authority am I done, pray?"

"Mine. Make no mistake. If you come at Edith again, you will be coming at my wife."

Malice showed in the man's eyes. "You'd make her a countess? Good God, man, don't you know I've been there before you?"

Niall gritted his teeth. "You're lying."

The sneer returned to Kilshaw's mouth. "Am I now? She has you fooled, has she?"

"Don't compound your villainy with further lies! I know Edith too well to be taken in."

"My dear sir, I know her a deal better than you might wish."

Niall's temper got the better of him. "Be silent! Or I'll bury my scruples and break your pretty nose!"

Kilshaw grinned sourly. "That's your trouble, Hetherington. Too many scruples."

Aware the man was merely trying to provoke him, Niall shifted his ground. "If you show your face in this district again, I will make your recent activities known to the world at large."

"What, and force Edith to brave the scandal? I doubt it, my friend."

"Do you? Then you don't know me, my friend." He strode to the door, but did not open it immediately. He looked back at Kilshaw. "By the way, I'll be writing to your royal patron. I dare say he will be interested to learn of your doings. More so to hear of my intent to make them public. They tell me the Prince of Wales is terrified of scandal. And you are one of his cronies, are you not?"

He had the satisfaction of seeing the smug expression wiped off Kilshaw's face, and knew at last he had found the chink in the fellow's armour.

"You need not be afraid." The words were grunted out. "I'm done with the wench. She's not worth it."

Niall eyed him with contempt. "She is to me. Remember that."

Turning from the sight of Kilshaw's pallid countenance, he opened the door and left the room, shutting it quietly behind him.

Chapter Thirty-two

The journey back to Itchington Bishops seemed to Edith a timeless interval. Wrapped in a travelling rug Niall abstracted from beneath the seat, she sat beside him in the curricle as he drove through the darkened countryside, lost in a dreamlike state where reality melded into nightmare.

The events of the last minutes of her capture replayed in her mind over and over again. She found it hard to believe Niall's assertion that Lord Kilshaw still lived. Yet for no consideration would she have gone back into that room to see it for herself.

The hood was up on the curricle, giving her an illusion of privacy within its cocoon. She knew, at the back of her mind, that Niall's groom was on the perch behind and the rest would be following, either on horseback or in the phaeton.

She recalled sitting in a public room downstairs, shivering on a bench, while young Peter Eddows conversed with his father. She could hear sounds of a struggle out in the hallway, with thumps and grunts betokening some sort of fight. Mr Eddows must have noticed her question, for he had approached her, laying a hand on her shoulder and speaking in a tone of reassurance.

"Don't trouble your head about it, Miss Westacott. Kilshaw's groom and the landlord and tapster here put up a spirited protest at our invasion, that is all."

She nodded, feeling dazed at the number of men Niall had brought to her rescue.

"Peter, fetch a tot of brandy to Miss Westacott. If the tapster or a waiter is not by, get it yourself."

Voices had been raised in argument. Edith recognised Peter's, barking quite in Niall's peremptory manner, which had induced a tiny smile. He returned presently and passed a glass to his father, who urged it upon Edith.

"Drink this, Miss Westacott. It will revive you."

She put a hand towards the glass, but did not take it immediately. "Brandy?"

"Just so. His lordship would advise you to drink it, I know."

"Advise me?" Edith's dazed state had lightened for a space. "Order me, more like."

Mr Eddows smiled. "Well, I will not emulate him, ma'am, but do take a sip or two. I truly think you need it."

Edith took the glass and tipped the fiery liquid down her throat. She gasped and coughed, but the effect was almost instantaneous. Warmth slid into her chest and the clouds in her mind began to dissipate.

She was alert enough on Niall's joining them for the horror of what she had done to resurface. He must have seen it in her face, for he did not wait for her question.

"He's alive, Edith. The wound was deep, but not fatal. I've patched him up and told his man out there to send for a surgeon."

Mr Eddows blinked at him. "You amaze me, my lord. After all that man has done?"

"He does not deserve as much consideration, but it will save trouble in the long run."

He had lost no time in bundling Edith into the curricle, saying he must get her home in the shortest possible time. He'd set as speedy a pace as the dark night would allow, and few words were exchanged between them.

Edith did not ask what had occurred after she left the parlour. It was enough to know she had not killed the wretch, and so need not fear the authorities.

Lulled by the rhythm of the vehicle, the regular beat of the horses' hooves, Edith's mind became cloudy again. The events of the night began to assume the aspect of a dream, and she woke with a start to find the curricle at a standstill.

Blinking into the lightened atmosphere, she sat up and looked about. The vicarage? She was home! Candlelight flickered within the downstairs windows, where the curtains were left undrawn, the shutters open. Her uncle must be up still, waiting for her.

Niall was no longer beside her and the groom was at the horses' heads. Leaning forward, she saw Niall at the open door of the vicarage and caught sight of her uncle, who came hurrying down the path ahead of him.

"My dearest girl! My poor Ede! I have been in a fever of anxiety."

He reached the curricle and put up his hands to clasp hers, gazing up at her with so much affection as to bring tears pricking at her eyes for the first time this night.

"Uncle Lionel," she managed and could not say more.

"Let me come there, sir."

Her uncle gave place, and Niall held up his arms. "Come, Edith."

Shakily, she prepared to alight. She was no sooner on her feet than Niall plucked her bodily from the curricle and swung her up into his arms. On instinct she threw an arm about his neck to steady herself, clutching his coat with her other hand.

"I could very well walk, you know."

He smiled down at her. "I know."

He bore her down the path and through the front door, where Mrs Tuffin came up and began clucking along with her uncle in the rear. Niall set her down at last on the day-bed in the front room, keeping an arm about her until she was settled.

"Hot milk! I shall fetch it at once," clucked Mrs Tuffin. But she did not head for the door, instead pushing in past Niall and seizing Edith into a suffocating hug, unaccustomed sobs choking in her throat. "Our girl is safe! Our dear, dear girl is home again!"

Edith's heart swelled and she returned the good woman's embrace with fervour, tears seeping from her eyes. Released, she smiled into the housekeeper's softened features, amazed and touched to find herself so valued.

Mrs Tuffin dashed at her cheeks, her tone rough. "Oh, look at me, the silly old woman that I am! And you crying out for something hot to drink."

Seizing her hands, Edith squeezed. "I am, and I'm so glad to have you to fuss over me, Mrs Tuffin. Only may I have tea?"

"Tea! I'll have it to you in a jiffy." Straightening up, she bustled off, calling to the vicar to let her know what his lordship might like as soon as ever he could drag himself away from his niece.

Her uncle was wringing Niall's hand. "There are no words to describe to you my heartfelt thanks, my dear lord. Without your intervention, my darling girl would have been lost to that blackguard."

"I believe not, sir, for she saved herself, you must know." Niall's glance strayed to Edith and she saw admiration in his eyes. "I will leave her to recount her part to you, but in truth I had only to harry the enemy after his defeat."

A shudder ran through Edith at the memory thus raised. But her uncle was moving towards her.

"Is it so indeed, Ede? What a resourceful child you are. How did you manage it?" He clasped her hand. "No, don't tell me now, my dear. I can see it is too raw at this present."

She gave him a grateful smile. "I would indeed prefer to tell it later, Uncle."

"I would not for the world distress you further, after all you have undergone this day." He dropped a light kiss on her hair and turned to Niall. "Only tell me if the danger is past, my lord. Is my Ede safe?"

"I believe so, Reverend. I threatened Kilshaw with public exposure, and I have every intention of writing of his doings to his precious friend, the Prince, as I told him I would."

"Good heavens! Will that serve, do you suppose?"

As startled as her uncle, Edith awaited Niall's response with a rise of real hope. Was it truly the last she would see of her Nemesis?

"It was certainly the one thing that wiped the complacency off his face. The Prince of Wales makes his own scandals, but I hardly think he will wish to be associated with a fellow who thinks nothing of attempting to abduct another man's wife. And a countess at that."

Heat leapt to Edith's cheeks and she cast an agitated look upon her uncle.

But the vicar was beaming. "Is it all settled then? My dear fellow, I could not be more delighted. And as for you, my dearest Ede," he continued, turning to her before Niall could respond, "it is no more than you deserve, and I wish you every happiness."

He swooped upon her, but Edith put up her hands to hold him off and Niall coughed behind him.

"I regret I am a touch premature, sir. Edith has not yet accepted me."

"Uncle Lionel —" She was given no chance to speak, for her uncle seized her hand again, holding it fast.

"But she will, my dear lord, she will. Will you not, my dearest Ede? You have my consent, for I cannot think of a better man to guard and keep you. In every respect, a most suitable match. And best of all, you will be close to me here, my dear niece. After this episode, I could not have endured the thought of you going out of my reach again."

Edith's throat ached and she could hardly get the words out. "Oh, Uncle, Uncle! You are too good!"

He patted her in the way he always did, beaming again. "And now I shall leave you, for I perceive my lord Hetherington here is impatient of my absence, are you not, my dear lord?"

A hearty laugh accompanied this effusion, and Edith blushed again as Niall cast her an amused glance. "I am, sir, but I wish you will call me Niall. I aim to be as near to your son-in-law as makes no odds."

The vicar was moved to wring his hand again, looking up at him all smiles. "My dear Niall, nothing could give me greater pleasure. Now, what shall I tell Mrs Tuffin? Will you drink tea with Ede or —"

"Tea will be most welcome, Reverend," Niall said, firmly escorting him to the door, and shutting it behind him as the vicar ambled out. He turned with his fingers still about the handle and looked across at Edith with a rueful grin. "It appears your uncle has your future sewn up, whether you will or no."

"It seems so indeed."

She swung her legs down and sat up. Niall came quickly across, putting out a hand.

"Don't get up. You need rest."

She took hold of his hand and drew him down. "Then sit with me."

He did so, bringing her hand towards his lips. But he paused, his brows drawing together as his eyes went to her wrist. "What the deuce?"

He released her and got up abruptly. A couple of strides took him to the mantel, where he seized the candelabrum there and brought it across, lifting a chair close to the day-bed at the same time. He set the candelabrum down on the chair so that it threw brighter light upon Edith.

She blinked in the glare as Niall squatted before her.

"Show me your hands!"

Edith held them out, watching his face as, with care, he pushed back her sleeves and examined the red weals for several moments. She saw a muscle twitch in his cheek, and his jaw line tightened.

"This needs a salve and bandages."

The tone was taut with held-in emotion. Fury, Edith thought. She spoke in as matter-of-fact a tone as she could command. "Mrs Tuffin will see to it presently."

Niall glanced up once and then his hands cradled her forearms, his hold gentle. He leaned his head down and planted a tender kiss on each mutilated wrist. His fingers slid down to grasp Edith's hands, his hold tightening as he looked up, regarding her with a riven look.

"I could kick myself from here to eternity. I failed you! I should never have left you alone at the Fair."

His voice was hoarse, and Edith's heart squeezed as a shine rimmed his eyes. Her fingers turned within his and she gripped hard.

"No, Niall. You took every precaution. I was foolishly negligent."

"You've been shamefully used in every way and I can't bear it, Edith!"

"But I'm safe, Niall. You came for me as I knew you would." She tried for a lighter note, though her voice was shaky. "Come, this won't do. Where is my conquering chevalier, who is afraid of nothing?"

A faint sigh escaped him, and he returned the pressure of her fingers.

"He's giving way to the terror he fought against throughout. I've never in my life been so fearful, I promise you."

"Niall, it is over!"

"But at what cost?"

"A trifling cost indeed. Come, get up and sit by me."

He did as she asked, settling beside her and putting his arm about her. "If I'd known that crowing cockerel had tied you up..."

"That was his ruffian."

"But he ordered it, I have no doubt."

"I don't think so. I expect he merely instructed the fellow to capture me and bring me to that out of the way inn."

"The one where I'd seen his groom," Niall put in, his voice a little more normal. "Thank the lord, for it could have taken a deal longer to find which way he'd taken you without that knowledge."

His hold about her tightened as he spoke, and Edith warmed to the evidence of the depth of his affection.

"I never doubted you would come for me, Niall. And to tell the truth, my discomfort in that cart was short-lived, for I did not regain my senses fully until we had well-nigh arrived at the inn."

"I'll have that ruffian laid by the heels," Niall growled.

"Well, you may try, but I don't imagine he'll wait about for you to find him."

Niall's hand captured her cheek and he turned her to face him. "You are mighty cool over it, Edith."

"Well, I have my knight to hand. What have I to fear?"

His laugh was a little harsh and he drew her close. His voice came low and vibrant. "If you knew the agonies I went through this night, my darling!"

She caught his hand and held it in both her own. "Did you fear you would not catch us?"

"No. I would have caught you regardless, for I would have followed to the ends of the earth, if need be." His convulsive grip told Edith more than the grated words. "I was afraid I might not reach you in time. That danger well-nigh killed me, Ede. That you should be subjected to his brute force…"

She sank against him and his hold gentled, cuddling her in as tender a manner as she could wish. "He did so intend. I believe he would not have travelled further. He meant, I think, to let you catch up only to find me ruined. And that would have been the end for us."

Niall's arm dropped from about her, and Edith found herself gripped by the shoulders. The fierce look in his face was matched by his voice. "Do you think I would have left you? Even had he done his worst? Do you rate my love of so little account?"

"No, but —"

"Don't dare tell me you would have chosen to go with him rather than come back to me!"

She put up her hands to grasp his wrists. "You're hurting me, Niall!"

His hold loosened at once and he took his hands from her shoulders, holding them away. But the fury in his face did not abate. "Edith!"

Her lips were trembling and she could barely speak. "I don't know, Niall, I don't know." The sudden disappointment in his eyes cut at her heart. She put up her hand and caught his cheek, feeling the ridge of his scar against her skin. "I can't lie to you, Niall. But know this. I had only one thought in my head throughout, and that was to prevent him violating me by any means I could find. I did nothing but hunt for weapons from the moment we arrived at that inn."

His face softened and he caught the hand resting against his cheek, holding it there. "I'm sorry. I'm being stupidly selfish. It doesn't matter."

Something squeezed in her heart. "But it does, Niall. It matters to you. And all I can offer you is my resolve to evade Lord Kilshaw because I wanted to come to you pure and untainted."

He took her hand from his cheek and kissed the palm, sending a shiver through Edith.

"That will content me." He smiled. "Does that mean you accept my suit? You will be my wife?"

Edith's eyes pricked and her voice was shaky. "With all my heart, my dearest knight errant."

She heard his indrawn breath and felt his lips on her hand, punctuating his words.

"My love, my darling, my precious Ede."

Edith's smile was tremulous. "Don't you mean to take the real kiss you've won? The dragon is slain, after all."

The lopsided curve to his mouth appeared at last and his arms slid about her. Edith's veins quivered and then sang as his lips touched hers.

A NOTE TO THE READER

Dear Reader,

With the current #metoo culture, it is hard to realise how vulnerable women could be in days gone by. Not so long ago either. So much has changed within my lifetime and I rejoice in the female freedoms so widely available. Sadly not in all cultures even today.

But I am here talking of women of the Regency era, and in particular those of genteel birth, yet less protected than their counterparts fortunate enough to be born into affluent circumstances. The Brides by Chance series follows the adventures of such women, and Edith Westacott is perhaps the heroine most affected by the disparities then existing between men and women.

A man with no visible means of support, without a patron to buy him a commission in one of the services, might still choose a respectable profession within the church, the legal or medical fields, architecture or science; attach himself in a secretarial capacity to a man of rank or politics; even enter the diplomatic service, albeit in a lowly capacity. As long as he was well educated and stayed out of trade, his options were actually better than those of the sons of the aristocracy with the more limited traditional choices of army, navy, or church.

For a woman, on the other hand, there were only three work options: companion, governess or schoolmistress. Historical romance aside, once you took up such a post, there was no going back. Instances of the governess or companion securing a husband were few and far between, though occasionally a prudent man would even stoop to marrying the cook to save expense!

The governess, like any female domestic, was considered fair game by the marauding male. A young and pretty woman would not be hired in a household where there were impressionable young sons, mothers being notoriously wary of scandalous goings on.

Imagine then, the situation of our schoolmistress Edith, entirely without protection and prey to the flattery of an experienced seducer without scruple or mercy.

It seems incredible, in our enlightened times, to think women might be subjected to such a determined and ruthless pursuit. But there is no doubt it did happen. The road to ruin took many an innocent down the path to prostitution, the all too likely future for a female who succumbed. To demonstrate that I do not exaggerate, in the late 18th century the statistic of criminals, for one year in London alone, labels 50% as prostitutes. How many of them chose the life?

Edith escaped, thanks to her knight, and that is the pleasure of writing romance!

If you would consider leaving a review, it would be much appreciated and very helpful. Do feel free to contact me on **elizabeth@elizabethbailey.co.uk** or find me on **Facebook**, **Twitter**, **Goodreads** or my website **www.elizabethbailey.co.uk**.

Elizabeth Bailey

Sapere Books is an exciting new publisher of brilliant fiction and popular history.

To find out more about our latest releases and our monthly bargain books visit our website:
saperebooks.com

Printed in Great
Britain
by Amazon